KILLING DONNIE

PART I

Written by

RAFAEL FRANCIS

Adapted from the Screenplay

Published in (US) English

Killing Donnie is a work of fiction. All names, characters, businesses, places, events, and incidents in this novel are either the product of the author's imagination or used in a fictitious manner. Any resemblance to actual persons, living or dead, or actual events is purely coincidental.

rafael-francis.com

CONTENTS

"Whoever fights monsters should see to it that in the process he does not become a monster. And if you gaze long enough into an abyss, the abyss will gaze back into you."

- *Friedrich Nietzsche*

Prologue

Shit happens.

That's what they all say. I can no longer recall the exhausting number of times I've heard those same words from mostly the same people. People I've loved and people I've loathed. It's all the same. It always means the same thing:

Stiffen up, don't lose sleep over it, you'll forget all about it tomorrow, or simply, *just shut the fuck up and keep your goddamned mouth shut.*

I navigated the Lincoln about nine miles south of the city and pulled up in a dark patch along a broken road. No lights. No signs. No people. I looked back at the Yankee Empire and wondered why the lights were so bright and so close, yet nobody was around. The perfect place to bury a secret. The perfect little trench for the city's problems to slide into, and the more they desperately tried to claw their way out, the more the sinkhole would dissolve them.

I lit a cigar I'd been saving for a while. A Churchill. Castello seemed nervous, neither indulging in his usual pack of donuts nor his favored jumbo shamrock shake. I needed to make conversation, a distraction from the obnoxious groaning and grunting from the rear of the sedan, accompanied by Johnny Cash playing off an old cassette tape in the car. We needed a breather after the day we'd had. The cigar was full-bodied—it had this indescribable sweetness to it. I knew it was a rarity, but I couldn't be sure how many more special occasions I had left to save it for. Castello enjoyed it, too, although he wasn't even a common smoker.

I exhaled. "You watch the Yankees play this week?"

Castello glanced at me, knowing I was finding any way to prolong the inevitable opening of that black steel trunk of the Lincoln. He nodded as I passed him the Cuban.

"They were up against the Dodgers, weren't they?" He was tired of it, too. The same old shit, week in, week out. He wasn't getting any younger either. Castello reminisced over having been to the City of Angels and not spending enough time to really see all there is to see. Unfortunately for us, we couldn't go back there no more.

We heard some thumping from the trunk. It sounded like a pack of starved, stray hounds attempting to scratch their way out after sniffing a well-cooked roast on the other side. I couldn't help but give Castello *the look*. After passing the cigar to me, he reluctantly snatched his keys and hobbled over to the back of the car. I needed another drag before meeting him there. Either the cigar was too sweet to waste, or I just needed another second.

The trunk swung open and there he was, with his patchy mustache and receding, oily hairline. *The skinny businessman.* I can't remember too well, but I think his name was Arnold. There's not enough room in my brain for useless information. Unnecessary data consumes valuable space. From the desperate look in his eye to the necktie covering his mouth, you almost wouldn't have noticed the fact that his pants were missing. Oh, you bet your ass he tried to plead, but back in the city would've been his last chance, if he had one at all. When you get out here, nobody can hear you, and nobody can see you disappear.

Castello made him well aware that there was no way out of this, emphasizing the vast emptiness that surrounded us. Before he could elaborate, a wad of saliva spattered onto his cheek through a gap in the necktie. *No emotion.* I think he expected it. He waltzed back to the car and opened the door. Most times, Castello was a calm, serene man. But like all of us—pushed to the edge—he can be a real relentless son of a bitch.

Arnold looked up at me from that trunk. "You. You're a good guy. I know you." He recognized me. Hell, he even knew my name. "The name's John, isn't it?"

He nodded, hoping he was right, hoping that I'd find something deep inside me, some speck of sympathy—some faint trace of humanity within the realm of my very being. Unfortunately for him, I've made that mistake before, and I wasn't about to make it again.

Castello returned from the car with a limited-edition baseball bat he'd bought specially for his nephew back in Niscemi. The bat never made it to young Georgie because it was left damaged after Arnold's skull was used for batting practice before being dragged by his legs onto the curb.

The blood made it onto my jacket and onto Castello's cheeks. Blood can be a real messy medium to work with. *It gets fucking everywhere.* Arnold could no longer move but his eyes were still darting between myself and Cas, still holding on to the glimmer of hope that he'd make it out of this alive.

After dyeing the baseball bat and everything around it in a deep-red glaze, Castello slipped on the puddle of blood beneath his feet. "Look what you did to my clothes!" Castello returned to his feet. "Fucking prick."

After one final, world-class strike to his torso, Arnold wasn't the same man he was before. Coughing up blood, his children wouldn't even recognize his face if they saw it. Still with the tightly gripped bat in his fist, Castello took a step back, gasping like he'd just run a ten-mile marathon. Arnold's eyes were locked on me. He was pleading without verbally speaking because he physically couldn't. So, with the cigar lodged between my teeth, I pulled the pistol from the rear pocket of my jacket and drove a bullet clean through the left side of his forehead.

How does somebody become so desensitized to this kind of lifestyle?

I'd have to take you back, say ten years or so.

You might think this was a pivotal moment, something I'd look back on for the rest of my life. But for us ... this was Tuesday.

Chapter One

The City of Dreams. The City of Nightmares.

New York City, September 1973. Don't ask me the exact date, I never carried a journal. When I stepped out of that subway station in Brooklyn, the scrapers towered tall above me. When you picture Manhattan before seeing it with your own two eyes, you assume it's just another city, an exaggeration, an overblown fantasy. Well, seeing it for the first time makes you feel almost microscopic—insignificant, like a drop of fresh water in the Atlantic. Nobody knows you, and nobody cares. You just blend in with the rest of them. Every direction turned, every street gazed at, every avenue walked, you'd never reach the end. Looking up would make you dizzy and for some newcomers, the only way to stay on your feet was to keep your eyes on the ground. The rich get richer … you know the rest.

I was seventeen. I had big hopes in the big city. Wall Street was booming and the only thing these sorry bastards were thinking about was cash. Couldn't say I was any better myself after my father passed away back home—*God bless his heart.*

Catania, I was a city boy over there, too. I was one of the only kids in my family with some kind of education. But I was hungry ... hungry for more, hungry for the prospect of being a *somebody*. And thirsty for the New York cash flow they'd raved so much about back home. The success stories, the triumphant tales of booming businesses in billion-dollar battlegrounds. It *lured* me, it *reeled* me in and convinced me that this is where I'd build my wealth, my worth. This is where Johnny Caruso would construct his great name. But before any of that, like anybody else, I had to start at the bottom.

***

"Big Johnny Caruso: CEO of West Quarters." *Doesn't that sound neat? Doesn't that sound fucking sublime? Imagine the business card— imagine the respect—Jesus Christ ... imagine the pay.* My initial aim was to eventually reach the peak of that totem pole.

When I walked into my first brokerage firm, I fell in love. I was in love with the idea of money and the promise of more money. America was my ticket to fortune and financial freedom.

Mind my youthful ignorance, will ya? I was brash, arrogant. Things change.

Tall with black hair, formal stockings, and those thick glasses that either come off as stereotypically geeky or in this instance, magnificently sexy. She leaned over my desk with a folder and a seductive grin. "Some onboarding papers to getcha settled in. Don't let the whales eat ya. It's a tricky industry for school fish."

I raised an eyebrow and leaned back on my chair, stretching an elastic band. "Oh, don't you worry, darling. Whales don't eat sharks."

She smiled, biting on a pen. "I'm Robin." She shook my hand.

"I'm Johnny. Johnny Caruso."

"Just shout if you need anything, Johnny." She placed the pen on my desk, glazed with her lip gloss.

Way back home, my family always told me I was a people person. I had a natural gift of charisma—I never stopped talking, and in turn, my relatives never stopped talkin' to me. So, naturally, this was the occupation for my skillset. I had my own desk, my own phone, my own chair, and most of all, a brand-new inked-up pen to scribble away with. Life here seemed as sweet as a Boston Cream Donut until that doughnut was abruptly stepped on, squashed, and splattered before I could even sink my pearly whites into it, and as such, my dreams of becoming an A-class stockbroker.

Louie Brucciani may have been a lean man but his shadow standing above my desk carried the weight of a thousand tons. In his gray tracksuit, it was difficult to take him seriously until you realized he wasn't wearing those garments because he was broke, poor, or on his daily power-stroll down Ocean Ave. It was on account of his *give no fucks* attitude. Somewhat disrespectful, somewhat admirable. He was a real hard-ass, starved by his parents as a child and forced to work on the rails. When he was picked up by the Caruso family after doing a few odd jobs and favors for them that only a kid could get away with, he revisited his folks and shot them both in the head with a .357 Magnum. At sixteen, he was already part of the business.

"Johnny? We work with your Uncle Don." Louie towered above me, his arms crossed. "He's got other plans for you."

He placed his hand on my shoulder which I swatted off like a ball of lint. "What plans? I ain't even been to the bathroom here, yet!"

He simply ignored the words I muttered and proceeded to introduce me to his short, olive-skinned sidekick, Carlo. Roughly a year older than myself, Carlo was one of the only men I ever knew who had a genuine, beating heart, aside from his comical escapades and the occasional fiery outburst. The only thing shorter than himself was his own fuse. Their persuasive attempt consisted of a superior living situation, higher pay, and a steady income. To me, that all sounded like a sham: *the typical sales pitch.* Upon my abrupt refusal, it was difficult not to notice the thick, glistening gold chain beneath Louie's collar. Even if they'd been telling the truth, I wanted to make it on my own in the big city. I wanted to write my own name in the sand. I wasn't interested in a free ride.

"It's a lot more than that, Johnny, it's—"

"Don't call me Johnny unless you know me, understand?" I pointed at Louie, curt. "Only my friends can call me that."

Louie looked down at the carpeted floor and sniggered. *What was he smiling about? Was I acting too much like a tough guy? Or was my attitude all too familiar to him?*

"Okay, *John.* Let me be frank. Don told me to get you. If I get back there without you, my day ain't gonna be so good."

I asked them if they were deaf *and* stupid. I already told them I wasn't interested. *Jesus Christ*, in retrospect, if somebody else spoke to them in that manner, they'd be clobbered to a pulp and clawed in the back of their skull by the rear end of a steel hammer. Maybe frustration was the culprit behind his laughter. He knew he couldn't touch me. Nevertheless, they sure did their homework. They knew where to find me on my first day. They knew what time my shift ended. They even knew how much cash I was making hourly.

"Look, Jon-Jon." Louie snatched a piece of paper off my desk, maintaining eye contact and somehow writing an address on it without breaking the bond of our pupils. "Why don't you do yourself a favor and after you finish up here, come by *this* address."

That part left a bitter taste in my mouth. See, only my folks called me Jon-Jon. Nobody else should've even known that about me. I felt as if all my privacy and sense of security was stripped away at that very moment. *Who the fuck did these guys think they were?*

He neatly returned my pen to the holder. And with a swift smile, he folded the note and slipped it into my shirt pocket, patting it. Carlo shot me a sincere nod before tailing Louie out of the office. I fished the note from my shirt pocket and disposed of it in the empty trash can beside my desk.

"You must already be a *somebody* in this town. That looked awfully important." Robin appeared, grazing her hand past my shoulder, forcing her delicate fragrance to charm my olfactory.

"Don't worry, it wasn't," I said, before biting on the same pen she'd left at my table. "Now, how about I take you out sometime and tell you more about *Mr. Somebody?*"

She inhaled deeply and turned, strutting away. "Just call my line."

As I leaned back on my chair with my feet up on my desk, something had already changed. The phones were ringing louder, the brokers were talking over each other like a swarm of Africanized bees. The printers, the staplers, the footsteps, the fucking door slams. I needed a breath, and a glass of cold water. *An instant headache.*

How can two minutes with two total strangers change my perception of the environment around me? An environment that I so deeply wanted to be a part of.

Over by the window, glancing down from the twelfth floor, I noticed Louie and Carlo stepping into a black Lincoln Continental parked illegally on the curb. Louie knew what he was doing, gazing up at me before his eyes caught the sun. As he slid his sunglasses on and squashed his cigarette on the concrete beneath, he stepped into the car.

"Hey, buddy. Customers ain't out that window," said the scrawny, bald manager with his cheap suspenders and nose held so high, I could almost see his brain. "They're on the phones."

As I made my way back to my desk, I couldn't focus—not one bit. I pondered over it. I stared at that note in my trash can for what seemed like an eternity. It was calling me, screaming at me. I almost ignored it, and sometimes I wish I had. As an apple core found its way into the same container, I had already made my mind.

***

Midnight in Harlem—the backstreets. Steam wafted from the sewers beneath the road and the rain came down sideways. In the middle of the back seat of Louie's Continental, I remember Carlo in the front, holding a gray briefcase with a silver lining. He was gripping it tight as if the entire night depended on whatever was inside. My skepticism must've been infuriating.

"Who the fuck works this late, anyway?" I said with a sneer. "And what's in the case? Drugs? *Are you drug dealers?* I bet you two've never worked an honest day in your lives."

Within ten minutes of the drive, Louie was already growing tired of my shit. "You got a mouth on you, Johnny."

"Just like his uncle." Carlo found it amusing.

"I told you, don't call me Johnny. You ain't my friend," I huffed. "Especially, 'cause I sure as hell ain't workin' a job that starts at midnight."

Louie needed a cigarette after that one. Carlo passed him the whole carton. As he snapped his lighter shut, the smoke slowly escaped his mouth while he gazed at me in the rearview mirror. I knew this wasn't a regular job. I think I knew that from the very second I laid eyes on them. Maybe I even knew it before I came to New York. Louie ordered Carlo to pass me the case. Carlo was reluctant but Louie shot him a reassuring nod.

"You're gonna walk this case over to that man over there, drop it at his feet, and get back in the car. Simple enough?"

I asked him if he was joking but he stared at me, his eyes carving me up like a jack-o'-lantern. As I stepped out of the car into a puddle, I'd never felt a colder breeze. I approached the hooded figure in the alleyway, leaning along the downpipes, smoking a cigarette. *What if this was the wrong guy? What if he had a knife?* Turns out he didn't have a knife ... he had a *gun*.

I cautiously placed the case at his feet, fighting my urges not to stare at that silver pistol strategically placed within his jacket. He nodded. "Grazie mille." A familiar term. I hesitated and responded, although I didn't need to, "With regards from Don Caruso."

I stepped back into the car, rattled. "Now, is somebody gonna tell me what the fuck that was about? That guy had a gun in his jacket," I raved. "What is this shit? You tryna get me killed?"

"You remember the last time you saw your Uncle Donnie?" Louie squinted.

As far back as I could recall, I must've been five years old, maybe younger. I couldn't even remember what he looked like. His presence was so heavily felt that you'd imagine he was fifty feet tall.

"If he wants me in this business so bad, then why don't he come see me himself?" I scoffed. "He's gotta send his *goons* over instead?"

Oh, I was really playing with fire when I cracked that one. Louie's lips were shaking like a pair of coked-up flamenco dancers. "Donnie's a busy man," Louie snarled. "And if you call me a *goon* one more time, I'll smack the next briefcase over your head so hard that you ain't lookin' like nobody's nephew no more." After a lengthy four-second interval, Louie cracked an unexpected smile and Carlo cackled along. He was yanking my chain—*busting my chops,* as it were—and this was something I simply had to get used to.

We pulled up along the street to a white building of Victorian-style architecture. The place must've been around for at least fifty years. "What do ya know? That's him up there now." Louie pointed. "The boss man himself."

On a balcony some twenty stories, *there he stood.* A silhouette swirling a glass of liquor. Donnie Caruso. My uncle. My zio. The most stubborn yet determined man you'd ever meet. I hadn't seen him since I was a child, nor did I remember his face. But there he was, standing on that balcony, looking down his nose at an entire city with his chest out like a lion and smoking a cigar the size of a fucking crowbar. As he inhaled that *Gran Corona,* he leaned on the balcony rails. I wondered what he was thinking about. What troubles could possibly be tormenting a figure of such stature. He was the lone pioneer of the Caruso empire in New York after his father—my grandfather—passed away. And I was the young wolf, looking up at him in awe, unaware of the dangers and lies lurking beneath that creature of a man.

The well-known tale in my family is that Donnie was the bad egg, the one that wreaks havoc, causes chaos, and was most likely to end up as a cashless deadbeat. *This was him?* I thought. *This was the guy that wasn't supposed to make it? Who knew a black sheep would stand at the top of the hill?* Maybe they were wrong about him. Maybe they despised him for leaving them behind for success? Maybe, just maybe, the rumour outweighed the truth.

I was interrupted by Carlo, flapping a fat envelope in my face.

"Little onboarding gift from Donnie," Louie said as he started the ignition. "There's more where that came from but for now, *get out.* We'll be in touch."

The envelope was packed to the brim with cash. It wouldn't even close—trust me, I tried. Within my spiral of confusion, I asked them how we made this cash when I barely lifted a finger.

"You got too much money or somethin', kid?" Louie sniggered. "Just take it and buy yourself somethin' nice."

Carlo nodded with a sincere smile—a welcoming one. "Who said you need to be pushing buttons or making calls all day to get some green?"

I stepped out of the car and glanced down at the mass of cash stuffed into the envelope. I couldn't help but chuckle. I took one last look at the balcony above. Donnie was gone.

After quitting my job and taking a raincheck on that date with Robin, I had a new job. I didn't even know what the fuck I was doing. I found myself tagging along on drives with Louie and Carlo here, there, and everywhere. Picking up suitcases and dropping off briefcases. Traveling from warehouses to alleyways, then back to warehouses and straight to the docks, then back *once again* to the warehouses and finding myself at the rear of the Yonkers Raceway and Empire Casino handing a heavy burgundy briefcase through the back window of a limousine to a man with a mustache and a full head of hair bobbing in his lap. They didn't tell you nothing, and the more you wanted to know, the less they wanted to tell. Carlo seemed to keep his mouth shut most of the time. I got the feeling they were surveying us to determine whether we could be trusted with sensitive information. As the cash kept rolling in, I knew I was home, exactly where I wanted to be. My primary goal in New York was to make money. Somehow, I was making it just by existing.

***

The city that never sleeps. I sat on the fourteenth floor of the Caruso building in an empty kitchen watching the city, alive in unity. It sang for me. It had a heart with a beat that wouldn't stop. From every flashing light to every horn beeped by every raging driver, this city welcomed you with open arms.

While eating Nonna Francesca's famous pasta ravioli, she asked me if I was attending an upcoming wedding—Francesco and Lucia's. I didn't even know these people personally but being a part of this community meant that you were a part of everything that came with it. While Nonna Francesca wasn't even my grandmother, we still called her that anyway. She was like the grandmother of the whole family. Short, wobbly, and frail but if you stepped just one foot out of line, she'd have her whacking-ladle at the ready.

As she boasted about her gorgeous granddaughters attending the wedding and her hopes of me rubbin' elbows with them, I couldn't help overhearing a conversation on the other side of the room. Two large men discussing a deal and the risks of getting caught with mention of the feds, the police—the whole shebang.

"Keep it down, ah? That's Don's nephew over there." Politely smiling at me with a little wave was Mattia, who you've already had the pleasure of meeting. Usually spotted eating or with some kind of donut in his hand, he was better known as Castello. He was a long-time member of this business and Donnie was one of his associates. Until Donnie inherited the business from his father and the word *associate* became *boss*.

And who could forget Vinnie Russo? Brought up only by gangsters, he belonged to this business just as a demon belonged in hell. At fourteen, he was already hot-wiring cars and reselling them under different plates in the Bronx. Aside from his brute weight and curly hair, the first thing you'd notice is the deep scar above his left eyebrow. Best not mentioned and best not stared at.

I strolled down the corridors of my newly inhabited building with my own last name stamped on it, wearing my new suit and tightening my necktie. I was able to finally put things into perspective. My Uncle Don—he was very, very rich. The building wasn't only a well-overpriced hotel, but we also lived there in luxury on the upper stories—*all of us*. Donnie would invite friends of his to stay in the spare apartments we had, to help with accommodation and such. As the newspapers piled up at the doors and the cleaners exited the vacant rooms, wringing the red water from their mops, I knew I could call this place home, *so long as I didn't ask questions.*

I would've thought I'd have to struggle to find work in the City of Dreams. Instead, I found myself belonging to a family that had a place for me with open arms. A purpose, just for me in their own business.

KILLING DONNIE

Chapter Two

Glitz, Glamor, and the Good Stuff

Among all the bars in all the hotels in all the city, there's not one place you'd rather spend your Saturday night. As I stumbled through the gaggling guests and laughing Larrys with a silver tray of champagne in my left hand, I was always shaking somebody else's with my right. The Caruso building had this bar in the penthouse just for Donnie and his guests, but these weren't just random visitors, you'd see the same faces all the time. Robbie Ciccone, Marco Fallaci, Jay-Jay Genovese. The makeup, the jewelry, the clinking of the glasses and the rapid ascent of the bubbles inside them. It all went hand in hand with the swing jazz playing on the small corner stage he had set up. In this room, the women were just as respected as the men, if not more so. These were people you'd never forget—Guilia Lo Conte, Mia Lorenzo, Cecilia Mancini— three women that you can't walk into a room without kissing twice on each cheek ... *whether you knew them or not*. And who could forget the fidgety one, Luca Toscanini? Better known as Twitchy Luca—*don't give him a gun, if you know what's good for you.* But even though it was just their routine, weekly Saturday night, these things were classy, and I mean gold watches, chains, rings, fur coats, diamond jewelry, none of which I'd ever been accustomed to. Everybody knew each other, and even if you didn't know them, they knew *you*. These functions alone made you feel like you were a part of something big. It was weekly, it was wealthy, and it was wonderful.

At first, I didn't speak to my uncle very much ... at all. As I approached his smoke-hazed table, he looked up at me. Although, he somehow still made you feel like he was looking down on you. In his mid-fifties, he was a slim man, hair slicked back and well dressed in a slender black suit. Whether you were swayed by the charming look in his eyes or his arrogant grin, you'd quickly be distracted by his collection of thick gold signet rings along his fingers and a watch that's priced higher than your life.

"Young Johnny," he said with a snigger. "Why don't you bring that sweet little ass over here and give your Zio Donnie a kiss?" I approached him with a gulp. "Now, get on your knees." The other hunched men around the table began cackling like a colony of seagulls. You'd expect one of them to drop dead from cardiac arrest at any moment. "Relax, Johnny. I'm just breakin' ya balls. It's only a joke—sit down."

I felt like his own personal jester. I had to match the pace.

"You know, every joke has a lining of truth to it?"

Noticing my smirk, Donnie's grin rapidly escaped him. Insulted, he stared blankly into the rocky depths of my soul. He could see my heart, sense my nerves, and rip the smiling lips off my face forever. The world stopped spinning for about three and a half seconds until Gigi, Donnie's frail accountant and longtime friend and confidant, cracked a giggle. And to my relief, the laugh rippled throughout the entire table.

Gigi pointed my way, nodding at my uncle. "He *mus*t be your blood if he's dishing out wisecracks like that, Don!"

"Everyone, I'd like you to meet my nephew, Johnny." Donnie wrapped a firm, embracing arm round my shoulder.

Family can be a word loosely thrown around in any business. But in this one, it meant what it meant. At the same table sat the Barresi brothers—identical twins. The only way to tell them apart was their hairstyles. We called them the Boston Connection. They'd only come down to New York about twice a month. And when they did, it was always a party. Celestino would always be sporting a mustache and curly hair, twirling his drink with a long teaspoon, while Riccardo, raising his glass to me, was usually clean-shaven with a short afro. Identical twins but their personalities couldn't be more contrary.

Unused to their antics, I took a formal approach, firmly shaking their hands with a masculine nod. "It's a pleasure to make your acquaintance, fellas."

"Woah, woah, *acquaintance?* We're movin' too fast over here,"

Riccardo jested. "You're not gonna ask to *marry* me, are ya?" He shook his head and turned to Donnie. "What the fuck is this? You raisin' a fucken lawyer over here, Don?"

To Donnie's delight, Celestino pointed directly at me. "You don't shake *our* hands, kid, and call us your acquaintances." Celestino glared, serious, dabbing his index finger on the table. "You walk in here, talk with *us*, have a drink with *us*. That means you're family. If Donnie's family, you're just the same."

It was the first time I felt some measure of acceptance. *Isn't that what we all want?* The feeling of inclusion. The satisfying embrace of being a part of something bigger than yourself. As Donnie raised his wine glass to me, I knew I was right where I belonged. But when you're a part of this business, you're a part of everything that comes with it …

The good, the bad, and *the real fucken ugly.*

***

Midnight. A couple miles from Franklin and just under an hour from Manhattan. Louie was driving the car as usual. Carlo was in the back with me. In the passenger seat was Tony. Around thirty years old, chubby, sweaty, obnoxious, and in-fucking-tolerable. He had a mouth on him the size of a pelican's—literally and figuratively.

"So, I get home from *you know where* and Audrey unstraps my belt to give me a *you know what* and guess what she says." Tony could barely hold himself together.

Louie tightened his grip on the wheel. "What'd she say, Tony?"

"Whose lipstick is that?" Before the soundwaves could even reach Louie, Tony had already belted out a laugh. I'd say it was comparable to a walrus in labor. "If only that bitch knew where I was the night before *that.*"

Louie and Carlo humored him. All I could do was roll my eyes so far to the back of my skull that I could see the road behind us. *It was painful.* He was out of breath from laughter.

"You're the prick of all pricks, my good friend." Patting him on the shoulder, Louie wasn't usually so tolerant. Something was off.

After we pulled into a dirt road under a rusted-out bridge, Tony had already invited himself to Francesco and Lucia's wedding after catching a whiff of it through the grapevine. Louie finally pulled the car over to a complete halt. He had turned both the engine and the headlights off. Complete silence after a half hour of mindless jibber-jabber. Louie glanced at me again in the rearview mirror. This time, dead serious.

The nerves crept up my spine and I gulped in fear. Assuming it was just another briefcase swap, we stepped out of the car. Although, there was no briefcase, and the presence of Tony should've made me question the situation much earlier.

Louie scanned the area. *Dead silence.* You could hear a pin drop. "So, we have a little problem, fellas."

Tony was confused, scratching his neck with a shrug. "What is it? Are the pigs on our tail?"

Louie gave him an unconvincing nod. "Say, Tony. Go check over by the water for me."

"I don't think there's nothin' over there, Lou." Tony seemed hesitant. "I'm freezin' my nutsack off over here."

Louie wasn't taking no for an answer. He never did. "Just go check it out, Antonio."

Carlo and I looked at each other, puzzled. I felt a small void begin to manifest in the pit of my stomach. Tony sighed and took a half-assed walk over to the stream that gently ran under the bridge. That's when Louie pulled out his pistol.

One shot in the back of the head.

Another in the back of the neck.

The gunshots felt like ice-cold shivers shooting straight down my spine. I'd never seen a body drop so quickly. It could've been because he was a morbidly obese prick, or it was likely the fact that all his nerves in his brain were severed by a single bullet speeding at around a thousand miles per hour. Either way, *he was dead.* His body kicked up a tremendous amount of dirt as he kissed the ground. That was the moment ... the moment I knew I was deep into some serious shit. Carlo didn't even flinch. Shit like that was normal to these fellas.

A few hours earlier, we were at an Italian restaurant, you know, one of the good ones with the checkered red tablecloth, eating pasta carbonara together and laughing like we were brothers. Tony was stuffing his face with garlic bread, piece by piece into his already full mouth, laughing himself to death.

I was shaken, staring at his eerily still corpse beside the water. This guy's last meal was a pasta carbonara and a bullet through his mouth the opposite way. I looked at Louie for some kind of answer, some kind of explanation, hoping to God that he only had those two bullets with him.

"I brought you both here for two reasons." Louie slid the gun back into his pocket. "To show you what happens to a snitch, and because I need a few hands to get this hippopotamus garbage in the ground."

Carlo and I looked at each other and went straight to work. Little did I know that at the time you die, you usually shit. And with a stench like that, in *that* situation, I'm surprised we didn't die along with him. As we dumped the body in the shallow dirt, I didn't want to look at Tony's disfigured face, but I somehow couldn't manage to look away. Only a few minutes earlier, there had been expressions, emotions, and muscles moving beneath it.

Louie slammed the trunk and that was the last anybody ever heard of *Talkie-Tony.*

What did he do to deserve such an execution?

It made me a paranoid. Paranoid that I could hurt somebody, piss somebody off, or even look at somebody the wrong way, and suffer the same abrupt fate. I couldn't help but wonder how many other bodies were resting beside Tony in that shallow mud.

I was beginning to question the definition of *family*.

***

After that night, they included us in almost everything, from bagging briefcases to counting cash. For me—that night was labeled as some kind of fucked-up initiation. For them—*that night* never happened.

So long as I was getting paid, I was keeping my mouth shut. Uncle Don had a whole lotta connections throughout New York. We ran and did business with a mass of shop owners. We took a little bit off the top, tucking shopkeepers' cash into our own pockets. A little bit off the bottom, helping ourselves to shelf stock from a general store we had in our protection. And a little bit through the middle, cutting off loose ends—which sometimes meant Vinnie and Castello chasing down a cheap fucker who didn't pay his dues. The penalty varied within the scope of breaking a couple kneecaps, to beating their heads in through an alleyway. As much as it made me sick to the stomach, I knew it was just part of the job. I ignored it and told myself it was necessary. I convinced myself that these people must've deserved it. I was there for all of it, waiting in the car and driving our boys back to the Caruso building every night.

But only in the nighttime would they creep up on me. I could still hear the faint echoes of those lost souls, screaming at me, shrieking in pain ... Turning on a TV managed to help me block those voices out. From then on, I never slept unless the TV was on—even if it was only static.

***

Businesswise, things were swell. Carlo had just turned twenty-one and it seemed like life was on the up and up. We hit the strip joint to celebrate, just him and I. Over a few glasses of straight Japanese whiskey, Carlo started yacking on about his dreams, mentioning that he aspired to be some kind of baker, with his own shop and everything.

I smirked at the proposal. "How many drinks've you had?" I couldn't help but imagine that little tough guy, Carlo, in an apron, rolling dough.

Carlo shook his head. "I'm dead serious, Johnny." He seemed to expect my amusement as if others had done so before. "That's my passion. I'm twenty-one tonight and I wanna start thinking about my own business. I'm gonna make the softest, spongiest, fluffiest fucking bread and bagels that you've ever laid your eyes on. Guaranteed."

To be truthful, I never really considered the aspirations of some of these guys. Just like me, they had dreams too. As financially rewarding as this life was, some people just wanted to escape it. And after what we witnessed in the car with Louie and Tony a few months earlier, I couldn't blame him.

"I feel like this is the time of our lives where we're supposed to find ourselves, you know? Find out who we are and what the fuck we're gonna be for the rest of our lives. Louie? He's a part-time security guard on the side. That *can't* be the best we can hope for, Johnny. Not here, not in New York." Carlo was desperate. He wanted out. It only took a few drinks to spill the truth.

"And I will come work with you at the bakery." I nodded to Carlo. "Either that, or I'll be dropping *you* briefcases every Monday."

The laughter continued. After that conversation, I knew that we'd have each other's backs, for better or for worse. It turned out to be a real good night ... until we heard the screams.

Gunshots—too many to count. Screaming waitresses diving to the ground, covering their heads. Two men strutting into the building with machine guns firing at both Carlo and me. We ducked down beneath our booth as the glass shattered above us. I crouched, blocking my ears while Carlo pulled out his own pistol, firing right back at the fuckers. One of the strippers on the podium was ducking for her life. The worst place to be, in plain sight of the shooter. I tried to get close to pull her down beneath the booth for cover but by the time I got within a few feet, she'd been shot three times in the torso, and once through her forearm. Prior to that, she'd been using a red ribbon as a prop to use with the pole, which somehow tangled in the whole ordeal and left her body hanging awkwardly against that oiled metal, reminiscent of a lifeless trapezist.

The multitude of glass flying in every direction throughout the room made me wonder if I'd be pierced by a bullet, or a rogue shard.

"Johnny!" Carlo yelled in my direction. "Get the fuck up!"

First off, I didn't have a gun on me; I never carried one and never saw the use behind it. Second, I was left stunned. The stripper's body leaned backwards in my direction. Her perished eyes seemed like they were looking into mine. A solitary tear rolled upside down onto her forehead, mixing with the blood and collecting eyeliner as she hung backwards. *I could've sworn she was looking at me.* She was only young. Her life was taken by no fault of her own. This wasn't the first time I'd be seeing something like this. *It was haunting.* Her skimpy outfit was drenched in blood, her body dangled there before me as the glass behind her shattered into a thousand pieces. I couldn't save her. I could slowly hear Carlo's muffled voice tuning back into my ears, screaming for me to—

"Get the fuck up! Johnny! C'mon, move!" Carlo gripped my arm and pulled me up from the booth.

The shooters must've been reloading. I don't know, I couldn't think straight. I was caught in a daze. My body felt cold when the gunshots continued. My adrenaline was so high that by the time we busted out into the alleyway, I wasn't even aware that I had a bullet hole in the back of my left calf.

Before I began living this life, I never witnessed any direct murder. At this point, after a few months on the merry-go-round, I'd already seen several and copped a bullet in the leg. I started to wonder whether this was really what I wanted.

Vinnie's bedroom. I had never felt a pain like it in my entire life. He was a big guy, but he was good with his hands and skillful with a scalpel.

"You're a stupid son of a bitch, you know that?" While I was writhing in my wounds, I had Vinnie giving me a professional lecture. I couldn't help but cringe. "Nobody ever told you that you gotta pack heat?"

"You ever been shot before?" I yelled to the ceiling. "It fucking burns! I think the bullet's fragmented!"

As he hand-stitched the wound, he looked at me, stern. "I've been shot three times before, so cram it. What would your uncle think, ah? He's gonna think you can't handle yourself, now."

It seemed I wasn't the only one conscious of Donnie's opinion of me. I told him it all happened so quickly—the truth—I didn't think. At that point, he lightly slapped my cheek and pointed directly in my face.

"I *know* you didn't think. I was supposed to be sleeping 'cause I got an early morning with the Barresi's, but I'm stuck here stitchin' your ass up for bein' stupid. You're lucky you had young Carlo with you. At least *he's* got his head screwed on straight." Vinnie seemed to have a lot of faith in Carlo, and with good reason. I wouldn't have gotten out of there if it wasn't for his swift heroics. "Now, we gotta get you some crutches and you're gonna look like a donkey at Lucia's on Saturday."

I didn't realize the wedding was so close. It was the first chance to meet everybody formally and I'd be on crutches. I'd have to come up with some other excuse for what happened. While picturing what I'd look like in a suit and crutches, I was welcomed back to reality by Vinnie pouring some clear liquid onto my gunshot wound. It felt like somebody stabbed my leg with a sword, then set the blade on fire and did it again.

***

Four days alone in my bedroom. No socializing, no drop-offs, no leaving the room. They didn't want any attention on the injury and for the most part, even if I wanted to leave the room, I physically couldn't. The time spent alone was more hindering than the wound itself. All I had was cigarettes and TV, cigarettes and TV, all day for four days straight. The same peeling wallpaper, the same dusty furniture. I even counted the number of stripes on the blanket and listed the twenty-nine imperfections on the walls. If you ever wanted an easy way to lose your mind, *this was it.*

Carlo visited me the day before the wedding. I wasn't in a chirpy mood, but could you blame me?

"I'm just sick of bein' cooped up in here like a fucken hermit. I need to be busy or doin' somethin'. I'm going insane over here, Carlo."

Carlo didn't have much to say. Nothing he could have walked into that room with would fix the bleeding, gaping hole in my leg. "I'm sorry about your leg. Does it hurt?"

Does it hurt?

Does it fucking hurt?

Of course it hurt. I think he was just trying to make conversation, but *Jesus Christ*, what a question to ask. I should have told him it didn't.

"I move two inches and it feels like somebody's stickin' their fingers in the wound."

Carlo sighed and nodded. "Either one of us coulda been killed that night. Louie told us to celebrate my birthday and take a few shots—I didn't think he meant it literally."

In the end, Carlo always knew how to make me feel better. I couldn't help but smile, probably over his weak jokes but maybe I was smiling because I was alive, still breathing, knowing I had the chance to laugh once more with a friend.

"There he is! There's that smile I've been missing!" Carlo got comfortable on the bed, repeatedly forgetting about my leg and knocking it numerous times—*excruciating was an understatement.*

He began to talk about work. It was a win-win. He'd have a chance to vent, and I'd get the juice. "We're still doing drop-offs by the docks. Vinnie and Louie have been at each other's throats, arguing like there's no tomorrow. I'm just waiting for one of them to shoot the other." Carlo then looked down at my leg. "You gonna be alright for the wedding tomorrow?" I shrugged, knowing it was going to be a tough ask to get out of bed, let alone attend. "I know it ain't easy sitting in this room alone. I'm here for you, bello—anything you need."

Carlo's the reason I went. Like I said, he really had a heart and that was a rarity around these parts. I felt like he wanted me to be there, like I wasn't some kind of burden. I was one of them. "Where can a guy get a suit around here?"

With midnight on the horizon, I hobbled through the halls of the

Caruso building, slowly getting acquainted with my crutches and moving at the breakneck speed of a snail. As the vulnerability kicked in, so did the pain of the crutches under my arms. I finally reached a door with the moans of a woman on the other side as if a grizzly bear had been ruthlessly smothering her.

"Awhh! Keep going, keep going!" You could probably hear this broad from Philadelphia.

And with Donnie's hasty response, "Shut the fuck up," I knew I had the right apartment.

I tried not to listen in, so I turned around to walk away, but one of my crutches manifested a mind of its own, finding its way to the floor with a loud *thump*. The moaning instantly stopped, and I couldn't walk without the crutch. I was stuck, stranded in front of Donnie's door, before I heard the dreaded footsteps approaching it from the inside. I hesitated, straightening myself up as if I were there with intention, not listening in like a common creep.

The door swung open, and there Donnie stood, puzzled and pulling up his pants. He looked both ways down the hall before addressing me, but I was there alone.

"Johnny? It's almost twelve."

"I was just about to knock but my crutch fell," I stammered. "I'm sorry, Zio. I can go—"

Donnie shook his head and sighed as he pulled a cigar from his pants pocket. "Don't ever be sorry. You're my nephew, I always have time to talk ..." He began looking for a lighter, patting his pockets. "You smoke?"

Considering the vast amount of chain-smoking I'd been doing in that room all alone, I happened to have one in my pocket. "Sometimes."

He glanced at the engraved flip-lighter and admired it. "Where'd you get *this?*"

"Francesca bought it for my birthday a few months back," I said under my breath, knowing he'd forgotten about it.

"Your birthday? Shit, I'm sorry, kid. I'm no good at birthdays." He lit the cigar. "I haven't been around much lately, have I?"

He felt like he let me down, but I wanted to prove that I didn't need him. I was independent, self-reliant. "It's no problem, I'm fitting in pretty well with the guys, anyway."

He nodded, glad to hear it, before we were both disturbed by the unseen flapping dolphin in the apartment. "Where are you, Big Daddy? I'm on the clock."

Donnie turned around and pointed into the room. "Shut the fuck up and wait there. I'm not done with you yet." He closed his eyes in frustration and calmed himself before turning back to me, taking an elongated drag of the cigar. "What can I do for you anyway, Johnny?"

"I need something to do, Zio. If I have to stare at those four walls for another day, I'm gonna end up breaking through it and killing whoever's on the other side." It was purely out of loneliness and the crippling frustration of boredom. I made it clear that I'm not the guy to sit around all day with my feet up. I wanted to show him I was eager, I wanted to prove to him that I could handle this lifestyle; more so I wanted to prove it to myself.

"Look, Johnny." He fiddled with his loose belt. "I'd love for you to help out, but anything we're doing includes physical work or driving. You need to recover. And on top of that, one of my old acquaintances is in town and I can't have a cripple gettin' in the way. Shit's really heating up at the moment for us and I need the more experienced guys on those drop-offs." Donnie was dead serious. He didn't want me working, whether it was for my reasons or his own.

"I can do the drop-offs, Zio," I pled. "Just let me prove that I can get shit done whether I have one good leg or no legs at all—" Before I could finish my sentence, I was yet again disturbed.

"Am I gonna screw myself, or what?" squealed the hooker, sounding like she was packing some kind of bag. After a quick, frustrated exhale, Donnie was about to blow steam from his ears.

"One second, Johnny." He turned back around and busted his own door open like the police, slamming it behind him as he entered the apartment. His yelling was muffled, but it made the walls seem paper-thin. "What part of be quiet don't you fucken understand?" You could just picture the colossal vein on his forehead.

"Geez, alright. I'm sorry," she said under her breath.

Donnie was stern. "Now, you stay here and wait patiently like the little slut you are or you ain't gettin' a single dollar outta me.

Understand?" Let's just say Donnie wasn't a top-notch example of chivalry. He returned to me in deep breaths. "Sorry about that, as you can hear I have a guest—who *won't shut the fuck up.*" He deliberately raised his voice loud enough for her to hear. I knew her night would only get worse the longer I stuck around.

"It's alright, I'll leave you alone. I'll see you tomorrow at the wedding, Zio."

As I turned around, Donnie placed his hand on my shoulder, and I faced him once more. He detached his gold chain from around his own neck and looked at me with sincerity. "I'm sorry I missed your birthday." Donnie passed it over to me. "This is twenty-two carats, direct from India. Don't lose it. I've had it since I was about your age." As he fastened it around my neck, I told him he didn't have to, but he insisted. "It's yours. Thanks for all the work you been doin'. I appreciate it. Your efforts are not goin' unnoticed." He took one last drag of the cigar and passed me the rest of it. "Finish that for me, ah? I'll see you tomorrow at the wedding—I've got a big speech prepared."

After a confident wink, he took a deep breath and neatened his hair before strutting back into his apartment, gently closing the door to continue his unfinished work. Immediately, I could hear the hooker being tickled to a high-pitched hysterical laugh. I looked down at my first Cuban cigar. The taste was bold, yet smooth, unlike any cigarette I'd ever inhaled. As the moaning resumed from the apartment, I hobbled a few steps down the hall until I reached a large, European mirror. I took another long drag of the cigar and ran my fingers along the gold chain which glistened under the hallway lights.

This is what I'd been missing.

I couldn't help but stare at my reflection, in admiration of my newfound stature.

Chapter Three

Marianne

I was dreading the reception but, in our culture, you don't miss a wedding unless you're dead, and I'm sure glad I wasn't. In the largest of the Caruso building function rooms, Francesco and Lucia celebrated their love in matrimony. Amid the dealings, the drop-offs, and murder without relent, these were the flickers of light, love, and togetherness.

Rosana, tall, blonde, mid-forties, and exceptionally gorgeous, approached me the second I limped in on my crutches. She had a stunning Italian accent, almost unchanged since she'd been living in America, yet polished enough to roll every word off her tongue in style.

"Little Johnny, is that you?"

Her surprised voice was croakier than I remembered. *Was it age?* No. Rosana was a star back in Catania. At sixteen, she was deemed to be the next big thing. She possessed the literal voice of an angel, and I mean enough to make any man collapse to his knees. Anywhere she sang, she made people cry to the heavens, even if they didn't know her. She had a talent nobody could match, performing in shows from Rome to Paris, sometimes with audiences of over thirty thousand people. Her voice was a silky slice of heaven ... until she met a boy. At eighteen, America came calling. This was her big break. The boy, let's call him *Jack*, didn't like the prospect of her departure. It was either jealousy—because he had no talent or aspirations of his own—or he was used to living off her like a parasite. One night, Jack became violent when Rosana seemingly chose her dream over him. And within a twenty-second struggle, he'd somehow knocked her down and supposedly stomped on her neck, crushing her vocal cords to bits. No doubt he knew what he was doing. He destroyed her voice, her dream, and her career. An angelic slaughter. Nobody heard that same voice again after the reconstructive surgery of her mangled esophagus. As for Jack? There were but few stories tossed around over his fate, but through Rosana's connections, her parents and family back home, one tale seemed to stick. We all heard that they tore Jack's own larynx out of his neck, along with his ears, his eyes, and his genitals, before dropping him off on the island of Grotta Dell'amore. Chances are he either fell off a cliff and drowned, or he simply starved or froze to death.

Anyway, let's not get sidetracked. I hadn't seen Rosana since I was about six, and she was still as beautiful as ever. Jack may have taken her voice, but nobody could ever take her beauty.

"Rosa? I'm seein' a ghost!" With a kiss on both cheeks, it was refreshing to recognize a familiar face within this new life of mine.

"What on earth happened to your leg?" She covered her mouth, staring down at my crutches.

I looked over at Donnie and Vinnie gasbagging in the distance. "Car wreck," I muttered with a shrug. "It's not all bad though. It means I can catch up on TV!"

She laughed. "Some things never change, ah?"

She then mentioned that she wanted to introduce me to her niece, Larissa, in hope that she could set something up, but I was in no way to think about women in the current state I was in. "You must at least meet her later. She's a darling!"

"Rosana," I smirked. "Anybody related to *you* would be."

She laughed, claiming that I was just as cheeky as she'd remembered. Carlo soon joined the conversation having not yet met Rosana. He looked at her like he'd look at a slice of rich, chocolate fudge cake. Before Rosana left me with Carlo, she said something peculiar, something I'd never forget. "If you need anything, anything at all, you let me know. I know how difficult Donnie can be." I think everybody already knew what kind of man he was. Except me.

As Rosana walked away, swayin' her hips, Carlo asked me why I hadn't introduced her earlier. *As if he had a chance.* She was married and he was twenty-one while she was nearing her fifties. She was old enough to be his mother.

Carlo placed his hand on my shoulder. "I'm glad you came, man.

Really."

"Of course. Can't miss a beautiful night like this. I also can't stand starin' at that fucking wall all day." I reverted right back to the depressed old hermit I was the night before. I was well in need of a couple drinks because I wanted to smile, I wanted to be better. I was never the type of person to kill a mood, and I wasn't going to let myself become that. The only feeling worse than avoiding somebody—is being the person who is avoided.

Carlo sipped his drink, leaving his arm around my shoulder and forcing a smile out of me. "I know *just* the thing to make you feel better. There're a couple dolls coming out to the bar upstairs tonight, I used to know them way back when I was younger—"

As much as I really wanted to listen to Carlo's story, my attention was wrenched by a figure across the room. I'd never seen her before. Young, maybe eighteen. Long, wavy brunette hair with beautiful big brown eyes and glossy, supple lips. Perfect in every way possible before I was even able to meet her. She wore a beige dress with an elegant cut right down the side. Traditional, but enough to liquefy you. She was playing the grand piano, talented but shy. I wanted to know more. She focused solely on the notes she was playing, pressing each key as if they were designed to draw me to her. As she moved her hair out of her face, she glanced at me with a short smile, before her eyes returned to the ivories.

As she smiled at me for a second time in succession, she took a sip from a glass of water. My future flashed before my eyes. *She was it.*

Apologies for the spoiler, but I end up killing her, along with her father ... I know that's not what you wanted to hear but that's how this story goes. I looked around that reception and acknowledged Carlo and Castello giggling together, the children chasing each other, and the newlyweds dancing for the first time, I needed to remember the rules of this game: *Never make close connections, friends or girlfriends.* One day, you're kissing her forehead, talking about your future, and the next, she's dead.

I nudged Carlo, interrupting his conversation with Castello. "What is it?" Carlo snapped.

"Who's the dame over there, by the keys?" I tried to be discreet by swinging my head in her general direction.

Carlo sniggered softly. He knew all about her. "Better be careful, my friend. If you're looking for a bad girl, then she ain't the one. She's the goody of the bunch. Her name's Marianne. I've known her since preschool."

I couldn't stop staring at her. I was mesmerized. As much as I wanted to look away at the risk of her noticing my stare, I simply couldn't muster the strength. Not in a million years would I give up a second looking at anything else. She was right there, it was unavoidable. She glanced at me again from the keys. I shot her a nod, to show that I was a human rather than the mannequin that I felt I was. She looked away again; I think she was shy, too. After a few seconds, she looked back and shot me a smile. My heart skipped a beat, and my lungs had to readjust. I blocked out whatever Carlo was saying because my mind could only focus on one thing. The notes she was playing were more dramatic at this point. She was playing my emotions, literally on the keyboard. She controlled my heart with every chord from every ligament that slightly moved within her forearms. When her song finished, the audience applauded.

Carlo chimed back into my ear, "If you got the hots for her, you needa know a couple things. She's a *Manzelli*. You do not fuck with the Manzellis. They don't care who you are or what connections you got." A crowd of people approached the piano where she sat pretty, congratulating her. "Johnny, if you plan to make a move with her ... you better make it count." Carlo was in my ear, but she was in my head.

Among the crowd of people around her, she looked directly at me, almost for some kind of validation. I remember smiling and raising my glass to her with a charming grin. And somewhere between her smiling back at me and closing the fallboard over the keys, I knew I wouldn't want anybody else, ever. I felt my heart beating out of my chest like some cheesy cartoon, accompanied by the love-heart eyes and a lengthy draping tongue. *I wanted her, and nobody was about to change my mind.*

The balcony of the function room was a peaceful escape from the roaring festivities inside. I leaned on the stone railing beside Marianne, gazing over the city and its glistening lights. When she was around, she seemed to brighten everything else, as if an aura of light was beaming onto everything surrounding it. It wasn't just looks either; she was the smartest woman I'd ever known. One of the first things you'd notice was her soft, delicate, and feathery voice.

"So, even back home you're a city boy?"

Even talking to her, I almost forgot I was on crutches. I was weightless, transcendent. "It's nothin' like this. The city's not as bright, the women aren't as beautiful." Which was a lie because back home, nearly every woman was a work of art but even *they* couldn't hold a candle to Marianne.

She looked at me with a smile, acknowledging how cheeky, yet cheesy that compliment was. "You're a talker, aren't you?"

"There's a lot more to me than that." I smiled. "Where'd you learn to play the keys that good?" She giggled to herself, modest. Her laugh rippled down my spine as if every bone in my body was elevated—or maybe it was just my vertebrae giving way from being on my feet too long after the injury. I probably should've had it checked out.

"My mother taught me to play when I was younger. I'm really not that good."

"Are you fucken kidding me? You were great. I couldn't take my eyes off you that whole time." She instantly placed her white-nailed index finger on my lips—so soft and slick that my lips felt like rocks in comparison. *The electricity began to conduct.*

"Don't swear. A man is a lot more attractive without the gutter mouth."

I sniggered at the comment. "What are you … my mother?" As I leaned in to kiss her, she pulled away.

"I'm sorry." She hesitated. "My parents are gonna show up any second and if somebody saw me kissing you ..." She was lost in a gaze, mid-sentence. "News spreads quick in a family like this, ya know?"

I sniggered again and glanced over the balcony. "Hey, look! That's them showin' up now! It takes approximately three minutes to catch the elevator up to this floor, which means we have exactly one hundred and eighty seconds before they blow my brains out."

Marianne giggled and raised her eyebrow with a smirk that'd make you jump right off that balcony, knowing you got to witness the greatest view of all time before your bone-crushing demise.

"You don't even know what my folks look like. And if you knew my father, he'd take much longer to reach us."

I persisted, "With that fact, you're only giving me more reason to."

She smiled, pressing her lips in thought before glancing inside to the party. She moved closer to me, as if hovering, levitating off the ground. "Well, I don't really think anybody can see us …"

My hands found their way to her waist as she gazed into my eyes. *Ecstasy.* No better feeling in the world. Before my lips could reach hers, the doors opened wide, and the loud music was reintroduced to the balcony.

Angela, about twenty, cake-faced with a sour grin—her clothes not leaving too much to the imagination considering it was a wedding—stared at us both. She had two other girls on either side of her. I let go of Marianne instantly, not yet having met these magnificently disruptive women.

"You wanna get your meat hooks off our Marianne?" Angela was a snappy, possessive little swine. Marianne rolled her eyes. She herself wasn't Angela's biggest fan.

"Leave us alone, Ange. We shut the door for a reason." As Angela completely ignored Marianne's comment, she continued gawking at me as if I were about to challenge her for Marianne's hand in a bloody Roman arena.

"Listen, new guy. You know who her father is?"

Marianne proceeded to scratch her head and ignore them by gazing at the tiled floor.

"Just be careful, Mary. He's a chatter-bug. Don't want him to be another victim of the Manzelli family." For some horrible reason, Angela leered at me, as if she was jealous of Marianne's interaction with me.

I simply gave up. I turned to Marianne with a sigh, yet a smile. I wasn't disappointed; in fact, I was glad—glad to have spent whatever few seconds we had together, knowing they wouldn't be the last. "I'll catch up with you some other time, okay? Maybe we'll get some *privacy.*" I grazed her chin with my thumb before collecting my crutches. Marianne scowled at Ange. Oh, she was satisfied with her work, breaking us up like that. She even managed to throw in a quick zinger before I made my way off the balcony.

"Look out for him, Marianne. These guys are always trouble. At least get a man that can walk on two feet." Aside from Marianne, the girls almost stumbled to the ground like a pack of hysterical hyenas. Instead, Marianne and I were in our own world, still gazing at each other as if those carnivorous mammals weren't there at all.

I rejoined the reception.

Back inside, Carlo interrogated me over my whereabouts.

"I knew you'd like her," he smirked.

"Am I *that* predictable?"

Carlo smiled daringly as he finished his drink. "I know your type," he said as he surveyed the group of girls. "You're too respectable to go for Angela—in other words, *cake-face*—but you're too experienced to go for Sophia. Plus, Marianne stands out in the crowd, and I know you like a diamond that shines."

I smirked. "You got a way with words, pal. Are you sure *you're* not in love with her?"

Carlo laughed obnoxiously and gestured across the room. "No, no, I have my eyes on my own beauty."

Larissa, Carlo's childhood crush, and, little did he know, Rosana's niece. To get the heat off my ass, I persuaded him to ask her out. He was shy but I knew I could sway him considering I had already made a move to show my own interest. *Peer pressure is a wonderful thing. Alcohol helps, too.*

"I've liked her for so long, man. I've just been building up the courage to ask her out." Carlo fiddled with his fingers, twisting a silver ring a hundred times like a ritual.

Larissa was, of course, gorgeous. She had this contagious smile that'd spread to whomever she spoke to like an uncontrollable, ineradicable disease. She was sitting at the table alone, occasionally looking over at Carlo. A very well-presented young woman with the posture of a seasoned nun.

"Well, she keeps lookin' at you, so either you're creepin' her the fuck out, or you stop talkin' about askin' her and actually grow some balls and *do it*."

Carlo batted me away, laughing. "Okay, Casanova, but not tonight."

"Carlo, if it's not tonight, then it's never gonna *be* the night. Just go tell her she looks beautiful, or somethin'." I was preparing myself to make a couple clucking noises but before I knew it, Carlo chugged another drink before setting forth on his quest to win Larissa, grabbing another drink to greet her with. All he needed was a push and he started up like an old reliable lawnmower.

Although my focus was fixed on Carlo, I couldn't help but glance at the balcony, where Marianne laughed with her friends. As much as they said what they said, and ruined the moment that they ruined, she was still forgiving and friendly to them. To me, that didn't sound like somebody who came from a deadly, vengeful, or spiteful family.

"You're a good friend to him." Castello appeared beside me with two cocktails. "He needs somebody like you."

"Can I ask you something?" I turned to Castello.

Castello stuck his finger in his drink after a fly fell into it. "What's on your mind, Johnny?"

"Who are the Manzellis?"

Castello immediately stopped fiddling with the glass. He looked up at me with one raised eyebrow. "That's a rusty can o' worms better left unopened, Johnny. Estevan Manzelli is a sneaky, slimy bastard. He's somebody that you ought to keep at arm's length ... maybe best avoided altogether."

What could be so dangerous about this family that even the Carusos would be afraid of?

"So, what about Marianne?" I asked, destined to get to the bottom of it—determined to find some kind of green light among the words and food scraps flying out of Castello's mouth as he bit into his fifth crusty cannoli.

"That's his daughter. She's a good girl, probably the most ambitious and academic outta all of them. Why the curiosity?"

I shrugged, sipping my drink. I didn't want to seem eager because I knew this'd be someone Donnie wouldn't want me fraternizing with. Castello made that quite clear. I could tell he already knew that whatever he could say wasn't going to sway me away from her. He leaned in, serious.

"Keep your nose clean, kid. If I have any advice for you at all, it's to *keep your nose clean as a whistle.* With anybody in that family, you're either all in, or you're all out."

He was deadpan, and I mean you would've thought he was having a stroke or something, and it lasted a couple of seconds, too. I realized he was waiting for some kind of acknowledgement of my understanding.

"I get it." That's all I could say. I didn't say I would take a chance, but I also didn't say I wouldn't.

As Castello placed his glass firmly on the table, I looked over at Marianne rejoining the reception with her friends. She looked directly at me. It was like she'd been walking in slow motion, floating, perhaps.

Castello whispered into my ear, firm. "All I'm sayin' is ... Play. It. Safe."

***

Speeding through the streets of Staten Island on a golden afternoon, the world melted into motion blur. Being safe was laughable when we were together. I gripped the wheel of the black convertible with the top down, the wind roaring like a wild hymn around us. Beside me, Marianne sat radiant—her brunette hair thrashing in the breeze like a banner for everything pure, reckless, and free. Her lipstick, bright as fresh blood, caught the light each time she threw her head back in laughter. She screamed—not in panic, but in euphoria. It was a scream of liberation, of being young and untouchable, like she'd finally been unshackled from the expectations wrapped around her like chains.

I stomped on the pedal, forcing the car to break-neck speeds, driving our adrenaline sky-high. I watched as the young, academic, traditional daddy's girl carelessly threw her arms to the sky, fingers splayed as if grasping the clouds—she was the very manifestation of liberty. I stole glances while trying to keep the car steady, watching her revel in the danger, in the speed, in me. It wasn't the kind of beauty you admire—it was the kind that consumes you. She didn't need the brakes. She needed the chaos. And I didn't just see her, I felt her in my chest, in the marrow of my bones. She wasn't a girl anymore; she was a revelation. Soft yet wild, sweet yet volatile, innocent yet unrepentantly dangerous. She made every breath taste like the first hit of oxygen after drowning.

When I was with her, there were moments where time would stand still. If you've ever experienced love before, you'd know exactly what I mean when I say that. The way her hair fluttered in the wind. The way her nose scrunched when she laughed, looking into my eyes. But most of all, the way she'd look at you like you've never been looked at by anybody else you've ever met before in your entire life. That look in her eyes will tell you that there is no other place you'd rather be. I could already envision our future in technicolor.

The current was alive. In motion. It was electric.

Chapter Four

Risk Over Reward

Castello always told me that this business was like playing a round of poker or blackjack. One day, you'd be winning—the next, you'd be two nickels from broke. The more you stick your neck out, the higher your risk of losing everything. Except in this specific game of poker, it wasn't chips you were gambling with—it was your life.

Angelo. An arrogant, bald recruit, and about the height of a fucken emu—with the brain of one too. Gambling with Donnie's dollar, his feet were up on the table—a fitting representation of the disrespectful bastard he was.

"Hit me."

I stood beside Louie and Carlo, checking our watches and shaking our heads at the amount this guy was throwing away. He tapped on the table yet again as a sour glare grew upon Louie's face.

"Hit me," Angelo squawked again.

In this business, with this amount of risk, you need to keep a straight face. You can't tell anybody what your next move is.

Louie was trying to keep his cool, but he usually had trouble hiding it. Angelo didn't even dignify Louie by turning around. Not even an acknowledging nod—nothing. I think he simply got too comfortable.

"Wait a minute, fellas. We'll go soon. I don't know why Big Donnie wants to see me so bad, anyway. He knows I'm good for it." And as Angelo stared at the dealer across the table, he said those dreaded words once again.

"Hit me."

It's all just a game of chance. It only depends on who the unlucky one is. You take one little risk in this business, and you could easily be the one that gets *hit*.

Angelo looked at the hesitant dealer with wide eyes. "Did ya hear me, asshole? I said *hit me!*"

As I drove the four of us from the casino, Angelo sat in the passenger seat. I knew we had to make a stop on the way. It was close to my old brokerage firm, a perfect little secluded alley, at the stroke of midnight.

"What the hell's goin' on? What's the big idea?" Angelo still didn't get it. He never would. Although, I could see the gradual emergence of sweat beads on his forehead.

As the car stood stationary, idling in the cold alley, the only thing other than the thin ice on the windows was the swift spray of blood painted on it from the inside. Carlo held the gun from the seat behind Angelo.

The noise is what got me.

Silenced or not, a gunshot in a confined space is so fucking loud that you'd hear ringing for the next ten minutes and wonder if you'd be deaf for the rest of your life. I glanced over at Angelo from behind the wheel. His head rested on the dashboard, blood still trickling from it. *My stomach turned.* Like I said, you can't even consider taking chances in this business. Louie caught Angelo gambling on Donnie's dollar at the casino. Once was bad enough, but this was a third offense.

Louie placed his hand on my shoulder, and I flinched, still startled by the incident. "Let's get 'im in the trunk."

"Lucky it didn't bust the windshield," Carlo said, unloading the pistol. These fellas were more concerned over the wellbeing of the car's auto glass than the man in the passenger seat with a gaping hole in the back of his skull.

Louie responded, "It's only a thirty-two, it probably didn't even leave his brain."

We stepped out of the car, making sure the road was clear in all directions before I gave the signal for Carlo to pull Angelo's body from the passenger seat.

"Johnny?"

My eyes darted to the origin from which the familiar, yet unexpected female voice had sounded. Robin, the seductress from the firm, stood there like a deer in headlights and high heels. She recognized me before recognizing the corpse being removed from the sedan. Her lipstick fell to the ground. She barely had time to react.

I looked at Carlo.

Carlo looked at Louie.

Louie raised his gun.

I shook my head. "No—"

Before I could even register the sound of the gunshot, Robin's body hit the ground. Her knees clattered on the concrete. Glancing back at Louie, the gun was aimed at her torso. My one good leg failed to support me, and I kneeled to the ground to collect myself. A hole resided in my stomach and felt as if it were getting bigger. *She was dead.* He'd killed her. Robin was dead. Carlo rushed back to work, shoving Angelo, and now Robin, in the trunk. I was still in shock, both hands clawing my own scalp in horror. Carlo scooped the lipstick she'd dropped on the ground, throwing it in the trunk before slamming it shut.

And just like that, Robin didn't exist anymore. Just like Angelo, she disappeared without a trace, never to be seen again. Just a statistic in this city full of statistics.

***

Marianne and I sat on the floor of my apartment bedroom, watching *Casablanca* on a small TV in the corner of the room while I played with her hair. I never understood why, but she loved it. Maybe it reminded her that somebody was there with her, that she wasn't alone. It was some measure of safety, some sense of security. Getting used to this life means getting used to the lines that cannot be crossed. Business and pleasure stay separated. This proved to be the most difficult part of it.

How can I be the same Johnny day in, day out?

I must've asked myself a thousand times if Robin's death was my fault, or just a cruel coincidence. Whether I'd known her or not, they would've shot her anyway. She would've witnessed it. But *I* was driving. *Maybe my subconscious brain led me down those familiar streets where I started at the firm? Therefore, inadvertently placing her in the crossfire?* I would have gone insane thinking about it.

I decided to suppress it like everything else. Cigarettes and TV.

Marianne and I couldn't tell anyone what we were doing but we couldn't keep away from each other either. She was perfection in a human being, and I promise, I really did fall in love with her. She was the kind of girl who would give you everything, so long as you did the same for her. But if you didn't treat her right, she'd up and leave. And God knows, I treated her right.

"You're missing home again, aren't you?" During my thousand-yard stare, I hadn't noticed she'd been watching me through the TV's reflection.

"Yeah … a bit."

I kissed the nape of her neck, and she smiled. It was a distraction, for her and for me. Although I couldn't see her face, I could feel the muscles on her neck stiffen and her jaw tighten.

I lit a cigarette I'd been saving from the previous night with the boys.

It was Vinnie's birthday the night before, and he wanted to go fishing, so Donnie had an old friend of his lend us his yacht. Well ... he said it was a yacht, but you'd sooner relate it to a fishing dinghy crafted from used, rusted tin cans. With Donnie, Carlo, Castello, Vinnie, and Louie, the boat barely had enough space for the fishing gear. And to make matters worse, there was some unexpected rain—heavy rain. I yearned for a cigarette, scabbing one off Louie, but the moment I'd light it, I knew it'd be swept by the waves or the spitting water, so I held it tight in my pocket and endured the miserable birthday of Vinnie's— leaving me never wanting to be out at sea again.

As the tobacco strands ignited piece by piece, I was back in my apartment with Marianne's silky hair in front of me. Such contrast, such comfort, content to be in such a warm, cozy environment.

"You know, my aunt has lung cancer." Marianne whipped her hair back. "And they say it's from smoking those cigarettes." She looked at the cigarette dangling from my fingers with disdain.

I couldn't help but laugh to myself as the smoke escaped my mouth. "If I had a dollar for every time somebody told me that, I'd be richer than my uncle." Her eyes turned downward, and I realized my insensitivity to her words. She was like an armor-piercing bullet. Nobody could change my mind like she could. No matter what she'd use to convince you, you'd always listen in the end.

"You don't want me to smoke no more?"

"I can give you a good reason not to," she smirked. "The smell of that cigarette's gonna get into my hair and when I get home, my father isn't gonna be so happy with me ... or *you* for that matter." She fluffed at her hair, knowing I wouldn't take another puff after that.

Marianne Manzelli had a power over me like no one else did. I must admit, I was a stubborn son of a bitch in my younger years but with her, I toppled over like a one-wheeled wagon.

"Kiss me."

"Your mysterious father might show up," I smirked.

She giggled and grasped my cheeks with both her hands. "Such a masculine jawline. Almost like it was sculpted by Rodin himself."

She pulled me closer and kissed both my cheeks, slowly making her way to my lips. Her eyes locked on mine. I was left hypnotized, like a drug that left me stuck in a solitary time-lapse that phased out any sense of reality. She quickly turned back around and tugged at her hair, expecting me to stroke it again. A tease. A welcomed torment.

She'd then asked about my mother. My mother died when I was younger. That's all I told her. I didn't want the hauntings of my past and the absence of my mother to burden the current perfection of the situation. I wasn't usually somebody to complain, or wail about the past, whether or not it weighed on my mind.

"I'm sorry. I just noticed there were no photos of her in here." She glanced around the room for any photo or hint of me even having a mother—or having a past before New York. I admit I made it difficult.

"I don't keep photos." I shrugged. "It's not healthy to dwell on the past." I wanted to change the subject. Talking about my mother would take me back to when I was younger. I didn't want to show too much emotion in front of Marianne—not at this point of our exchanges anyway. That didn't stop her.

"What did she look like?"

I looked up to the ceiling, thinking of my mother. "Beautiful, like an angel, only bringing warmth when she came around ... before God blessed her with wings."

Marianne looked at me. I had struck a chord somewhere inside her. "You're quite the poet, Johnny Caruso. Do you talk like this around Carlo?"

I laughed at the idea of it. "If I talk like that, I'll probably get whacked."

"Well, you can be yourself around me. And that counts for something." Marianne understood the sensitivity of the topic, but she also knew how important family was, and that's what I loved about her. It wasn't all about the glitz and glamor of the good life. It was personal, the human touch. Her eyes were trained on me. I could almost see her mind working. "Why wouldn't you put up a photo? It's not about remembering her ... No man will ever forget his mother. Photos can be a tribute of how special she was to you."

She had me. I did think about my mother that night, for the first time in a while. The fire, the screams, the suffering ... the confusion of it all. I even thought about my sister. I needed to be stronger than this.

Why is it that I can only reflect on the bad things?

I lightly nudged Marianne's nose with my knuckle. "Boop!"

She batted me away, giggling. "Johnny!"

I continued playing with her hair and watching the movie. But I couldn't focus, only looking down at her, content that she was mine and mine only. The resurfacing of these emotional memories somehow strengthened the bond with Marianne. In any emotional state, you usually latch on to the closest thing that understands.

Marianne was a smart girl, different from the rest. How many teenage girls can you find who actually know who Auguste Rodin is? She didn't want me to think she needed me, but more like I needed her. She was a privilege, not a right.

***

Thursday night. It was a surprisingly cold evening considering it was nearing summer. Castello had picked me up and we headed north of Manhattan toward Connecticut for a special delivery

Castello tried to make conversation to break the silence after the week I'd had. "So, how's the family back in Catania, anyway?"

"Look, Cas. I don't mean to be rude, but I don't feel like small talk. I still keep seeing Robin's face." I stared out the window, watching the storm clouds approaching the east.

"What do ya think I'm tryna do, Johnny?" Castello shrugged. "Shit happens, and small talk is the way we deal with things around here. Without it, we'd all go insane in the pits of our minds."

I turned to him. He was right. This was partly why these guys spoke so much shit all the time. Conversations that seemingly went nowhere.

"So? *How's the family?*" Cas focused on the road.

"It's only my sister over there. She's two years older than me and she has schizophrenia." I sighed, leaning my head on the passenger window. "And she's got this druggo boyfriend who's a gambler. So, not too good."

"You ever think of goin' back? Takin' care of things?" Castello seemed genuinely interested in my family back home. I glanced at him and sniggered. He then pointed at me. "Just remember: Family comes first, Johnny. I'm not saying go over there and save the day but if you can, send her a couple hundred a month to get by, you know?"

I understood what he meant. My sister and I hadn't really connected since our early teenage years. I didn't want to remember the past. I trained myself only to look ahead, but I think Castello was trying to get me to remember where I came from, and not get so caught up in this life that I forgot who I was.

"What about you?" I asked.

Castello shrugged. "What *about* me?" He was happy to ask me questions but seemed to dodge them when the pendulum swung the other way.

"You got family over there?"

"Nope, haven't been to Niscemi for over twenty-five years."

"Then what about here?" I persisted.

"What *about* it?"

I couldn't help but laugh. "You got a family, or what, Cas?"

Castello finally broke his silence. "I got a pregnant wife and a stepdaughter." I was surprised and with a burst of happiness, I nudged him on the shoulder. "Ouch! Watch it!"

I congratulated him but he stood me down immediately. "Just keep it to yourself, will ya?" I protested, claiming that this was something to celebrate but he responded abruptly, "No."

Castello took a few seconds to gather himself and after a deep breath, he looked over at me. "When you're in a business like this, you do a lotta things you regret, kid ... Unintentionally, you make enemies, and all those enemies start to know your name." Castello was serious but it wasn't that that worried me. It was the dull, empty look in his eyes that sent chills down my spine. "How do you get revenge on somebody that killed one of your family members?" I couldn't answer. I could only stare into his hollow eyes as he explained. "You might think you'd kill them, right?" I nodded, assuming that was the answer, but he shook his head. "Wrong. That'd be too easy, you'd be letting him off the hook. The way to make a man pay for his sins, is to not attack his heart, but attack everything surrounding it. You strike at everything he holds dear, to make him live the rest of his life in misery, wishing he could erase that *one* second of his life that he spent pulling the trigger on that *one* family member he stole from you. Destroy the armor, and the heart will deteriorate. And that's why, Johnny. That's why I keep my family well away from this shit. I don't need that happening to me."

As we arrived at an abandoned warehouse, I offered my personal, dampened congratulations on the pregnancy, and this time he accepted gracefully. "Thanks, Johnny. You're a good kid, you know that?"

"Thought of any names yet?"

Castello cracked up and waved his hand at me. "Okay, now you're gettin' too personal. Drop the subject." We had arrived at our destination.

As we stepped out of the car, the only sound we could hear was the wind whistling through the trees. I felt the hackles on my neck rise. I grabbed my crutch, only needing one after the few weeks of recovery. The only sound heard was the loose gravel beneath our shoes, crumbling together as we approached the shady warehouse. Castello walked slowly behind me.

Something was off. "What are we doin' here so late, anyway?" I shivered. "We ain't got any briefcases."

Castello sighed. "This isn't a briefcase swap, kid. Donnie wants to have a serious talk with ya. There's a little problem he's been meanin' to … discuss."

At this point I was ready to shit my trousers and get the fuck out of there. For sure, Donnie knew about Marianne. For sure, it's impeded the family—for fucking sure, I was a loose end they were about to cut off. This was the end of my story. I was the problem he was about to *sort out*.

I hobbled to the side door that Castello led me to and entered cautiously, unknowing of whether I was going to be ambushed by a barrage of bullets or strangled until my veins popped.

Castello and I opened the door to find an empty warehouse, with a man taped to a chair in the center and a plastic bag over his head. You could see the bag moving from the quick breaths he was taking. He was still alive. Donnie then made his magnificent entrance, strutting in from a back room with something hidden behind his back.

"What's going on here?" I couldn't make heads nor tails of the situation.

"Johnny, how's the leg?" Donnie said in his gritty and arrogant tone. He revealed a baseball bat, gripping it tight with his right hand as he approached me.

I felt a trickle of fear creep up my spine, backing away and guarding my leg with my crutch. "What's that for?"

He instead laughed at me, spinning it in his hand. "This ain't for you. It's for *him*." He pointed the bat directly at the man strapped to the chair. "He look familiar to you?"

I shook my head. "Not at all, Zio."

"Not one tiny bit?" Donnie was sure I knew who it was. At that point, the man started struggling in the chair. "Where the fuck do you think *you're* goin'?" Donnie strode toward him and tore the bag right off his head. He was in his late twenties. A beard-covered face. Turkish, I'd assume. Donnie forcefully gripped the man's chin and directed it toward me. "You remember that? You fucking scumbag. That's my fucking nephew!"

The taped-up man instantly shook his head. "I don't know what you're talking about! I swear! You've got the wrong guy!"

Donnie raised the bat, ready to swing. "Say that again for me. Do it."

"You've got the wrong guy! Please? I don't know why I'm here!"

One swing, a crack to his leg. The man screamed, looking directly at the ceiling above.

"Say it again, you lyin' prick! You're only makin' it worse for yourself!"

You could tell the man was already tasting blood. "Please? Stop!" His eyes begged for mercy. Donnie proceeded to slam his leg with the bat, over and over. The sound progressed from the solid sound of knocking wood to a fleshy, pasty thumping. Every hit with the bat, I'd cringe more and more. I wanted to close my eyes but more so, I wanted it to stop. If Donnie saw me close my eyes, I'd look weak in *his*. Castello stared blankly at the beating. He was numb to these things by now.

"You gonna apologize for this? For what you did to my nephew's leg?" The man looked up at him as the tears streamed down his face and the blood streamed down his leg. He couldn't even support his own head. Donnie wasn't finished. He punched him. "Look at me!" He struck him again. "Was it a random hit, or do you know who we are?"

The man shook his head, too startled to speak.

"Answer me, you worthless fuck! Was it a random hit, or *do you know who we are?* 'Cause if you knew who we were, you wouldn't have fucked with us, am I right?" Donnie gripped the bat once more.

The man spoke through fear. "We were just robbing the place! It was nothing personal, it was nothing personal!"

Donnie sniggered to himself. "So, you *admit* it was you? Then why'd you say it wasn't?" He gripped the man's hair, pulling his head backwards. "Why did you say it wasn't? You said you didn't know anything about that! So, you're a liar now, too? How the fuck am I supposed to believe any of the tripe that comes outta that mouth?" He gripped his hair tighter and yanked it sideways to lock eyes with him, grinding teeth as he spoke. "Look at me when I'm talkin' to you!"

Donnie snatched a concealed pistol from his back pocket. He aimed, point-blank at the man's head. He turned around, looking directly at me. I knew I was going to have something more to do with this. He spoke softly. "Johnny, where were you shot?" He lowered the gun and instead aimed it up and down the man's leg, like some kind of circus game. "Johnny. Where was it?"

I had to say something. I couldn't help but stammer. "It was just in my leg, Zio."

Donnie nodded with frustration, shutting his eyes, impatient. "I know, but which part?" As the pistol moved slowly up and down the man's leg, my eyes darted between Donnie's psychotic grin and the taped man's pleading face, begging me not to speak with whatever persuasion he could wring out of his dying eyes. "Pick a part, any part, Johnny. We ain't got all fucking night." The man breathed in, nervous as the gun began moving faster up and down his leg. The quicker the gun moved, the quicker my hyperventilation kicked in. "What, are you fucken deaf, Johnny?"

I had to spit something out, worried that one of those bullets had my name on it. "The back of my calf," I stuttered.

Donnie then employed a daring smile. He had his answer. He just required one more piece of information. "Which one?"

I took a long, deep breath before taking a sincere glance into the man's desperate eyes. I looked away. "Left."

The man's left calf was blown to bits. I'd never heard a man scream louder than that. Blood and bits of adipose tissue puddled the floor around him. The squealing almost sounded like setting fire to a fucking pig.

Donnie stood back up, wiping the blood off his own face and punching the man once more. He continued to scream.

"Shut the fuck up!" Donnie pointed.

How could the man have possibly been expected to control his screams under such agony?

"Shut your fucken mouth!" The impatient Donnie snatched the plastic bag on the floor and wrapped it over the man's face. "Keep screamin', I dare ya!"

You bet he kept screaming. But soon his screams began to disappear as his legs flailed in every direction, suffocating and shaking his head as if possessed. Donnie still hadn't had enough. He gripped the baseball bat once again.

"Stop." I couldn't take any more of it.

Donnie paused, insulted by his own nephew for whom he was doing this. He looked directly at me, exhausted, wiping the blood off his cheek and neatening his ravaged hair. "Pardon? Did you just tell me to stop?" He dropped the baseball bat on the ground and approached me with his cocky strut, seasoned for intimidation. Even in a situation like this, he'd still be on his high horse.

"If you want him dead, just get it over with ..." I didn't want to see any more of it. The man had suffered enough. This was too far, and it was the first time I could see how monstrous this man could be. The stories told no tale to what reality Donnie had lived. Any other man would fall sick before finishing the job. The taped man continued to suffocate, struggling with the bag over his airways. Castello looked away instantly, crossing his arms and steering clear of Donnie's imminent outburst.

"Fine." Donnie poked a hole in the bag, introducing the air back to the man's weary lungs. *Relief.* He gasped rapidly, breathing once again. I thought it was over. He thought it was over. *Poor bastard.*

Donnie approached me and I gulped. He moved uncomfortably close to my face, staring directly into my eyes at point blank. "I always knew you were a soft bitch, ever since you were young." Those words struck like a bolt of lightning to my chest. Before I could respond, he placed his pistol firmly against that same chest. "I'm gonna watch you. I want him dead, now."

"I can't." I coughed the words out with the air escaping my exhausted lungs.

"Excuse me?"

"I can't do it." I looked over once more to the man taped to the chair, bent forward, defeated. He was already more than halfway down the road to death, dripping blood onto the concrete beneath him, as if red oil were leaking from a car.

"You can't do what?"

I looked down at the gun, then to Castello, hoping he'd say something to help me escape the situation, but his eyes averted mine.

Donnie willfully entered my sight. "*Don't* look at him. I'm the one talkin' to you."

I had to stall him. "Are you sure you even got the right guy?" Donnie didn't move one bit.

"Pull the damn trigger."

He was clear as day. There was no way out of this. "There were two guys. It coulda been the other ... Why are you making me do this?"

"You said you wanted to prove that you can get shit done, am I right?" Donnie tilted his head. I could feel his hot breath against my cheek. "Or am I just wasting my fucking time with you?"

The man on the chair knew his fate the moment he was taped to that chair. He looked up at me. "I'm sorry." He could barely speak amongst the blood exiting his mouth. "I'm so sorry." He sobbed as the red tears fell directly from his eyes onto the floor.

"You're a part of us, now. This man wronged you. End him."

I cocked the gun and took a few steps toward the man. Donnie stayed where he was, anticipating the release of the inevitable bullet. I took aim, pointing a gun for the first time at another human being. I was about to stop his heart from beating. His legs were soaked in blood and his face was sunken, annihilated. I hyperventilated, faster and faster under pressure. The man looked up into my eyes, pleading for his life. I began sweating and my fingers began shaking. I could still feel Donnie's intense stare, pushing me to a psychological limit.

"What are you waitin' for? Do it."

As my finger stroked the trigger, there was only one way out of this. One last tear rolled down the man's face as he looked away, accepting his fate.

Donnie yelled out once more, *"Do ittt!"* The barrel shook in my grasp. I took a deep breath. The only thing louder than his piercing voice in my ear were the bullets exiting the barrel.

Two gunshots echoed loudly throughout the warehouse. The rippled soundwaves that returned shook the bones within me.

The deed was done.

Chapter Five

To Believe in God, One Must Believe in the Devil

The water cleansed my hands as it turned to a pinkish red, spiraling into the sink, leaving my stomach turning the same way. I was the reason for that man's death. He was dead because of me. As I snatched the white hand towel and dyed it red with my fingernails, I looked up to the mirror, staring into my own eyes as if I were somebody else.

My father once told me to stop every now and then, look in the mirror, and ask myself, *"Am I a good man?"* Most of the time, I liked to think I was. But sometimes, I wasn't sure. Maybe I was just lying to myself. When you take somebody's life, it doesn't feel like you think it'd feel. Suddenly, that person doesn't exist, and you must live with it. You can't go back and change it. They'd lived their entire life up until that moment, from birth, to childhood and aspirations, relationships, growing and striving to be the best version of themselves—all until one point, the closing of their lives—that life that *you* put an end to. You never dictated their birth or how they were brought up, which friends they were to make, the other lives they were to impact, or who they were going to be—but you dictated their death, therefore forcibly closing what they didn't know would be the final chapter of their lives.

Back at the warehouse, I stared down that steel barrel and closed my eyes. But I lowered the gun. Turns out, Donnie had another pistol in his back pocket. He took two shots. The bullets found their way directly into the man's chest. Castello joined in, clipping the man in the neck as the blood rapidly spilled from it. I was just a spectator, a bystander. It was a show, performed by the Great Donnie Caruso just for me. I was the only audience member. The chair fell backwards, and the man lay still. Donnie walked up to me and relinquished the pistol from my grasp.

"I knew you didn't have it in you." I broke eye contact, ashamed to have disappointed him. He turned and looked at Castello. "Clean this shit, then take 'im home. He ain't ready for this."

Donnie left after that. I stood there, staring at the victim of execution before my very eyes. Castello bit his lip before untying the lifeless man, pulling him by his arms and dragging his body to the back door. I think his name was Lucas. I wasn't even sure if he was the right guy, but due to his whereabouts on the night of Carlo's twenty-first birthday, it was enough evidence for Don to strike the blow.

"Ay, gimme a hand with this, will ya?" Castello was already exhausted.

I didn't know what to feel. He died either way. If I had killed him myself, I would've at least earned some respect from Donnie. I knew I didn't want to do it. I couldn't. These guys were trying to dip my hands in cold water, but I hadn't even fired a gun before.

***

The cathedral bells rang out as I tagged along with Donnie and Castello to the weekly service. I still needed one of my crutches to get by as I hobbled behind them. As the organs sounded, the guests waited outside the church, greeting Donnie with handshakes, kisses, bows. I wouldn't have been surprised if they began dropping rose petals before his feet as he walked. I couldn't hide my emotions. I was dead inside and would continue to be for the next few weeks or so, considering what had happened, and I was somewhat afraid of what was to come. Donnie and Castello were all smiles and waves. You couldn't guess in a million years that they'd just executed somebody strapped to a fucking chair in a warehouse some forty-eight hours before. And there they were, about to enter a place of worship. I hoped my face wouldn't give away the fact that my bones were rattled, my blood felt cold, and my fingers were still trembling vigorously from the few nights before. Not even the TV could drown this one out. These things were swiftly swept under the rug, although I was left to wonder if the blood would eventually sink through.

It only got worse at the cathedral. People were lining up to kiss Donnie's hand like he was royalty. He ran his fingers through their hair like some benevolent king. They nodded to him, blessed him, almost falling at his fucking feet. You'd think he was Jesus Christ himself. Some asked him to pray for their sick children, others for luck, for fortune. I noticed a tall, pale man in a long black trench coat lean in and whisper something in Donnie's ear—just him. Nobody else. I always wondered what those men said. All those ghosts in human form, slipping in and out of his world. In a place built on mercy, they came asking for vengeance. To bankrupt someone. To make someone bleed. To make someone disappear.

We hadn't even taken our seats yet when a frail old woman shuffled over and leaned into me. "You're a very lucky young man," she said, like it was a prophecy. "To be in the safe hands of Donnie."

Did she know what I knew? What kind of man he really was? Or did everyone know—and moreover worship him for it?

I felt I had to say something. "He takes care of all of us." The words felt cultish, automatic.

Donnie's hand, heavy with rings, landed on my shoulder. "Let me take you to meet someone."

He walked me straight to the priest—Raffaele. A short, bald man, revered by the congregation for his wisdom, his kindness, his grace.

Outside church hours though? He was a chain-smoker and a gambler. Underneath the vestments and the sermons, he was just another flawed soul. Another sinner wrapped in silk. "Wonderful to see you at today's service, Don," Raffaele said with a nod. "And who's this handsome fella?"

I extended my hand. "I'm John. Nice to meet you."

The priest smiled and shook it. "It's an honor to have you here today, John. Welcome to the family."

As we made our way to the back of the church, Donnie pulled out a thick wad of cash held tight by a single elastic band. He handed it over to the priest—quiet, discreet, like it was routine. A donation? A payoff? A favor? I didn't know, and by now, nothing would've surprised me.

By the time we returned to the pews, a fresh wave of worshippers had circled Donnie, kissing his hands, offering praise, basking in that glow. Donnie was adored in this city. There was always a kind of warmth around him—commanding, magnetic. People wanted to be near him. To be on his side. Even if it was for all the wrong reasons.

***

My safe place. My sanctuary. My home. It would only be a few hours a week that I could embrace the peace and comfort of being in my own bedsheets with Marianne's head resting on my chest. With Roy Orbison playing on one of the few records I had in my bedroom, I couldn't stop myself from staring at her, even after the month or so we'd already spent together. Aside from the Caruso work, I'd only spent my time with her and nobody else. And that was exactly the way I wanted it.

"So, when am I meeting your parents?" I asked, staring deep into her eyes, yearning to spend my life with her, imagining my first meeting with her father over a cup of coffee and panettone, watching her little nephews and nieces chase each other eagerly through the garden.

She giggled at the idea. "Let 'em get used to the idea of me *with* a boy first. It's probably driving them insane." She moved her hair out of her face. I could only explain so much of the unlimited and unbounded beauty in the depths of her pupils and the crinkles at both ends of her lips every time she'd smile. "Have you had any other girlfriends before me?" Her face straightened, anticipating my answer.

"You want the truth? Or a reassuring lie?"

Marianne was serious, awaiting an answer that she feared would be in the hundreds. "I always want the truth, Johnny."

"Back in Catania, I talked with a few girls here and there but other than that, I never actually stuck with anyone, at least not for long." You see, I could've pretended I had all the experience in the world. I could've told her a lie, but I trusted her, and I knew that whatever answer I gave her, she'd be okay with it.

As she unbuttoned my shirt and climbed on top of me, a devilish smile danced on her lips "I have the feeling that we're different, you and I."

She kissed my neck as I gripped her thighs. My blood began to simmer with her body straddling mine. Her lips slowly moved from my chin down to my chest as she looked up into my eyes while sliding my boxers off. She stood up, eyes locked seductively on me, spinning around and unclipping her lace bra. Everything about her. Every micro detail—every single look and expression upon her face tantalized me to the point of salivation. As her bra tumbled down her legs and onto the floor, she turned around with a daring smile and covered her breasts, knowing well she was a sight to behold as she climbed onto the bed, brushing up beside me and smiling. Innocence, but not without mischief. I stood up, removing my shirt, yearning for it to leave my sight so I could catch a glimpse of her again in case she disappeared, in case she wasn't real. She laughed to herself and rolled onto her back with her head and hair hanging from the bed while her legs dangled high in the air. At that point I wondered whether she'd done this before, whether this was her routine, whether other men had beheld such a sight before. She was simply too good at it. *Surely, she was mine and mine only*, I thought.

"I think I love you," I murmured.

She giggled again, suddenly shy. She was still a human after all. She tried to maintain her poise. "Strong words, pretty boy. Be careful how you use them with me." She crawled toward me as I leaned back on the bed. "If you tell me you love me, you need to *mean* it." She raised her arms, tangling them in her long hair as I observed the perfection of her sculpted figure. "Show me you mean it."

"I mean every word I say, doll face," I whispered, mesmerized, yet trying to maintain my masculine aura.

She began removing what was left of my clothes, once again straddling me, staring deep into my eyes, but as soon as her hand stroked by my pelvis, I hyperventilated and scrambled away from her. *What the fuck just happened?* My initial thoughts.

She looked at me, thinking she'd done something wrong, almost embarrassed. "You okay?" She backed away, assuming she was the problem, but I wanted it, I wanted her.

"Yeah ... I dunno what the hell that was." I forced out a smile, hoping for it to go away and hoping she'd continue. She did, quickly forgetting about it before re-employing that sexy smile, running her fingers up my leg once again. *Take two.*

The problem with an issue like this is when it happens—you try not to think about it in an attempt to get it right. We humans have a way of obsessing over things like this, further hindering us from overcoming the real problem. *Our brain is sometimes our greatest enemy.* I tried to ignore it, but it was suddenly all I could think about.

I flinched. This was getting fucking ridiculous. She sat up quickly, this time frustrated. "Seriously, what's the problem?" It was the first time I heard the tail of the Jersey accent whisper through her teeth. I ran my fingers through her hair, attempting to reassure her. I was just as confused as she was, if not more. Before I had time to heat things up for a third time, she'd already reattached her bra. I'd disappointed her. "I can't stay turned on forever." She sighed, "It's okay, Johnny."

I sat up, covering my lower body with the sheets as she gathered her clothes. "I don't know what's wrong, I'm sorry."

She didn't even respond. After she was dressed, she just sat down beside me and stroked my large hands with her slender, painted nails. It almost seemed like she was trying to remind herself that I was a man, as emasculating as that might sound. The night was over. I didn't know why I had trouble with it. I'd never felt that way before. Of course, I wanted it. Who didn't? But when she touched me, something was off, and I didn't know what the fuck it was.

***

"So, you can't get it up, huh?" Carlo wasn't shy in the wisecrack department. "You know what I do to get in the mood?" he said as he stuffed his face with miniature donuts as we made our way to a pizza shop.

"You wanna swallow that before you continue your sentence? I can practically see your stomach lining."

Carlo laughed, swallowing his donut before continuing. "Have a glass of orange juice, my friend."

I was confused. "Orange juice?" I thought he was just pulling my leg as usual. "With ice," he added. "You'd be surprised, man. It gives you that little spark of energy. You should try it, sometime. Just don't forget the pulp!" I laughed but Carlo shrugged, swearing on every word exiting his mouth. "Who knows? Maybe you'll just get over it. You've fucked heaps of girls, right?"

"Of course. *I'm Johnny Caruso.*" I winked. "Who do you think I am?"

"Then you should be able to work through it," he whispered as he patted my back. "Because you gotta satisfy your woman, my friend. *Everybody* knows that."

"Keep this to yourself, alright?" It was already too much that Carlo knew. "I don't need nobody else hearin' about my sex life."

Carlo laughed, flapping his arms. "Don't worry. Nobody wants to."

Mama Vero's Pizzeria. Co-owned by Donnie himself, we ran into a familiar face. Veronica Marini; she made the best pizza in New York. I don't mean to boast, but we *were* on the Italian side of town. She was about sixty-five when I first met her, and her accent was as strong as if she were still back home. Her pizza pie was the pinnacle of flavor, the cornerstone of our roots.

Proper, wood-fire pizza. Thin, extra-virgin olive oil crust. Sauce that was stirred to perfection with basil, oregano, fennel, and garlic. She even used real cheese like stracciatella or Mozzarella di Bufala straight from the water buffalo itself, back in Campania. As she effortlessly threw the spices into the pot, there was never too much or too little, it was like magic. She had a sauce that nobody could replicate and only used toppings that came direct from the old country. She even chopped up real tomatoes instead of those diced ones from the cans. The toppings sizzled as she extracted the pan from the wood-fire oven and placed it right in front of you—right under your nose. Even though the sauce was made to be savory, there was always that little something sweet about it. This was one of Carlo's favorite places in the world.

"You ever been in love with a food before?" he asked in awe. I laughed, grabbing a steaming slice for myself and watching the cheese stretch back to the pizza like its life depended on it.

Veronica hung her apron up and ruffled both of our hair. She was a family woman and again, just like Nonna Francesca, treated us like her own grandchildren. However, business was still at hand. Carlo straightened himself up as he surveyed the restaurant.

"Mr. Caruso's been pulling some heavy strings lately to keep this place running, Vero."

Veronica shrugged and gestured to her obvious lack of customers. "Business been no good lately. The other shop open across street and the children been spraying the walls with graffiti!"

"Wait, wait, slow down," I snapped. "Another pizza parlor?"

Carlo's eyes darted to me. "In our territory? I think we should pay them a visit, don't ya think?" Carlo was fuming, knowing this meant trouble. "Those fuckin' scumbags can't get enough."

Veronica proceeded to whack her finger in Carlo's face. "Ay-yayay! Language!"

We stepped out of the car in front of the new pizza joint. Bright colors, shiny and brand new. Too sanitary to be any good and the prices were too low to prove quality. *Disgusting.*

Carlo spat on the sidewalk in front of it. "Looks like this is the place. Won't be near as good as Veronica's, that's for sure." We entered Big City Pizza to meet a friendly Asian fella behind the counter, eager to make a sale. Carlo was skeptical from the get-go. "This guy's Chinese or something. They can't make pizza." The so-called pizza man tried to upsell by adding a drink for an extra fifty cents. Carlo nodded, pointing to the fridge behind the man. "Yeah, whatever, gimme a coke ... Need something to wash this stuff down."

Out in the car, we tried the pizza. Surprisingly, it was fucking delicious. Carlo was finding any way to deny the quality. "They come to New York to make money and then they go puttin' cheese in the base? Shameful." But eventually, Carlo had to face the music and admit it was good. "I thought the Chinese didn't know how to make pizza and now they're taking our business."

I tried to correct his ill manners. "I think he was Japanese."

Carlo shrugged. "What's the difference?"

I laughed. "There's a difference."

Carlo shook his head as he continued to devour the sloppy slice hanging from his palm. "Well, either way, it's good. Ain't no Chef Boyardee but it's *good.* Which for us, *isn't* good."

I knew we'd have to report this to Donnie, and that nauseating pit in my stomach returned. "We're gonna have to let the guys know." I looked at Carlo as he started the car and glanced back at me.

"Bet you anything we'll be back here tomorrow."

Carlo was wrong, we were back there that *same night*. As the sun came down, we returned to Big City Pizza. This time, through the parking lot in the rear. There were only dumpsters and stray cats in the vicinity, and it was just past midnight. Carlo had a brown paper bag in his lap.

Donnie always made his moves fast. Within hours, he could get the names and records of any employee in any restaurant in the city. How much coin they make, the hours they worked, and the names, business partners, and stakeholders of any fucker running any joint.

As I lit a nervous cigarette, we waited in the car for the place to close up. Carlo's eyes were glued to the store with anticipation. After about ten minutes, a pizza employee exited through the back with a set of keys in his hand. He had just locked up and was ready to go home, jerk off, watch a movie, and go to sleep. On the way to his car, Carlo appeared from the darkness.

"Can I help you?" The employee stopped.

Carlo slung his pistol. "Listen quick and shut the fuck up."

The employee dropped his backpack and leaned up against his car. I was taken aback by Carlo's swift action, but I had to play along.

"Please, man! I don't have any money on me! I don't own the place!" I hobbled over with my single crutch and tried to de-escalate the situation.

"We're not robbin' you, bud. We just need you to do us a little favor." I held up the small brown paper bag.

"What favor?" he stuttered. "This asshole's got a gun to my head!"

Carlo aggressively pushed the pistol harder against the employee's sweating mustache.

I needed to get this done fast. "You like money? You like cash?" The quicker we did this, the sooner we'd go home.

The man desperately nodded. "Who doesn't?" Talking quickly, every word was a plead for mercy.

"Good." I flipped out my wallet. "How does three hundred bucks sound?"

"For what? What are you tryna do?" He couldn't help but stare at the cold metal barrel against his upper lip. I opened the bag to show him the contents—cockroaches, hundreds of 'em, squirming and crawling. "Roaches? What the fuck are they for?" He looked directly at the pizza shop, knowing well what they were for.

"You're gonna take this bag of roaches, keep it in a safe place inside your shop where your manager won't see—"

"Are you fucking retarded? What is this shit?"

Carlo whacked him across the face with the pistol. I took a deep breath as he held his red right cheek. This time I was stern. "You're gonna *keep* this bag in a safe place. You're gonna make sure your manager *don't* see it. Then while you're working, you're gonna add *one* roach to every *second* pizza you make. Kapeesh?"

His eyes darted between the both of us. "You people are fucked up. It's a fucken pizza joint, for Christ's sake!"

I rolled my eyes. "Here's three hundred bucks for your troubles. When we start hearin' the reviews, you'll see more of it." He looked at me, then down to my wallet. I needed an answer and didn't have time to waste, so I dug deeper into my wallet to retrieve more cash but before I could reach for another Ben Franklin, we heard a rattle by the dumpsters. That's all it took That's all that we needed to hear. That's when everything went south—south of the fucking border.

Carlo turned his head from reaction. The employee launched at Carlo, and it all happened so quickly.

The gunshot.

The employee's body sliding down the car door.

The blood gushing from his neck.

I looked at Carlo in sheer terror. The first thing going through my mind was how the fuck we were to explain this. The second, which should've been the first, was that this innocent man was about to lose his life on account of us.

"What the fuck was that?" My lips quivered.

Carlo dropped the gun, shocked just as much as I was. "I—dunno. He moved and ..."

"Holy shit ... holy shit, man!" I immediately put my hands on my head and looked in every direction for possible witnesses.

Carlo was stuck trying to explain what happened, but he could barely speak. "I heard a noise, Johnny. I flinched. I heard a noise ... Fuck."

I pointed to the dumpsters. "There were cats over there before ... Didn't you see 'em? It was a fucking cat."

Carlo didn't want to believe what had just happened. This wasn't petty crime, this was murder in cold blood. "It was just a reaction. I didn't mean to pull—"

"A reaction?" I interrupted, "A fucken reaction—are you kidding me? He's dead. He's dead, Carlo!" I became dizzy, looking around, paranoid that somebody was going to show up any second. Carlo and I were quite literally red-handed.

"Gimme the roaches," Carlo snapped. "Gimme the keys." I'd never seen Carlo so agitated in my life. "We gotta finish the job." Carlo snatched the employee's keys.

I tried to stop him. "He's fucking dead, man! Where the fuck are you going?"

He turned to me, pointing in my face. "Keep your mouth *shut*. You wanna be seen?"

"When you hear a gunshot, you gotta go, Carlo." I began to worry about the police. "That was a gunshot. We need to get the fuck outta here."

He proceeded to approach the back entrance of the restaurant. "We gotta do something. Get the car started. One thing that *doesn't* fly with Donnie is unfinished work." Carlo was right. It would only get worse if we spent our night arguing over a corpse. I had to get the car ready while he threw the open bag of roaches into the restaurant. I looked down at the employee, still pinned against the car. His shift was over, and so was his life.

"I'm sorry. I'm so sorry," I whispered to his unresponsive corpse.

As Carlo locked the restaurant door, he rushed back to the car. On the way, he threw the set of keys back at the employee and jumped in the passenger seat as I turned the ignition, knowing we were in some serious shit. Not only had we taken somebody's life—an innocent life— but we had to face the unforgiving wrath of Donnie for the consequences. "What do we do? We can't just leave him there!" I was beginning to freak out, thinking about jail time, thinking about my life being over with Marianne.

Carlo shoved my shoulder. "We leave. We come back in three hours. If he's still here, we hide the body. If there are police, we drive past. Understand?"

I looked at him, shaking my head at the half-baked plan he'd conjured. "That's the worst fucking plan I've ever heard."

"What, you wanna be here at a fresh scene? Don't think about it, just drive," Carlo yelled.

Before I could step on the pedal, I couldn't help casting a glance at the innocent employee lying dead on the floor of the pizza shop car park. We did that to somebody. We did it.

"Drive, Johnny! Drive!" The tires screeched and we were out of there in four seconds flat.

***

"He's dead?"

At the bar in the Caruso building, the closest friends of the family were having one of their weekly get-togethers. Marianne was sitting cross-legged on the floor across the room with Sophia and Angela. Carlo and I pulled Donnie aside to inform him of the situation. Marianne glanced at me, knowing something was up. She was always good at spotting these things.

"Do either of you recall me telling you to off somebody tonight?" Donnie was furious but subtle, knowing he couldn't make a scene— which was probably the best time to spring something like this on him. "Who was it? *Who* pulled the trigger?" His eyes darted dramatically between us. Carlo sheepishly raised his hand. "Thought so. Where'd you shoot him?" Donnie knew I didn't have the balls to off somebody, even by accident.

"At the pizza parlor," replied Carlo with a hanging head. Donnie rolled his eyes, asking which part of the *body* he was shot, not the location he was shot at, the latter being obvious.

"The neck."

Shooting somebody in the neck would leave them with about a four percent chance of survival, maybe less. Other than the brain or the heart, it was the next deadliest location on that list.

Donnie nodded, biting his lip. "Why was the gun loaded?" He was eerily calm considering the circumstances, but it felt more like a hydrogen bomb just waiting to blow us to smithereens in a matter of seconds.

"What do you mean?" Carlo was clearly getting nervous and buying time to think.

"If you weren't wanting to kill nobody, then why was the gun loaded? Simple question." Donnie crossed his arms. There was no way to make this look better than it was. Plain and simple.

"Just in case ..."

Before Carlo could finish, Donnie cut in. "In case of what? He pulls a gun on *you*? This is a kid workin' at a fucken pizza joint, Carlo. Is your brain in the right place? What the fuck were you thinking?"

Carlo never responded well to criticism. I looked away to Marianne, still chatting to her friends. Talking to her was heaven compared to the conversation we rolled ourselves into. I just wanted to be back with her in my apartment, alone.

"The gun was just for intimidation." Meanwhile, Carlo was still trying to cover his ass.

Donnie wouldn't have a bar of it. "When you load a pistol. You load it with intent to *kill*. Now, this poor boy's dead because of a pizza feud. How pathetic is that? That's no way to go." Donnie seemed to feel remorse for this boy's death, as if his fate rested in Donnie's hands and he was to blame. He shook his head.

I tried to save Carlo's skin a little, but it only made matters worse. "Donnie, he attacked us. He was about to take the money. He was gonna do what we asked. He made a sudden move and it just … happened."

Donnie put his palm in my face, halting my words. "That's not my fucking point." Carlo and I fell silent. "I don't care that he attacked you. You need to defend yourselves and that's fair. But that kid's got a fucking bullet in his neck now over something that wasn't worth dyin' over. Once again, I raise the question, *why was the gun loaded?*" Donnie ground his teeth. "It woulda been okay if the rounds were in your pocket or the car. Or even the fucking magazine. You had the bullet loaded, inside the chamber, ready to fire? What the fuck is that shit?" Carlo's lips were trembling. He had no ammunition. He could only stare at the ground, wallowing in his own resentment.

Carlo looked up at Donnie, hoping for redemption. "After the heat's off, we're gonna go back and clean it up—"

Donnie instantly shook his head, laughing in disbelief. "You're doing *what* now? You're staying right the fuck here, that's what *you're* doing. I'll be sending Vinnie and Louie out there ... You two have put us through enough trouble tonight as it is. At least *they're* well capable of a simple task." Donnie crossed his arms. There was no escaping our mistake. "Now, did you even do anything with the roaches? Or is that *still* my problem?" Donnie was ready to explode if we didn't give him the right answer.

"Emptied them into the store," Carlo muttered with his eyes pinned to the ground.

A flush of relief swept over Donnie's sour face. "Okay ... finally did somethin' along the lines of what I asked. Now, get the fuck outta my face. I need a brandy."

Donnie walked away as I tried to console Carlo by asking if he wanted a drink. "Fuck this, man." He stormed out of there as I sighed, turning to Marianne. She was still in conversation with Sophia and Angela. I walked over and stopped halfway, struck, even by the way she adjusted her hair. A sight to drop dead for every time. Usually a man becomes accustomed to his woman, finding nothing new—but

Marianne was ever gorgeous, and I could never get enough, almost to the point of paranoia that another man might feel the same way.

Sophia was only eighteen. She was known as the foolish one. She was Vinnie's niece and all she'd ever talk about was the reckless hijinks she got up to on the weekends.

"So, he picks me up from the theater on Friday," she says as she picks her nails. "I'm there expecting to go to the drive-in to watch a movie or ... you know, get *bizzay*. And you know what I find?" The girls both sipped their drinks, intrigued, waiting for the imminent kicker. "Some other girl in the car!"

Angela cringed. As much as she was a cake-faced lunatic, she still had a few straight bones inside her. "Are you serious? Who does he think he is?"

Sophia giggled and shrugged. "He expected me to just be okay with it! I was hopin' for an explanation, like—maybe it was his sister or somethin'—but turns out he wanted a double hookup!"

Marianne shook her head. She'd rip me to pieces if I ever pulled something like that. "Tell me you walked away, Soph?"

Sophia shrugged again after Marianne's question. She had a habit of shrugging whenever she was guilty; even if she'd been shaking her head, the shrug always told the truth. She smirked. "Well, what was I supposed to do? I wasn't doin' anything else that night." Marianne and Angela cracked up laughing. Sophia was quite well known to get around town, especially with men that were significantly older than her. I'd always catch the secondhand gossip from Marianne when we were alone.

Something I loved about Marianne was when we needed each other, we both knew it. Even if she was with her friends, I'd just have to look at her, flick my head in any direction, and she'd jump up from whatever she was doing, and we'd go. It was something only *we* did. She'd do the same with me; even if I was talking to the big guys, she'd have that power over me. At this point in our relationship, we were equal.

We got into one of the parked Lincolns in the Caruso garage. For a few peaceful seconds, we sat there in silence. It felt like the first break I'd had in weeks. Marianne grew serious. It was as if she could physically see the thoughts and emotions seeping out of my head as I desperately tried to cram them back in.

"What's the story, Johnny?"

I didn't know what to say. All I knew was that I needed her with me. I wasn't allowed to talk to her about my business or the work we did. I lit half a cigarette I had tried to smoke earlier, but was too nauseous to inhale, considering the circumstances.

"I thought you weren't gonna smoke no more."

I held my palm up to her, inhaling every last bit of that first drag. I didn't need a protest. I just needed a break. "Not right now, please?" Marianne crossed her arms. "You pulled me away from my friends for a reason. We were talkin' about weird dates. It was a fun conversation that you cut short for me, Johnny." I exhaled, planting my forehead on the leather steering wheel. I couldn't stop thinking about him. The employee. Dead in the car park. If he were still living with his parents. If they were up waiting for him. If they didn't know that their son wasn't coming home because two clumsy clowns put a hole in his neck. I could barely speak, and shedding tears in front of her was the last thing I needed. I'd already let her down in the department of masculinity prior. "Johnny, what's wrong? You're startin' to worry me."

I closed my eyes. I couldn't look at her. "We were no good today." My voice cracked.

She placed her hand on mine. "What do you mean?"

I looked up at her. That beautiful, innocent face, unknowing of the dangerous monster that I felt I'd become. My eyes began lightly streaming like a leaky garden hose. "I don't wanna be a bad person." I gulped, trying to speak, trying to elaborate but my throat kept closing up.

"Nobody says you have to." She was doing her best to make me feel better, knowing nothing about the situation. I needed another drag. "Johnny, what happened? You can tell me. Can't be *that* bad. Can it?"

I looked back up at her, wondering if she'd ever forgive me for something like this. I turned away from her, reluctant to see the look on her face upon hearing the truth. "It was an accident. He was just an employee. I don't know what to tell you." My mind began to spiral, possibly prolonging what I was about to tell her. "I don't even know how much I *can* tell you or if I should even *be* telling you anything at all …"

Marianne stopped me, with her delicate hand on my shoulder. "Johnny … I think I know what your uncle does. I'm pretty sure I know what business you're in. We girls—we're wiser than you think." She wasn't stupid, I can tell you that.

Feeling some measure of comfort, I leaned up against the car seat and exhaled. "I just need you here, with me, that's all. Even if we don't talk—it's better than being alone right now."

After a few short seconds, it must've been circling Marianne's mind. It probably had her thinking the worst. Although, I'm not sure how much worse it could've been. "Were they young?"

I looked up. "Who?"

"The employee."

I took a deep breath and nodded. "Early to mid-twenties."

Her hand flew to her mouth, and she looked away. "You didn't *do* it, did you?" She must have been weighing up whether she still respected me the same way. She took the cigarette from my fingers and inhaled for some time before letting it escape her lips, still unable to look me directly in the eye. It wasn't her first cigarette. There were still things I didn't know about her.

I shook my head. "I can never do that. I can never kill nobody. That's not me, Marianne. I promise you—that's not me."

Marianne suddenly threw on a fake smile, chirpy. "How 'bout you and Carlo go out this week? For a boys' night or somethin'. Get your mind off things."

"What good's that gonna do?" I shook my head.

"You need a breath of fresh air. This job of yours is getting to your head." Marianne wound the window down, letting the smoke escape into the car park. Not only was she trying to make me feel better, but I assume she was trying to distract herself from the reality that her boyfriend did something heinous. Marianne placed her hand on my lap, gesturing back to the building. She returned my cigarette. "Now, you gonna walk me back inside? Or am I gonna walk all by myself in the dark?"

As we stepped out of the car and I lifted my crutch, I walked her back inside as if nothing had happened. I knew she was my safety net. When you love somebody so much, you wonder what the fuck you'd do without them. As I finished the cigarette, squashed it on the asphalt and followed Marianne, I realized that nobody understood me like she did. She wasn't only my partner, but my best friend. My everything.

It only left me pondering to what extent she'd tolerate the deeds I did. How far is too far?

Chapter Six

The Thin White Line

I couldn't sleep. I couldn't stop thinking about him. That employee. *Was I gonna pay for this? What are the repercussions?* I needed to make it right. *But how could I make it right when I couldn't turn back time?* I needed to speak to somebody about it. Somebody who knew exactly what we do, somebody who wouldn't snitch.

I visited Priest Raffaele at the cathedral. I caught him smoking a joint as he got out of his car. "John? Good morning!" He quickly butted out the spliff on the asphalt, startled. "What can I do for you?"

"Father, I need to get some stuff off my chest."

His face changed. He knew exactly what I meant. He'd seen it before. "The church is always here to accept you wholeheartedly, so long as you're willing to accept it." He unlocked the side door to the cathedral.

"I need to talk to *you*, Father."

Raffaele sighed and looked up at me. "You're a part of Don's family.

I know what you people do. If you want to ask forgiveness for these ... *deeds,* you do it in there." He pointed to the pews, but I couldn't do it by myself. It was too much for me to handle alone, and I'd never spoken directly to God before.

"You know what? I'll see ya later."

He placed his hand on my shoulder before I could turn around. "The church will always be here for you, son. No matter how difficult times may be, there's always a place for you in the arms of our Lord." I nodded, turning around again, until he mentioned my uncle. "Keep your uncle close to you, son. He's an ally."

I stopped and turned around. "What do you even know about Donnie? You only see the giver him, the donations he makes and the hands he shakes ..."

"I know him better than you do." Raffaele bit his bottom lip. "You don't think he's ever come to confess before? You don't think I've met the targets that he makes disappear?" Raffaele had a sour squint in his eye. "Some of them were my *own* people." He leaned in close to my ear, quick and erratic. "You don't think I've ever asked him any favors of my own?" A long silence followed. There was shame, desperation, and hatred in his voice. "We all do things we need forgiveness for. But for those specific deeds, you ask forgiveness in *there*. I can't help you on my own. Not me. I'm sorry, son."

It wasn't the fact that he wouldn't help me, it was that he couldn't. He'd committed these sins and required forgiveness for himself, so much that it would seem hypocritical to ask forgiveness from God on somebody else's behalf over the same deeds.

"I'm not telling you to keep Don close because he is a good man." The priest tightened his white collar. "I'm telling you that it is better to fight *with* the sword than *against* it."

***

Castello had a job and needed a spare hand from me in the Caruso building basement. You almost wouldn't recognize it as the same building. If you were locked down there and told it was a dungeon, you'd believe it from the raw bricks that enveloped the walls, the dust in the air, and the smell of iron moisture.

"How'd things turn out at the pizza joint?" I asked.

Castello shrugged. "The cops got there before us. So, don't be surprised if you notice the pigs snoopin' around. Keep your nose clean. You didn't see nothing. You were here, having drinks with us the whole night." Castello pulled a string, turning on the basement light. "Listen, Donnie told me to show you somethin'. He wants you to know exactly how we make our money here."

We reached the bottom of the stairs to an empty room with large tiles lining the floor. An old couch was placed neatly in the center of the room. I gazed around, disappointed, as if I had expected a clan of elves printing money. "It's empty."

"That's right. To you, it's empty. That's how it *should* look." Castello then pushed the couch against the wall, clearing the tile that the couch had covered. I was more than confused when he pulled out a small cornice tool from his back pocket and got on one knee.

"You came all the way down here to propose to me?" I joked. "Ah, geez, Cas."

"Don't make me laugh, kid. I got asthma." He chuckled.

As we slid the tile over, it revealed a neat cache of white powder in rectangular packets. "The hell is this?"

Castello raised an eyebrow. "What does it look like? Wild guess."

"Is that cocaine?" I was shocked at the amount. There must've been at least twenty keys in there. "This has gotta be worth thousands."

Castello chuckled once more. "Think bigger, Johnny. *Much* bigger." I didn't want to guess, worried I'd look stupid if I guessed too low or way too high.

"Tell me how many briefcases you've swapped this year." Castello crossed his arms.

"I dunno. Probably like eighty to a hundred? Give or take a few."

Castello nodded. "One hundred and twelve cases since the start of the year. Each case we collect has roughly three hundred and fifty thousand dollars in it." He grinned. "Give or take a few."

I picked up one of the bags. Weighty and thick. "The fuck do we do with it here?"

"Have you noticed that some of those briefcases are a little heavier than others?" I looked down at the solid key in my hand as Castello replaced the tile to cover the rest of the cache. "We don't only collect cash, but we collect the product. It's all a cycle. A very fucking profitable cycle."

Let me introduce you to what we actually did here in New York. It's the city that never sleeps, but there's a reason it doesn't sleep.

Cocaine was the game. We were only the gears that moved it. The product starts from the ground in the north-western parts of South America. For us, we were mostly utilizing Bolivian coke, calling it Perico or Yayo. After our sources in San Borja would very carefully collect the leaves, they'd spread them out, grind them up, and soak them in gasoline. It would take nine hundred and fifty pounds of these coca leaves to produce a single kilo of coke, which is two point two pounds of pure Bolivian angel dust. The workers add various household chemicals like bleach, cement powder, and battery acid to extract the substance ... some of which you'd find under every sink in every fucking kitchen in the United States. After they siphon the clear water cocaine from the mixture, they separate it and add a splash of ammonia to solidify the product. And when that process was complete, our work began.

We had a system that was foolproof. Each case location was

randomized and organized only fifteen minutes before drop. Each location had a one-word code that our trusted connections had already written down prior pickup. It wasn't our business how they smuggled it into the country, whether it was transported in liquid form or strapped beneath cars; as long as each case arrived at the right date and time in its solidified state, we were ahead. We bought the product, case by case, through those Bolivian connections. We gave them what they wanted for it after production and raised that price by six hundred and fifty percent, sometimes even seven hundred if the right buyers came along.

This was where our Boston connection came into play. The Barresi brothers would take our product over to Beantown. They'd send it on to their partners, who sent it on to *their* partners, eventually supplying every major city on the east coast in adequate numbers. The advantage of working with these guys was the fact that there were no middlemen. They simply collected the product direct from us and distributed it themselves.

We weren't even the ones dealin' the stuff. We had carefully selected pushers who had close connections to the family. The same faces, the same amounts, but different locations every time. Our product was then distributed throughout each entire city. We'd even get it into other cities like Chicago, Vegas, and Los Angeles because our coke was simply better than the shit they had over there. Our Perico was ninety-seven percent pure, which was far better than most, only getting to the right people for the right prices. The cash flowed like nothing you've ever seen before. The only rule was never to touch the stuff ourselves.

We had one aim: Stay under the noses of the feds and shoot it up the noses of the wealthy.

Later that day, I went to lunch with Castello in Brooklyn at a restaurant we'd never been to before. These things didn't usually happen. When you know all the good places, you usually stick to the same ones, the trusted ones within our connections. So, when a spot is unfamiliar, you'd know you're not just there for the Eggs Benedict.

As the poached eggs were placed in front of Castello, steaming all the way up to his face, I was curious about our dealings. "So, how much of it is ours?" I scoped the area so nobody could hear us.

"In New York?" Castello looked around immediately. A sensitive subject. "Most of it." I fiddled with the miniature coffee cup in front of me; I knew this was a big fucking deal. Cocaine? New York? The worker-man's drug in the biggest central business district. It couldn't get any bigger. Castello continued. "Four years ago, we owned somethin' like eighty percent of all the product in the city. Rough figures." He sighed. "But that was four years ago. It's declining. You see, these days, the price is the highest it's ever been. More sellers wanna get in on the action to make a dollar or two. Everybody wants the white stuff. They wanna move as fast as the numbers do."

Donnie was bound to be undercut by street dealers working on their own merit, but their stuff wasn't the same. You'd shoot our coke, and you'd feel like a much more focused and efficient version of yourself on a wave of success—well, that's what I'd been told anyway. But if you take a street dealer's coke, you could suffer a heart attack, paranoia, nausea, a million different side effects, and in a lot of cases, get poisoned and fucken die because someone didn't extract the battery acid.

However, the street dealers weren't the problem. The percentage of coke distributed by us had dropped to about sixty to seventy. Street dealers? You wish. I asked Castello if the dust we had in the basement was the entire city's stock and he laughed in my face.

"No, Johnny. That's just the Yayo that's ready to go. The rest of it is stored safely in a flour mill outside Salisbury, up north in Connecticut. About five to ten percent is all from independent parties. These fuckers cut the product with all sorts of shit. It'll make you sick hearin' what they put in there. But they can do whatever they want as long as they're off Donnie's turf."

Like I mentioned, that ten percent or so a year that we were losing wasn't to mere street dealers. Castello then asked me if I'd ever heard of a man named Blackjaw. I shook my head, oblivious to the significance that name would have on my life after that conversation.

"Never mention that name to Donnie. They used to work together and had a falling out. Blackjaw supplies the rest of the product in the city, slowly overtaking our numbers. He doesn't care who he fucks with as long as he makes his money."

This really got me thinking. Donnie had an enemy. These are the things he ponders over on that balcony of his. This must also be the "old friend" he had mentioned that came to town a couple months before. Things were changing and they were changing ever so quickly. "So, are we gonna do anything about this guy or just let him walk all over us?"

Castello shrugged. "That's the problem. This guy's a ghost. He slips through your fingers." This guy was beginning to sound like an even bigger player than Donnie.

As Castello left the money on the table, we got up to leave. Castello tapped the waiter on the hand before he cleaned our table. He'd left a case beneath it. I glanced back as we left, noticing the waiter collecting it.

***

Just as Marianne had suggested, Carlo and I hit the downtown pool joint to clear our heads and clear some tables. At this point I was walking quite well and didn't really have a use for the crutches, but still brought one with me as the pain varied from time to time.

Leaning on the mahogany bar, Carlo couldn't keep his peepers off a group of squawking girls walking past and sitting at the booth. Something was up with Carlo. Maybe it was Donnie that set him off, maybe it was the stress of the business or the remorse over the employee. He was just somebody else that night.

"You ever try the stuff?" I nudged Carlo. "The ... dust?"

Now I'm a curious man, so my mind had been revolving around this one topic like a fly on dog shit since I was with Castello that morning. Carlo looked at me, running his finger along the empty glasses in front of him. "Nah, man. That ain't me. I heard Frankie's tried it, though." I didn't even know who Frankie was. I guess there were still a few folks I hadn't met yet. "Louie's nephew. He works part time at one of the mattress stores in Brooklyn."

"You ever heard of this Blackjaw, jerkoff?" I asked.

Carlo's eyes widened more than usual the second he heard that name. "You always ask this many questions after a few drinks?" I could see I was becoming something of an annoyance. We went to the bar to *forget* our problems, not to discuss them. "Never heard of 'im." Carlo wasn't having a bar of it as he dug his fist into a bowl of salted peanuts.

"Castello told me he's the competition. I just wanna know who this guy is. Donnie hasn't mentioned him at all."

Carlo took a shot and shook his head, beginning to crack his knuckles repeatedly. He was nervous. I'd spent enough time with him by this point that I could interpret his body language. "There shouldn't be no competition. We're just tryna make a few bucks and live our lives here, man. So long as I get my bakery one day, I'm as happy as a clam." He continued popping his knuckles, even the ones he'd already cracked.

"Hey, stop cracking your knuckles. I heard it gives you arthritis." I gestured to his fingers before sipping the drink in front of me.

He shook his head, "Man, that's just an old wines tale …" I couldn't help but laugh. He seemed defensive. "What … what is it?"

"Old *wines* tale? It's an old *wives'* tale." I pursed my lips to hold in the laughter that was desperate to escape my mouth.

Instead, he was puzzled, gesturing to the wine bottles on the wall. "What? An old wines tale, like a story told by some Irish drunkard."

I smiled. "No. It's something to do with false tales passed down from generations of women from the fourteenth century or some shit."

Carlo shrugged. "I'm too tipsy for a history lesson."

I decided to focus on enjoying the night rather than turning it into work, or a lesson in history. After all, we were there to get away from it all.

Carlo looked over once again at the same group of girls that had danced in earlier, leering at them as they giggled and pointed. I wasn't sure if they were actually falling for his pretentious grin or just cackling over how ridiculous he looked. "Look at them, man. They want it, I can tell. They want a slice of Monte Carlo." I was confused, remembering that he said he'd only wanted Larissa, Rosana's niece. Like I said, on this specific night, he was a different man. "There's nothin' wrong with a little messin' around."

Carlo wanted to have some fun that night, even if it meant a little trouble. "Alright, I'll wait here for ya. Just pick one of them before you go there, or you'll look like a chump," I tried to warn him.

"Nah, nah. I got a better idea. I'm gonna make them want *me*." Carlo then proceeded to pop his collar. "Carlo don't approach nobody. Females approach Carlo." I couldn't help but chuckle over his excessive confidence.

"You talkin' in the third person now, big man?"

Carlo stood up, neatening his shirt and winking at the girls before approaching a table of men similar to us in age. He called the next game of eight-ball as he slapped a wad of cash onto the green felt. Carlo's cocky grin forced my eyes to roll to the back of my skull. He was then gawked at by a grinning posh, clean-shaven white boy in a bomber jacket who stood on the other side of the table, leaning on his pool cue.

"I've never seen *you* here before." He looked down on Carlo, much shorter than he was. "Put your piggy bank money away. Don't waste your time, kid."

His group of friends laughed and snorted like a pack of savage chipmunks. They were obviously unaware of Carlo's short fuse. At this point, Carlo kept his cool, seeing as he was still attempting to please the chickie-babies over in the booths. "Did ya hear me? I said next game."

Mr. Bomber Jacket's friends referred to him as Richie, encouraging him as he sighed with an eye roll. "I'm not taking your milk money ... Now hop on outta here, toots."

As his friends continued to laugh willfully louder, the girls over in the booth looked away as they sensed Carlo's embarrassment. I could imagine he felt like a child in a playground being pushed around by a bigger kid. "Listen here, shit-face."

It began. Suddenly Carlo met his match as Richie puffed his chest out, unafraid. "What did you just call me, you guinea pig fuck?"

Although Carlo didn't reach the literal heights of Richie, his attitude surpassed the challenger. I grabbed my crutch, knowing this could get ugly. "You're too fucken scared to play me 'cause you know you'll lose in front of your faggot friends," Carlo poked.

Richie was egged on by his ravenous chums before nodding. "Alright. You want a game? You got yourself a game. Rack 'em up, eight-ball."

One of Richie's friends rounded up all the balls. Carlo giggled.

"What's funny, short stack?" Richie was confused.

Carlo chimed in. "I like your friend's nickname. What's yours? *No balls?*" Jesus Christ, Carlo was having a field day with these guys.

"Real funny, asshole. How much we playin' for?"

Carlo pouted, putting down fifty. Richie nodded and placed another fifty down, "Alright two fifties," Richie announced. "So we're playing for a hundred big ones."

"Slow down, Pythagoras." Carlo still couldn't keep his mouth shut, burning over that first insult.

Richie threw him an old, faded cue. He decided to break up the balls himself, calling it a home team tradition. But of course, before the cue ball even moved, Richie winked at Carlo.

"Cocky bastard," Carlo murmured.

"What'd ya say?" Richie stood up straight.

Carlo rolled his eyes. "Nothin'. Just shoot the damn ball, coglione."

Richie began potting, already knocking two balls in the pockets. "I'm smalls."

Carlo muttered, "You sure are."

Richie then pocketed two more balls in quick succession. "Show us what ya got."

Carlo approached the table as this game was starting to gain the attraction of other guests and spectators from the bar. As Carlo aimed his cue, one of Richie's friends blew air obnoxiously into his fist before Carlo could shoot, and he completely missed the pocket as they broke out in a riotous laugh. "That's bullshit!" He gestured to the culprit, who was almost pissing himself.

Richie smirked. "What's the problem? House rules, pal." Carlo's face went red. I knew there was a bomb somewhere in Carlo and detonation was imminent. Richie then knocked two more balls into the pockets with ease. It was Carlo's turn again. "If I get to seven balls, you know the rule, right?" Richie was now razzing Carlo for fun, walking around the table, lifting his shirt and brushing his skin. "Public place. You'll have to do it. Or else you'll be deemed a bitch forever."

"Not so much as your mother." Carlo walked up to the table, already six balls down.

I clapped, attempting to motivate him. "Come on, Carlo. Show 'em who's boss!"

Carlo knocked one of the balls in. Richie tuned in once again. "Oof! Saved your ass." Carlo then knocked in another two. A bead of sweat glistened on Richie's face, reflecting the lights above the table. "Couple of lucky shots but I'm on black. As soon as you miss, your ass is done."

Carlo looked up and smiled at Richie. "Only thing I'm missing is your sister and her bed." Even Richie's boys cracked up over that one.

Richie leaned over to his buddy. "How does this asshole know I have a sister?"

Carlo overheard his whispers. "Lucky guess. Or maybe 'cause she showed me how to handle my stick." I let out a laugh and I looked around. I was not trying to attract attention to myself—the last thing I needed was to be caught in the crossfire of words, get into a scuffle, aggravate my injury, and make a public spectacle of myself. Carlo then skillfully rebounded a ball twice off the sides of the table and into the pocket. The crowd erupted. It was like we were at a confined baseball game and Carlo had just hit one out of the park. Even the girls in the booth began cheering him on. He had one left, but it was behind the eight ball.

Richie grinned. "Looks like you're snookered, pal." As everybody in the house watched in anticipation, Carlo took a deep breath and lightly tapped the ball. It rolled, slightly tapping the black ball and knocking the colored into the pocket. "Game over," shouted Richie, cutting the silence.

Carlo spun around, outraged. "What? It's in the pocket, isn't it?"

Richie shook his head. "You hit the black first, dumbass. Take your lunch money home with ya. You probably need it more than I do." Richie effortlessly knocked the black ball in. "That's game." He showboated for the rest of the bar; he and his cronies chugged beers in celebration. It was time to cut our losses.

"Let's go home, bello." I patted Carlo on the back. "You did good. These guys are seasoned. They're obviously here every week."

Carlo shook his head. "It's bullshit, man."

And how stupid was I?

How naive could I have possibly been to think that this was the end of our night?

As we turned to leave, one of Richie's friends emptied the remainder of their beer, hurling it at Carlo and I. Carlo received most of the blow. Carlo turned around, his nostrils flaring. "Who was it?" He stomped back toward the table as Richie giggled to himself.

I grabbed Carlo's shoulder. Anything to avoid a brawl. Creating a scene meant all sorts of trouble—especially in this business. "Let's go. They're not worth it. Don't fuck around, don't gain attention."

Then Richie opened his big mouth. "What are you gonna do? Better be careful, kid. You might end up like your friend over here." He gestured at me and my crutch.

The hair on my neck stood up. "You wanna take that back, you son of a bitch?" I pointed at him.

Richie laughed. "Oh look, crutches-kid finally spoke a word. I was beginning to think you were a mute. You know, you gotta use a cue to play pool, not a crutch. You also gotta stand on both legs to reach these tables." He and his boys had burst out laughing once again, prolonging their laughter as I took a deep breath to contain myself.

Carlo couldn't. "Don't you speak to him like that, you fucken slimebag."

"Didn't know he was your boyfriend, fag." At that point, Richie hadn't realized what had happened, but he found himself wiping blood from his own lip.

Carlo's fist dripped with the same blood. "Talk your shit once more and it'll be the last thing that ever comes out of that sorry mouth o' yours," Carlo spat.

Richie launched at Carlo. It all kicked off. They were grabbing each other, throwing each other, clawing at each other. I think Richie sunk his teeth into Carlo at some point too, but before it could become a full-fledged bar brawl, the bartender yelled.

"Break this shit up! Either separate or take it outside." Richie raised his eyebrow to Carlo in question. By this time, the girls Carlo wanted to impress were long gone. Carlo and Richie's primal male tendencies took over and soured the environment.

"Wanna take this outside?"

Still wiping the blood from his lips, Carlo gestured to the alleyway. "After you, prick."

Richie and his boys waited outside for us. Some part of me wished they'd just leave, but another part of me wanted to witness what was about to happen.

We stepped outside and Richie turned around, butting out a cigarette, "Ahh ... here they are. You lost fair and square, my friend. Like I said, house rules, pal." But what Richie didn't notice was the pool cue, gripped tightly in Carlo's left hand. "Woah, woah! What the fuck?" Richie's crew backed up instantly before the cue swung, whacking Richie across the face with the thick end. He fell to the floor, holding his mouth with a muffled screech. "Fuck! You just broke my fucken teeth! Fuck!"

Carlo didn't flinch, helping himself to another shot. Carlo whacked him a few more times in the head with the pool cue, over and over, and with every grunt spattered more and more blood. By this time, Richie's so-called "friends" had already fled the alley, dropping their bottles and cigarettes on the wet pavement. Carlo reached his point of no return, tilting his head and screaming into Richie's ear, "You like that, ahh? You a big fucken maaan?"

Richie was flailing his arms all around after the yell of saliva that had spat onto his face. "Ah! You're a fucken psycho!"

I looked at Carlo. This guy was taught his lesson, humbled. He had

had enough. But Carlo still hadn't. He snapped the cue in half over Richie's back. He then snatched my last crutch and used that as a weapon of mass destruction over Richie's head. The crutch also snapped, and Carlo decided to voice his opinion on the industrial cue manufacturers. "Cheap, Chinese shit!" Carlo kicked Richie a few more times in the torso and finally stopped after he ran out of breath.

Richie, who was minutes earlier an arrogant son of a bitch in a bomber jacket, was now a mere scumbag, lying in his own puddle of blood on the ground of an alleyway. He spat the red stuff on the pavement and looked up, barely able to express emotion with his facial muscles. "We—we were just playin' around, man."

Carlo, for good measure, got one more zinger in to complete the night. He leaned into Richie's face, nice and close. "Street rules, pal." He spat on Richie and stepped over his ailing body.

Richie still had the audacity to return to the big man he was inside the bar. "I'll fucken get you for this! I remember both your faces!"

Carlo quickly turned around. I thought he was going to kill him, right then and there. "What do ya remember? You stay on that fuckin' floor, or I'll make you remember *nothing!*"

Richie backed down. Can't say he didn't deserve it. He was one of those guys built to push people to the edge. They never seem to learn until something like this happens where they only have themselves to blame.

We walked out of the alleyway together. Goddammit, I needed a few cigarettes after that one. Something that many people didn't know about Carlo: He was a sore loser. He didn't like being beat. He made that quite clear.

Chapter Seven

A Demon That Wears a Smile

"You know how special you are to me?" I ran my fingers down Marianne's thigh. A half glass of iced orange juice sat neatly on the bedside table with condensation.

She looked up at me. "How special? I wanna know in words." She crossed her arms, giving me that unforgettable pout that makes you yearn to meet with those perfect lips with a strong vermillion border, never to let them leave yours. Lustfully intoxicating.

"Well, let's just say if the sun was important enough to brighten my day, then I'd say you're like a thousand suns to me." Looking back, it's difficult not to cringe at the words that escaped my youthful mouth. But what can I say? I was young.

Her smile quickly faded. "Are you saying I need to lose weight?" I thought I had carelessly stumbled upon a can of worms, but it turns out she could be quite a jokester too. As her smile gradually came back, she covered her mouth with a laugh. God, I fucking loved that about her.

"I'm kidding! You gotta grow a sense of humor! Shoulda seen your face!" She pointed at me and I removed her hand from her mouth as she looked back at me, shy.

"Don't cover your mouth. The world needs that smile. So, don't take it away."

She kissed me. Still the softest touch by anything I'd ever feel. "I think we should tell everybody about us. At least our families," she suggested.

"What are you, *nuts?*"

She bounced onto her haunches, taking my hands in hers. "I'm sick of actin' like we're just friends around everyone. Hear me out—my father is very close with your uncle. I think if anything, they'd be proud of us. Don't you think, Johnny?" Her eyes were alight. She simply wanted our love to be known, accepted, and celebrated by the people who loved us. *Why wouldn't I want to give that to her?*

I kissed her forehead. I had to agree with her. Her heart desired it, and I discovered that I crumbled easily when it came to what she wanted. There was simply no point in concealing the way we felt about each other, and no point in restricting it from flourishing into something bigger. We both knew the feeling was right; I mean, why come down to earth when we're so high up in the stars?

"Okay ... if that's what my doll face wants, then that's what she'll get." I think showing my seriousness over her triggered some kind of chemical reaction that led Marianne to leap onto the bed and straddle me.

"I want it *now*, Johnny." She kissed my neck, unbuttoned my clothes quicker than she could think, almost as if deprived.

I gripped her thigh with one hand and had her hair in my other hand. But, like before, as soon as she grasped my crotch, the shivers came about and I pushed her away, once again. I didn't understand it. "I'm sorry …" I muttered to calm her down before she could say anything. It was too late.

"What the hell is the deal, Johnny? I can't even have sex with my man?"

"I don't know what it is! Fuck!" I slammed my fist on the side table.

Marianne jumped off me and instantly began dressing herself, no doubt feeling embarrassed to be naked in front of me.

"I gotta go." Those words stung me, knowing I was the problem again.

I jumped up, trying to slip my socks on, balancing on one leg, but she was halfway out the door. "Talk to me! Stop leaving whenever this happens, for fuck's sake. Communicate!"

She gestured wildly. "Maybe you needa see a doctor about this or something."

"A fucking doctor, are you kidding me?"

Marianne shook her head. "Don't swear, Johnny. You know I don't like it—"

I cut her off, furious, but she had every right to feel the way she did.

I just couldn't handle being the problem. "The fuck sort of doctor am I supposed to see?"

Her temperament damped. She wasn't expecting me to be so defensive. She gestured at the door and spoke under her breath. "A psychologist or something …"

The more she spoke, the less a man I felt. "A shrink? I'm no fucken fairy!"

The first tears I ever saw greeted her big brown eyes. "What do you want me to do? You get me all turned on and then you freak out." Marianne threw her handbag over her shoulder. "I mean, should I wear more makeup or something? Am I not trying hard enough to attract you anymore? Tell me what it is about me that turns you off!"

I sat down, deflated. "This has nothing to do with you. You're perfect. Fucking perfect. Just don't leave. Why can't we just sit down and talk about this? I'll make you some tea—we can discuss how to work on it." Marianne sighed, wiping her eyes with the back of her wrist. She couldn't even look at me. She sat down beside me and leaned on my shoulder in silence. It was bad enough that I had this problem, but if it meant she was doubting her looks and spiking her insecurities— something had to give.

After a half hour of nothingness, she went home. I felt like I was losing her. I kicked the side table and stubbed my toe … It hurt like a sonofabitch. That was our first-ever argument. Even though it was a small one, it wouldn't be our last, or our worst.

***

We were celebrating Louie's thirtieth year in the business. Donnie held a special event for him in the bar on the upper floors of the Caruso building. All the oldies were there. The soft jazz in the background attracted mature, quiet conversation and the only loud table in there was that of my uncles.

At the usual smoke-hazed table sat Vinnie, telling a story to Donnie, Gigi, Louie, and a few other men. Vinnie had had a few drinks before I walked in with Marianne, so his tongue was already loose.

"So, this guy bursts into the diner, takin' three shots at the waitress ... misses every shot. He fires a couple at his main target, which was Larry Zafferano ... Clips the fucker in the jaw with one of 'em—*he* goes down."

Vinnie was a typical Italian. He couldn't speak two words without gesturing with his hands in some direction or rotating them in any way, whether it was a salad fork in his hand or a gun. Donnie sat back and watched, drinking his wine. That was Donnie's idea of living. He loved to be around people. He never yearned to be the center of attention but without saying a word, he seemed to have a much denser gravitational pull than anybody else.

Vinnie continued. "Next thing you know, this dumb motherfucker slides the gun back into his pocket while he's still standin' in there and—*bam*! He blows a hole in his own fucken leg!"

The entire table erupted, and I mean banging their fists on the table, leaning on each other, crying. Even Vinnie could barely hold himself together. "So, you've got a waitress that's probably pissed 'er pants, hidin' behind the counter. Zafferano chokin' on his own blood in the booth and this stupid dumbass, Angelo, squirmin' on the floor with a hole in his knee!"

Donnie shook with laughter. "Can't believe I had this guy workin' for me," he said, shaking his head and swirling his wine.

Vinnie slammed his hand on the table. "Then the cops get there, and young Ange is screamin', 'The shooter went that way!'"

Gigi nearly fell to the floor from giggling as the others ran out of breath. A few drinks in these fellas and you can knock 'em dead and still have time for a cigarette and a piss.

I approached the table with Marianne, shifting the overall atmosphere to a serious few seconds of silence. Donnie calmed everyone down with a nod. "Hey, hey, relax for a second. There's a young woman over here. Keep it appropriate, alright?" Vinnie quietened down and dug into his steak.

"Johnny, you made it. Take a seat with us, will ya?" Donnie gestured to the only empty chair at the table.

"I just wanted to let you guys know that Marianne and I are an item now." Marianne bit her lips in anticipation of Donnie's response. I needed to be as blunt as possible. I told them what she wanted me to, but I also didn't want to make a big deal out of it. These fellas wouldn't understand love. They measured their lives in success and loyalty. And if they ever did experience love, they simply wouldn't bring it up. To people like Donnie, falling for somebody was a sign of weakness and a lack of emotional control.

Donnie shook his head. "Oh Johnny, there's better ways of introducin' her than that. I don't even know what this is gonna be like for business." There it was; I'd been waiting for a comment over how my personal relationship would affect the gears and conveyor belts of Donnie's business.

"Mr. Caruso, I promise it's gonna be fine. You're stressing too much. My old man is very fond of you," Marianne reassured Donnie. That was pivotal. She wasn't some dumb broad I was sleepin' around with or just a filler girl. She had a voice and wasn't afraid to use it.

Donnie stared at her for a few seconds, surprised by her confidence. "Glad to hear it." He sat back with his wine glass. "I may have a talk with him tomorrow. He still on Fraser Avenue?" Marianne nodded. "Good." Donnie looked at me. "For now, we toast to the new couple. An incredibly good-looking couple, if I do say so myself."

As everybody on the table raised their glasses to us, those feelings came back to me. Acceptance and belonging. This was our family, and we shouldn't have felt so embarrassed or intimidated to share the news about ourselves with them.

Gigi nodded at me with a smile. "Very, very proud of you, my boy."

"In the name of love, compassion, comfort, children …" Donnie then glanced directly at me. "And in blood. We celebrate the new couple." A comfortable applause warmed the table as Marianne looked up at me. We were strong, together. Donnie then shook Marianne's hand and kissed it. She smiled, shy. He held her hand longer than usual. "You've got beautiful, soft hands." I could tell that she felt it was a few seconds too long as her smile faded, and she gulped uncomfortably.

"Nothin' like mine!" Donnie chuckled. "All chapped up and swollen!"

Marianne's smile reappeared as Gigi winked at Donnie. "It's from all the hard work over the years, Don!"

Vinnie looked over at us, keeping the attention on the news. "A new couple! It's beautiful, really, it is."

Marianne squeezed my hand with excitement. She was talking to me without saying anything. I squeezed hers, too, and she smiled. We made our way to another table to deliver the news.

Vinnie shrugged. "Can I continue my story now, or what?" Donnie gestured for him to continue but as Vinnie spoke, Donnie's eyes were still locked on us.

Nonna Francesca sat with Larissa, shifting the hair from the nineteen-year-old's face. Larissa was the youngest out of her, myself, Carlo, and Marianne. Even though we called Francesca our Nonna, Larissa was her actual granddaughter. She'd have a flare that'd make everybody else around her smile and even if they didn't want to smile, she'd have that spark that brightens a room without lights. Larissa was born in Chicago and moved to the big city with her parents when she was quite young. We barely saw her parents, but nobody really knew why. Some people said they were secretive and didn't want anybody to know where they were. Others said they got wrapped up in government conspiracy bullshit. But I say they didn't want anything to do with this business, given the burdens and demons that come with it. Larissa worked downstairs in the lobby of the Caruso building, so she was a part of us whether she wanted to be or not.

Francesca kissed us both twice on each cheek when we bent down to greet her. She liked to speak Italian most of the time to try and keep the old country in our day-to-day lives. "Marianne! Come stai?"

Marianne nodded. "Molto Bene, Nonna!" As they spoke, I thought her English was the height of her perfection but listening to her speak in her true, native language, another tune, gave me a whole new perception of her. I fell in love with her all over again, and the best part was: This woman was mine.

After hearing the news of us being an item, Nonna Francesca placed her hand on her chest in grace, calling me bello and gripping my cheeks, shaking them around, causing Marianne and Larissa to snigger at me.

"Ha ha, okay, okay! You've embarrassed me enough!"

Larissa yelled and jumped up, hugging both Marianne and me. She was known for her cuteness and playful appeal, and I could see why Carlo had a deep interest in her. At this time, their subtle exchanges were still behind closed doors.

Marianne had to slow her down. "Ha ha! Relax, it's not like we're engaged"—Marianne looked at me—"... yet." I know she wanted it now. She made it clear. I was going to marry her, I didn't know when, but I was sure of it.

"Vieni qui." Francesca looked up at me and gestured for me to come closer. She whispered in my ear in Sicilian that this one's a keeper. Marianne was the one. She didn't have to tell me twice.

Larissa joked about throwing a party for us to celebrate, but I couldn't help but wonder if she had an ulterior motive. "What do you think, Johnny? You gonna throw your lady a party, or what?"

I grinned, glancing at Larissa. "I think you're only asking 'cause you're hoping Carlo will be there, huh? If you'd just ask, we can go for a double date and get some ice cream at the drive-in theater."

She seemed to quieten down, embarrassed. I hit the nail right on the head. Larissa gestured over to Nonna, making sure I didn't spill any beans on her new crush.

Francesca spoke to Marianne in secret. Marianne smiled and looked at me. She held both my hands. "She told me to tell you not to underestimate women because when males act on impulse, the females watch and learn." I laughed, knowing it was only banter but also realizing how true that statement really was. Almost every death or close call I'd witnessed so far were males—the perpetrators and the victims. The girls didn't slip up as often, only if they'd been in the wrong place at the wrong time.

"Don't worry, she's just tryna scare you," Marianne said with a wink.

A hand gripped my shoulder from behind and I jolted. It was Donnie. "Johnny. Relax, nobody's gonna hurt you. But I like the reflexes."

I sighed. "What do ya need?"

He shook his head; his face was long. "Johnny, I don't just come and see you when I need something, okay?"

He greeted the women and only spoke to Francesca in Italian as he knew she'd preferred. He had asked her about her grandson, and she said he's growing into a handsome young man. For me, this wasn't Donnie being kind or courteous. Others liked to see it that way. I knew what he wanted, and that meant more boys, more people within the family to involve in his dealings. You may not choose this life, but sometimes this life chooses you. A group of men entered, shaking Donnie's hand and whispering in his ear about their own wheelings and dealings. There was still plenty that I didn't know about this man. I was especially curious considering they wouldn't involve me in some of these conversations, whispering to each other with small papers changing hands.

"Ay, Johnny. Come have a chat with me for a minute."

I stepped out onto that balcony, and I was greeted with the sound of violins. Someone practicing across the street in a window parallel to us. Donnie stepped out behind me. This was serious. He'd never asked to speak in private.

"What is it?" I turned. He wasn't at all happy with the manner of my question.

"Don't talk to me like you don't know me, okay? I've known you since you were born." He gestured to the ground. "I used to babysit you all the time."

I rolled my eyes. "Okay? What's the deal?" I knew it had to be something about Marianne.

"Ain't no deal, Johnny. I want you to be careful with this broad. Her father and I are a little rocky lately. The timing wasn't the best, I must admit." I knew he'd make it about himself.

"This has nothing to do with business, Zio."

He clicked his tongue. "Actually, it is. This might be a good thing because you are gonna help get her father and I back in good graces. I'm gonna need you to step up your game. You're not a kid anymore." I sighed, watching over the balcony as the woman played her violin as if a full-scale orchestra were her backdrop. "This ain't just about that doll in there. I want you to take a responsible part in this family. I wanted you to kill that fucker last year because I need you to show the others that you belong here."

Turned out it wasn't about Marianne but about my position in his future plans. "Alright. And what does that mean for me?" I asked, leaning on the balcony railing.

"It means that Carlo is looking more of a man than you are." And there it was. Donnie had a way of telling you things or asking favors—not by simply asking, but by way of insult.

"What the hell does Carlo have to do with this?" I scoffed.

"You two are the young ones, the next generation to move up in the business. You want him to be your boss one day? 'Cause it sure as hell ain't gonna be Frankie."

I shook my head and stepped away from the balcony. "Are you kidding me with this shit? Is this your way of telling me you want me to take your place?"

Donnie shook his head, still and forever on his high horse. "Nobody can take my place, Johnny …"

"Is that why you brought me over here?" I snapped. Donnie realized I was touching on a sensitive topic and became stern.

"You're here because your father died. Don't you forget that. Your old man never wanted a part in what we did. He was selfish, but smart. He was able to have a son, and I never had children, meaning you're the only family I've got."

"My old man was a good person. Selfishness had nothing to do with him." As much as he wasn't around, he'd have raised me a million times better than Donnie ever could have. Donnie pulled out a cigar and a lighter.

"If he didn't pass, you wouldn't be here, with us, makin' this money. I wouldn't wanna see my own blood on the street. No man belongs there. Especially, not from *my* family. I've been there, trust me. A man is merely nothing without his family, Johnny, so I've brought you here to give you the life you deserve."

He ignited the cigar. I tried to believe him. He seemed sincere for a moment. But I couldn't help thinking about my father. "I think I'd rather still have him around, so I can talk to him again ... I would trade all the green in the world to see my father one last time, Zio."

He only stared at me for a few seconds before leaning over the balcony with his glass of wine and cigar, staring at the violinist across the street. The silence was eerie before I turned and stepped into the building again. I made it clear that I was my own man, not a puppet. He needed to know that I couldn't just be anything he wanted me to be.

Chapter Eight

Blackjaw

"Hold still." Carlo aimed the polaroid camera. "Say provolone!"

The first real photo of Marianne and I, snapped with joy in our first apartment. We were still head over heels for each other and there was no reason to wait any longer to move in together.

"Can you grab those few boxes over there?" Marianne gestured to some boxes of clothes as she carried a large one full of photo frames.

"Geez!" I lifted a clothes box. "You got rocks in here?"

She shook her head with a giggle. "It's called quality material."

Even when she was sweating with her hair tied up, she was still the most breathtaking sight I'd ever seen. She wasn't afraid to get her hands dirty and that's what I loved about her. The motivation, the independence without relying on anybody else to give her what she wanted out of life. The love between Marianne and I was so powerful that I considered her my soulmate. You understand this finally when it makes you feel like there's a great power between you and this other person. As if nothing else in the world matters. Nobody else. It's as if all the world's electricity is surging through these two bodies. As if the whole world was made only for you and her. She was placed in your life for a reason, and you, for her.

As the sun beamed through the windows of our new apartment, the boxes piled up, ready to unpack. The floorboards and the empty appliance spaces in the kitchen were enough to call home, a fresh start. Marianne had even brought over her blank canvases and a heap of paint tubes and brushes. A new fresh space meant new dreams, beginnings, and aspirations. You see, times change, and expectations do, too. Back twenty years earlier, we'd barely be *kissing* each other until marriage. One of the things that made it acceptable was that we were bunking in the Caruso building, under the protection and watchful eye of Donnie and the others.

Carlo and Castello proved helpful, bringing in coffee tables and gifts from the family. As I helped Marianne unfold her easel, she stood on her toes, and I kissed her forehead. There was nothing like it. No other feeling. The view of the city, the sun reflecting off Marianne's skin. It was a reflection of love. It was like living a dream and I didn't want to wake up. The sight of Marianne and the smell of fresh paint and varnish.

Even Donnie showed up during the move to offer a bottle of celebratory champagne. When he realized he couldn't change me, he decided to accept me, which brought us closer than ever.

I even began to see signs of growth in Marianne, aspirations and the yearning for new experiences. She had signed up for a ballet class two blocks over. In a good relationship, ineptness doesn't exist. You grow with the person you're with. You're not afraid to try new things.

A good relationship also isn't without its occasional arguments.

"I want my easel to be next to the window, Johnny." Marianne followed as I carried her easel into the living room.

"Why can't you paint in the living room?" I asked. "There's more space for your things. I don't want you near the window."

Marianne protested, "I want natural light—it's the best for painting. The view gives me inspiration, too. I don't wanna stare at a wall all the time!"

I slammed the easel down in frustration and gestured to the open window. "I don't need creeps watching you paint in your underwear! The whole fucken city can see you through that goddamned window." She chucked her set of paints on the table with attitude and left the room. I sighed, knowing I'd been too coarse with her.

Aside from these short-lived, meaningless arguments with Marianne, everything was where it should have been, and it stayed that way for a few months at least. The only thing she and I would really fight about was the whole sex thing. I didn't know what the fuck was wrong with me, but the issue persisted, and it didn't get any easier.

***

"Why won't you fuck me, Johnny?" Standing in the kitchen, boiling a pot of water on the stove, Marianne yelled at the height of her lungs.

I gestured wildly. "What the fuck am I supposed to tell you?" I hadn't had an answer for her. And when she yelled, it riled me up to do the same.

As she gestured to her breasts, her Jersey accent stood out once again. "Am I not good enough for you? Are my tits not big enough or somethin'?"

I had both palms in the air. "You're perfectly fine. Perfect." I looked around for the TV remote to escape this situation as quickly as I could.

"Be a fucken man for once and have sex with me! Don't just stand there with your dick between your legs! Do something about it! Any guy off the street would kill to fuck me."

Now, the problem with me was, I didn't like nobody talking down to me, whether it was Donnie, Marianne, or the almighty God himself. And when somebody would insult my manhood ... that shit really pissed me the fuck off. I slammed my palm on the benchtop, startling her. "Then go *fuck* those other guys on the street! I'm sure they're *much* richer than I am, considering they're on the fucken *street*!"

Marianne flung the tea towel on the floor. She still wasn't pushed enough to the edge to actually break anything. That's more than I could say. "Don't yell at me, Johnny! I could leave you right now."

Another thing that sets me the fuck off is when somebody threatens me. I threw a handmade vase across the room, and it collided with a cabinet and shattered to bits. "Then fucken leave me, bitch! I bet you can find someone *waaaay* fucking better than me!" Oh, it was awful, the way I spoke to her. The things I said. The faces I made. Fucking shameful at best. There was no excuse. Maybe she was right. Not only could she do better, but she deserved better. I think my anger came from my own sense of accountability.

She fell to her knees, crying. Turns out she wasn't crying over what I said, but that vase I hauled was her late grandmother's. She sobbed as she picked up the pieces off the kitchen tiles. "Fuck you, Johnny! Fuck you! That was my grandmother's vase! Fucken prick!"

I mean, what the fuck was I doing? I'd never spoken to a woman like that in my life ... This wasn't acceptable and I wasn't about to let this become a habit. It felt disgusting, like a fine layer of slime had built up over my skin and I needed to wash it off before it solidified. As she ran out of the apartment, I put my hands on my head and exhaled. Something needed to change. I spoke to Carlo about this situation, seeing as it was a sore subject with Marianne. He agreed with her about seeing a doctor. Not just about the whole sex thing that was causing these arguments, but also how I'd been treating the woman I loved. I was convinced with my heart and soul that I was meant to be with her. Aside from these issues, we were perfect. We were meant to be together

… weren't we?

***

With a cigarette lodged between my fingers, I exhaled slowly and glanced up at the brick building near Brooklyn. Without anybody knowing, besides Carlo, I started seeing a shrink to find out what was wrong with me. Marianne would either be cooking dinner or attending her new ballet lessons on Wednesday nights, thinking I was just running jobs, like usual. I couldn't tell her I was actually getting help. After an enormously deep inhale of what was left, I squashed the cigarette and approached the building. *What else did I have to lose?* A relationship with the girl of my dreams had cracks in it—I didn't want those cracks to widen.

Dr. Kumar was about thirty-eight. A very well-spoken, well-dressed, and well-educated Northern-Indian man. I remember his bright white beard and his glasses, always looking up at me as I spoke, before adding to his notes. He spoke English better than any English person spoke English. I made sure multiple times that this was confidential. I didn't need people to find out, not Marianne and especially not Donnie and the gang. They'd get suspicious, thinking I'd be spilling information in regards to what we do for work or slipping up and throwing my own men under the bus. If they found out, they'd investigate, and I'd have to tell them the real reason I was seeing a shrink. It was also seen as weak in those days, cowardly. Even if they knew what I was there for, they probably wouldn't have believed it anyway.

Dr. Kumar reassured me. "These sessions will be completely confidential. Your information is not distributed to anybody outside of this room ..."

"This room?" I said, still not entirely convinced. "What about your other clients?"

Dr. Kumar sniggered. "No, Abraham. My other clients have their own issues, and they'd prefer to talk about themselves, not you. Everything we talk about in these sessions is strictly between you and me. If I disclose details about you to any third party, I could, and will, most definitely lose my job." I sat back and crossed my arms. With the money I was paying him, I couldn't take any chances. "I was offered this position in the United States for my expertise and there isn't much I'm going to do here without it. If confidentiality's a problem, we can scrap your documentation after our series of sessions are complete."

It was the safest bet. "Okay, let's do that."

He asked me where I'd like to begin but I really didn't know. *The part about the intimacy? The extremely foul way I had expressed my emotions to Marianne?* Both were embarrassing and to me, plain shameful. I straightened up and took a deep breath, starting from the beginning. "I'm gonna be straight with you, Doc. It started with sex."

He wasn't surprised. "Many issues with the brain can affect your intimate life, Abraham. Now, let's begin from when this first occurred and what you experienced."

As I bled my guts to him without spilling anything incriminating, it turns out I went to the right person. We hit the fucker right on the head. Dr. Kumar said it looked like something related to my childhood. I wasn't sure what the fuck from, but through a couple of exercises, we dug through it.

The next session, he'd set up a blackboard and drew up some diagrams which helped me to pinpoint ways to structure my thoughts.

"Okay, Abraham. So, with this exercise, we are going to undergo a few different ways to attack the source of this trauma. I want you to revisit your earliest memory possible for me."

As he waited, I desperately tried to think. I didn't have much from my childhood and couldn't figure out why.

"Uh ... at first thought, I'd say I can see my mother telling me to take a shower when I didn't want to. And then my mother shut the shower door, and my pinkie finger got jammed."

He wrote these things down as if they had some kind of significance or relation to my current issues. "Any memories you can think of before that?" He studied me in deep thought. "What age would you say that was?"

"I'd guess about three, but I dunno. Could be four."

He looked puzzled, removing his glasses and cleaning them before readjusting his chair. "So, you'd say that was your earliest memory? Nothing before that?"

I bit my bottom lip and shook my head. "That's the first memory I can think of. The only one. After that, I just remember goin' to school."

Dr. Kumar seemed concerned before clearing his throat. "School? You only have a single, solitary memory from your childhood before you began your schooling years?" I nodded, extracting as much as I could from my brain and coming out with bupkis. "Interesting. Although, not unheard of." He shuffled his papers. "I wouldn't lose any sleep over that if I were you. That could be your brain simply finding it more difficult to store memories than usual. *Or* your hippocampus doesn't regard your early childhood to be all that important to keep record of." He opened his book to another client's page and leaned back on his chair. "Unfortunately, that's all the time we have for today. We'll dig deeper and find anything we can relate to this trauma over the coming sessions. Between now and our next meeting, I'd like you to try and remember more of your childhood, even if you're just lying in bed or waiting for a train. Try to let your mind wander. You'll be surprised how many memories are buried in the depths."

***

After three drop-offs and a meeting that went on for hours, I returned home to the apartment thirsting for a beer and a cushion to lean my head upon. Marianne would usually cook dinner before I got home, and we'd sit and have dinner together, talk about our day and such. She didn't have to work, not for me, not for anybody. I was making enough dough at the time that it was carrying the both of us. Not to mention, it helped that we lived in an apartment owned by Donnie without the hassle of rent. This was Donnie's way of caring for us—no embraces, no emotional conversations—just an ease of living. Maybe it was the only way he knew how to show affection.

I pinched Marianne's cheek with a smile as she cooked. "You lose track of time with your girlfriends again?"

She poked her head up from a cupboard with a pair of tongs. "Yeah, so what?" Every day I was with her, her attitude climbed like a mountain goat. She placed her hands on her hips. "I have a life too, Johnny." She was buzzing for an argument, just waiting for me to say that trigger-word that'd set her off.

I didn't want Dr. Kumar's sessions to be in vain. "Okay ... just thought you might have some food ready, that's all." I got undressed and hung my suit in the bedroom, noticing the makeup scattered all over the dressing table.

"Gimme fifteen minutes, alright?" Marianne called from the kitchen as she switched on the stove.

As we ate dinner at the unusually long dining table, I could feel something had changed. I didn't know when or how, but it hit us like a bus going ninety miles an hour. The only sound heard at dinner was the obnoxious ticking of a grandfather clock in the corner of the room.

Is she falling out of love with me?

Tick-tock.

Am I trying to save a sinking ship?

Tick-tock.

"When are we gonna get rid of that damn clock?" I complained. "It's earsplitting!"

Marianne placed her fork down, insulted. "Johnny! Francesca bought that for us as a housewarming gift."

I gestured to it. "I can barely sleep at night with all that ticking. *Tick -tock,* it's like a bomb's about to go off!"

"Johnny, she spent a lotta money on that clock for us." Marianne clicked her tongue. "Have some manners, at least."

I know it was slight bickering but at least we were talking. For me, that was more comfortable than plain silence. "I'm sorry. I'm just a little stressed and overworked." I took a breath and continued eating the pasta. She'd worked prawns into the recipe, and it was a great success on the taste buds.

"It's okay. If you don't want the clock there, we could put it in another room." She still tried to compromise, even after my coarse words.

"No, no, it looks good. I'm grateful for it and I appreciate it. She coulda just got us tea towels like the rest of them." I pointed to the massive stack of checkered red tea towels on the table in the kitchen— gifts from acquaintances. "Fifty-six fucken tea towels. Gonna have to start wearing them as clothing if they keep stackin' up like this." I finally made her smile. "Anyway, how was your day? Tell me about it." I tried rolling the ball, capitalizing on the slight wave of conversation we'd steered upon.

Marianne reverted to answers of only a few words. "It was okay ... yours?" Little to no information. It's like she wasn't interested in talking at all. According to her lack of conversation, she sat there staring at the stains on the walls all day. Although, her makeup in our bedroom implied otherwise.

"Was fine." I was blunt, mirroring her attitude.

About a minute passed and we were just eating in silence again. I couldn't tell her about my day because I was with Dr. Kumar, and she wasn't in the mood to talk about hers. She then acted ecstatic. I suspected she was scrounging a conversation from the depths of her brain to fill the silence. "So, I hear Carlo asked out Larissa!"

I matched her tone. "*Is that right?* Fucker hasn't even told me. So, are they a thing now?"

She just shrugged and stirred her food. It's like she only wanted to kick off the conversation so I could finish it. Apart from the food on our plates, nothing about this dinner felt authentic. It wasn't.

"I don't know. She said she really likes him, so I assume they are."

I stirred my food, too. "That's good for him ..." I nodded. "Real good." The silence became deafening once more. I continued to eat, wiping my mouth with the scrunched napkin, which reflected the current state of our relationship. Carlo's barely developed relationship with Larissa somehow seemed superior to ours.

I showered straight after dinner to escape the interaction altogether.

***

Sometime that November, Donnie had given us a task to confront this scumbag stockbroker that Donnie trusted to invest in who knows what. The investment didn't matter. The return did. Apparently, he sold Donnie a cock-and-bull story that every dollar Donnie paid him, he'd return four dollars back. Quite a wager, and quite a risk—especially if this chump didn't know who he was dealing with. As suspected, we had no return, and Donnie had already given him more than enough time.

Carlo and I wore suits as we strolled into the office. They were all in cubicles; it was like a full-blown pig farm in there.

"Where's the briefcase?" Carlo whispered. I stopped and looked at him. "I thought you grabbed it."

Carlo shook his head. "It was between your legs in the car, dude."

I sighed, frustrated. "My mind's been somewhere else lately, man. Sorry."

Carlo huffed with annoyance. He couldn't afford another slip-up with Donnie. "We can't fuck this one up, Johnny. Don's been a real flat tire lately."

"Look, we'll just tell this guy we have the briefcase out back." I shrugged, hoping Carlo would agree. He nodded as we approached the cramped table of a skinny businessman, Arnold. He was still breathing air at this point in time.

"Hey, chump."

Arnold barely acknowledged Carlo. He seemed to have an unearned chip on his shoulder. "What is it? You can't see I'm busy?"

"Heard of Don Caruso?" Carlo muttered. Arnold instantly scanned the exits. "I'm not standing over there, fuckface. I'm right in front of you." Arnold's body trembled as Carlo had that killer look on his face again. He may not have wanted to be in this business anymore, but by God, he was good at it.

"What do you want from me? Of course I've heard of Don Caruso, who hasn't?" He was shaking in his boots.

"It seems Donnie invested fifty grand into your account." I leaned on the table for intimidation. "He's got no return. Where's the money?"

"I told him multiple times; it would take at least a month." He seemed somewhat sincere. I don't think he was trying to fuck nobody over. I think he was just a little sloppy, that's all. But Donnie doesn't do sloppy.

"It's been nearly *two* months." Carlo leaned down to Arnold's face. "Cough it up or that pencil in front of you is gonna be so far up your ass, you'll be writing essays with your tongue." Carlo was always the one to create a mental illustration.

"Jesus Christ. You'll get your money." Arnold shifted away from Carlo in fear. He didn't expect that kind of treatment on the first visit. But fifty grand was a lot of money, and you couldn't fuck around, especially if it wasn't yours to fuck around with.

"Tomorrow," I demanded, pointing into his mustache-ridden face. I stroked my fingers over a photo of him and his wife with a baby.

"I'll try my best. If not, the day after." Carlo wasn't satisfied. He snatched Arnold's finger and pulled it all the way back until a crack was heard. "Fuck!"

"Tomorrow, or I'll cut this fucking finger off and make you swallow it. You understand now, or do I need to pay your wife a visit?" Carlo was gripping his finger, tight. By this time, the scene drew attention from the rest of the office.

"Loud and clear ... loud and clear." Arnold was left in shivers. We turned and walked away. He looked around in embarrassment, loosening his tie and nervously chuckling in a desperate attempt to reassure the firm that there was no trouble. "Hehe, they were just playin' around ... funny guys, ya know?" he stuttered. As everybody else continued their work, he picked up the phone and continued his day job with a shaky hand.

"So you let him go?" Donnie sat at his office desk with his back turned, peeling a mandarin and leaning on the chair.

"That's the only way we get our money," Carlo reasoned.

Donnie turned around and glared at both of us. "So, this prick-ass, piece of shit, degenerate-fucker, is holding on to *my* money?" Donnie banged his finger on his own chest.

I stepped forward. "He's gonna give it up tomorrow."

Donnie leaned back on his chair. For a moment, I thought that was that ... for only a moment. "*Oh, good.* So, I can wait another day with my finger in my ass?" he ranted. "I got people to pay. This fucker is walkin' around Manhattan with *my* money."

Carlo once again spoke up. "Boss, we'll get it ..."

"Tomorrow, I know." Donnie sat up. "Whack him when you're done." Donnie then kicked his feet up on the table. He made that seem like a simple task and I was shocked to even hear it.

I objected. "Zio, he didn't even ask to get into this mess."

Donnie sat up again quickly. "Who's the one that asked for my money? Him. So, he plays by *my* rules, or he's dead. In fact, I want *you* to do him in, Johnny."

He stared into my eyes, deep. He was trying to do it again. I thought he understood the first time that I didn't want to kill anybody. "What the fuck are you gonna get outta that?" I threw my arms up in frustration.

Donnie stood up and Carlo stepped back, afraid. Donnie placed his cigar in the ashtray and approached me, shoving my chest, again and again. "You like that, Johnny Boy?" Another shove, followed by a harder one as I kept stepping back, but he kept moving toward me. "You like how that feels, you coward?" Then he slapped me across the face. My lips quivered and my fists tightened. Carlo looked away. "How 'bout that? Did that hurt?" Donnie stared deep into my pupils. All I could see was his eyes, and the smell of bourbon wafted from his lips. I was being provoked, knowing I had no choice but to let him treat me this way or banish me completely. Once again, he moved to sarcasm. "Oh, I'm ever so sorry if it did. Do nothing, don't retaliate. I could do this all fucking day and your sorry ass won't lift a finger to do anything about it!" I was mute. Nobody had ever done that to me. "Well, this man hurt me, Johnny, and he also hurt this family by takin' my money. That also means takin' the food outta my family's mouths. You want that? Is that a man you're willing to let live among us?" He then pointed intensely into my face, staring. I couldn't bear to look up at him. "You know what? I'll give you some time. Make it *Thursday*. It's not a decision anymore. If you don't hit this guy, there will be severe consequences. Consider this a final warning. Protect your blood or fuck off altogether." Donnie then looked over to Carlo. "Carlo, make sure the job gets done. Thursday is your deadline. You've got four days to do this which means no fucking excuses. Understand? I don't wanna see any of your faces until this prick's in the dirt."

Carlo nodded. He knew what he had to do. "Yes, Boss."

Donnie waved toward the door, retrieving his cigar. "Now get the fuck outta my face until it's done. Do I make myself clear? 'Cause sometimes, I fucking wonder with you two."

***

Solitary driving. No music. It was midnight and I couldn't focus. The streetlights went right over the windscreen, one by one. Sometimes, I needed time to process my thoughts. Marianne was argumentative, work was stressful, and Carlo was out with Larissa most of the time. They were fresh so they couldn't keep away from each other. This was the only time I could really take a breath and leave any confrontation to the daytime hours. I thought I'd just take a drive, have a smoke by the water, and head back home after Marianne was asleep, so I could rest without disruption. I realized that the night had other plans for me when I noticed a set of lights on my tail.

"The fuck are these assholes?" I whispered under my breath.

As soon as I braked, their headlights went out. This meant trouble and it was confirmation that they were tailing me. Before I could lose them, they came up beside me and forced the car quickly to the side of the road where I was almost on the sidewalk, erratically dodging postal boxes and streetlights. I thought it was only one car until another appeared ahead and gave me no choice but to swerve into a tight, secluded alley. I immediately had to stomp on the brakes to avoid crashing into a white Rolls Royce blocking my path. The door of the Rolls opened and out stepped a man in a white suit. He walked into the light with his heavy, black beard. It went down to his collarbone. He was about sixty with tanned skin. Before he even came close to the car, my rear doors were opened, and two thugs got into the backseat. One of them held a pistol to the back of my head as I froze up. I thought this was it. I thought I was dead, right then and there.

The man in the white suit stepped into the passenger seat, calm and collected. "What the fuck is this shit?" I yelled. The pistol was forced against my head.

Even though his suit was white, his face was still in the shadows of the car. "You've got quite the temper for a man with a forty-four mag to the back of his skull," he said in his slow, croaky voice. "I'll be the one talkin' … Johnny." I closed my eyes, but he pointed at the side compartment of my door. "Now, slowly hand over that pistol you got next to you. But no sudden moves ... You wouldn't want this beautiful windshield painted red, would ya?" I had an idea who it was, but I was reluctant to believe it. I handed over the pistol and he opened the magazine. Empty. "Nothin' in the chamber. What in God's name were you expectin' to do with this?"

He cackled and his goons joined in. My eyes frantically darted to every corner of the car for some way out of this. More men were outside.

"Do you know who I am, Mr. John Vincenzo Caruso?"

I looked up at the ceiling of the car, shaking my head. "No ... I don't." I couldn't help but stammer.

"Shame. You probably woulda known me better if it wasn't for that meddling uncle of yours." The sweat began rolling down my cheeks. He sighed, loading my pistol. "They call me Blackjaw." He leaned closer, revealing his face under the moonlight with a daring grin upon it, ravaged by age and grit, intensely staring into my eyes.

"And you, my young friend, are gonna do me a little favor."

Chapter Nine

Come Pleasure, Come Pain

My hands were gripping the steering wheel tight as Blackjaw looked deep into my eyes with my own gun aimed at myself and another pressed firmly at the back of my skull. Any sudden moves and I'd be the one that was painted on the windscreen.

"Tell me you understand. I wanna hear you say it, Mr. Caruso." After a short pause, I realized I had no choice. "I understand—"

"Sublime. That's what I like to hear." Blackjaw nodded as he reached into his pocket. I expected the worst.

A pair of clippers to send a finger of mine to Donnie if I didn't comply?

A knife to carve something into my skin as a warning?

No. It was a small bag of sunflower seeds, salted.

"You're not afraid of me, are ya?" I stared straight ahead. He giggled to himself as he leaned back to his goons. "He doesn't wanna say yes and seem like a pussy. But he also can't say no because I'd probably kill 'im." He turned back to me and his smile vanished. "Are you scared of me, Johnny? Answer me." He snapped a sunflower seed between his teeth.

I replied with a stutter, "I don't know—"

"You don't know? Well, I guess we know what kind of people Donnie Caruso works with these days. People who aren't sure of themselves." He leaned back to his goons again. "This little operation might just be easier than I thought, fellas."

"What do ya want from me? Whatever it is, just get it over with," I spat.

He emptied his sunflower seed shells onto the carpeted floor of the Lincoln. He grabbed my jaw with a tight grip and turned my head toward him. "You're gonna let us record every fucking thing that happens in this car. I wanna know what goes on up in that big castle of Donnie's. This is my town and you … insects … are just infesting it. And what better way to extract information than from the only man with the same bloodline? I'm sure he trusts only you with his big secrets." I shook my head. He had it all wrong. Donnie didn't trust me any more than he trusted the price of gas. He then held my own gun under my chin. One shot and my thoughts would've gone through the roof. "You're gonna do this for me because you care about your life, don't ya? When somebody's in this vehicle, I want you to force the information out, so I can hear it nice and crisp. For example, if you're purchasing goods, I wanna know *what* you're buyin', *when* you're buyin' it, *where* you're buyin' it, and *who* you're buyin' it from. Understand?" I kept staring directly ahead of me. The less I spoke, the sooner I'd get the fuck out of there. "If you don't, you won't mind me puttin' a hole in your brain." I nodded quickly and he clenched his hand—wrapped around the gun—into a fist. "They don't only call me Blackjaw from the color of my beard, you know?" He nudged my jaw with his fist, followed by a smile. He handed the gun to one of the goons and stepped out of the car. One of his men began installing a recording device in the glove compartment. Blackjaw poked his head back in the window. "Tampering or removal of this recording device or any of its attachments will result in your termination. So, don't touch it or there will be severe consequences. Sorry, kid. It's just business."

I sat there for another fifteen minutes or so while his men installed the device. It felt like an hour. And I felt like a traitor.

***

As the small strands of tobacco from my cigarette were ignited, I sat in the car and waited for Marianne to walk out of the medical center in

Soho. I was wearing sunglasses and letting the smoke escape my mouth and stream through the gap in the window. Two shop owners were arguing in Greek across the road. It was interesting, attracting pedestrians to catch a raw glimpse of free entertainment. But I couldn't. Nothing was distracting me from that beating glovebox a few feet from me. I knew what was in it. Nobody else did. It was my secret to keep, and it was listening, all the time, as if it had a heartbeat of its own. I had only met BlackJaw for about ten to fifteen minutes and I'd already become a slave to him. My entire life tipped upside down. I could've sworn I'd heard the device beeping, but it wasn't, at least not from where I was sitting. It was in my head, beeping faster as my breathing struggled to keep up with it. Breath after breath, inhale after exhale.

The car door swung open. My focus was broken by Marianne abruptly getting into the car and slamming the door shut.

"Let's go." She placed her handbag on the floor, and I stared at her, waiting for some kind of news as to why she'd been feeling under the weather.

I took my sunglasses off. "You okay?" I asked. She just nodded, strapping her seatbelt on. "What did the doc say?"

She didn't even look at me. "Nothin' serious." She glanced into a small makeup mirror at herself—a distraction to get me to stop talking. I wasn't satisfied. I blew off lunch with Carlo and Castello to take Marianne to this doctor. "So, what's the issue?"

She then clicked her tongue and sighed, looking at me. "I got a UTI."

I shrugged. "The hell is that?"

She crossed her arms. "Urinary tract infection."

"How do you even get that?"

She rolled her eyes and shrugged. "I don't know, Johnny. It just … happens."

I gave up, losing a battle to her sheer bluntness, "Alright, alright, whattaya need me to do?" I tried to be as helpful as possible. To me, it was just her own personal issue that she wanted to deal with herself. I tried my best to be hospitable. "I can get you some stuff from the drug store, if you want?"

"Just take me home, will ya?" she snapped. "I'm not in the fucken mood." I was confused at the sudden reaction. Marianne didn't curse often either, so it came as a surprise.

"Look, drop the attitude. I just care about you and wanna know what's goin' on."

"Johnny, just let it go." She slapped her hands on her lap. "It's a simple infection that you don't need to keep askin' me about!"

This was a common occurrence between us, which is why I thought nothing of it. "Okay, okay. I don't know why you're bein' so defensive." I turned away, dropping the subject to avoid elongation. I flicked the ash of the cigarette out the window and onto the road.

"Had a good enough look?" Marianne struck with an accusatory manner. I turned to her, confused. At first, I didn't even think she was talking to me. "Did you enjoy checkin' out that whore across the street?"

I didn't even see anybody walk by. There just happened to be somebody there in a tight skirt. "Are you kidding me with this?"

"No, I'm not. You turned to look at her so quickly your neck coulda snapped."

I couldn't help but smile from disbelief. I found it utterly ridiculous. "What, the one in the skirt? I didn't even notice she was there."

Marianne already had her arms crossed before I could finish the sentence. "Well, you seemed to notice she was wearin' a skirt, didn't ya?"

I shrugged and shook my head. This was getting to a whole new level. "Just because she happened to be in my line of sight, that doesn't mean I was checkin' her out. Are you crazy, or what?" She shook her head and grabbed one of my cigarettes. Only the second time I ever saw her smoke. "And when did you become a smoker?" I admit it was a spark for yet another argument but at the time, I needed to strike back with something, considering she'd just fired in all cylinders over something completely outrageous. She rolled her eyes and ignored me. She had a way of keeping the conversation on a topic she wanted it to stay on. I protested, "And how could you just call somebody a whore when you've never met them?" I should've thought these things through.

"So, now you're defending her?" She started sarcastically clapping her palms in my face. She knew she was boiling my blood, and she liked it. "Congratulations. You're really helpin' *your* argument."

"I just can't win with you, can I?" I gave up. She must've felt powerful—maybe that's what she needed at the time. Or maybe she just used that argument as a front to vent some frustration out on me.

"You know what, I don't wanna talk right now. Just take me home, please?" I knew it wasn't about the girl across the street at all. I gave her space as I started driving. I tried to comfort her, placing my hand on her thigh like I always did. She swept it right off, as if she was disgusted. She stared out the window, but I couldn't just leave it at that. I gripped the steering wheel tighter and ground my teeth.

What would Donnie have done in this situation?

Sit back and let her cool off? *No.*

Tell her she's right and take a loss? *God, no.*

Straighten her the fuck up and show her who wears the pants in the relationship? Reclaim my masculinity? *That's Donnie.*

To prove to her that I was the man, I had to take charge.

I took her bowling. The Harlem Bowling Alley was the place to be for an entertaining night out. The music, the drinks, the crowds. But this time, it was only her and I. She wore this sparkly pink skirt for a night on the town. I think she needed it. She needed to look in the mirror and feel good about herself. To feel the confidence that she'd felt before and reclaim the same feelings from when we first met. I wore a neat, white shirt as I handed her a colorful drink while the disco music played on the speakers. The setup was perfect.

"So, what's the occasion, pretty boy?" She looked at me with a smile. Well overdue.

"Doll face, the occasion is that you are the most beautiful woman I have ever seen in my life." I wasn't lying. Nothing came close.

She giggled and covered her mouth. "You know, having a UTI means I should be resting and staying hydrated, right?"

I gestured to her seat. "You're sitting down, and you have a cold drink in your hand. What more could you ask for?" I said with a cheeky smirk.

"You always seem to know what to say, don't you?" She looked sincere for the first time in a while.

"Look, I'm sorry about today. I didn't mean to put any pressure on you."

"Oh, Johnny, relax. It's nothing." She swept it off but I needed to make her feel okay, to feel like she could talk to me about anything.

As I already said, she wasn't just my partner, but my best friend. "You deserve privacy and I respect that in a woman. You don't need me on your back about anything and everything."

She nodded. "Johnny, you make me happy and that's all that matters." She was forgiving. Any speedbumps, mountains, or potholes in this long and windy desert road—she'd try her hardest to plow through them, if it meant we were still together on the other side.

I cockily grabbed a purple bowling ball and felt my childlike capabilities flooding back to me. I winked at her. "This one's for you."

I bowled it, expecting something close to a strike but it was destined to be a gutter ball. She laughed at me, teasing me. For a moment, it felt like we were back to normal. For a moment, we were younger. As she laughed, I watched in awe. It's funny how just a burst of laughter from a human being can make you feel so much happier. She was my world. As I stood there, stunned as she continued to giggle, she stopped to take a sip from her drink through a curly straw. Perfection in a single moment, paralyzed by time. The feeling where nothing else matters but that one person in front of you. She was my escape, my liberty, my freedom. I walked up to her as if possessed, having fallen in love with her for what seemed to be the forty-seventh time.

She looked up at me, halting her laughter, confused, but the smile remained upon her lips. "Are you alright, my love?"

I needed the reassurance. "Do you love me?"

"Yes, Johnny. I love you." She giggled.

I stepped closer. "Do you trust me?"

Her giggling stopped as she became serious, now lost in my eyes. "I trust you."

I proceeded to retrieve a shoebox from beneath the booth seat. "Open it."

"Oh, you didn't have to, Johnny—I know I wasn't in the best mood today but that don't mean you gotta buy me something."

I gestured to the door. "You want me to take it back? I can do that. It'll save me a couple bucks."

She held the box tight, pulling it close to her chest. Nobody was taking it away from her. She pointed her nose up at me. "Nope! It's too late!"

Marianne excitedly began opening the box and discovered a pair of pink ballet shoes with a solid gold lining along the sides and gold embroidery, displaying the words "Doll Face" on them.

"Oh my God! These are gorgeous! Where'd you get them?"

I gestured to the shoes, hoping to God that they fit her. "Try 'em on. See if they fit." She was about to stick her foot in before I stopped her. "Wait, wait! Check if they put that scrunchy paper shit in there first!"

She looked confused. These ballet shoes weren't just any ballet shoes you'd get from the store. They were custom-made and probably the most expensive pair of their kind in the United States. But there was something inside the shoe that surpassed them in terms of value and sentiment. Reaching inside the shoe, she paused for a moment. Her eyes grew wide as she looked up at me, unsure whether to believe it or not. She pulled out a solid gold engagement ring with the diamond the size of her fingernail on it. A six-claw, princess-cut solitaire. The tears greeted her eyes immediately and she jumped up at me, embracing me like she never had before. A love reignited. A marriage in prospect. Even the bystanders in the alley took a moment to pry. You don't see this shit every day and to them it was storybook shit. As she took her seat, I took the ring and slid it gently on her finger. A perfect fit. She stared at it in awe, speechless. I waved at the manager in the distance, and he nodded at me. I had the whole thing planned out. Trust me, when I wanted something done, it was done. And it was done in style with nobody fucking anything up. The manager played "Sea of Love" as I looked down at her and extended my arm.

"Take my hand, my love."

She heard the song and smiled, throwing her hand in mine with trust as I pulled her onto her feet and led her onto the bowling lane. She was cautious, worried she'd slip and die of embarrassment, but for me, there was nobody in there but her. I held her arms with reassurance. I wasn't going to drop her in a million years. I pulled her close within the safety of my chest as we danced slowly. Cheek to cheek, I swayed with her as my pointed shoes took their steps along her heels in perfect synchronization. I looked deep into her eyes and that's where my eyes would stay for the next few minutes. She looked into mine. I could tell it was the moment she fell in love with me again. It became almost abstract. We were going round and round in circles, swinging one way or the other as if there were no limits, even though we were bound by the bowling lane. We were dancing in space, the very fabric of thin air, the deep realms of our hearts combined in what would be an eternity of unconditional love and embrace. The bowling balls were still rolling in the background, hitting the pine like thunder. Other bowlers watched on but to us, they didn't exist; nothing else did. Nobody else. I couldn't even hear the music anymore. Our souls combined at that moment. I didn't have to ask. I knew it just by the way she was looking at me. I looked into her glistening eyes, and she was lost in mine. I could never forget it. That night, her smile was like all the lights in the city of New York shining right back at me. I didn't want to forget it. We both felt it. Little did I know that after that night, we'd never feel it again.

***

I sat in the passenger seat of the Lincoln, staring at the glovebox yet again. It was listening, taking in every word, every breath that exited my mouth. I couldn't think straight amongst the paranoia.

"Can't believe you're getting married." My focus was broken, and I was yanked back into reality by the voice of Carlo. "You alright, Romeo?" He could tell I wasn't myself.

I looked down and forgot I was holding a cigarette. The ashes were piling up at the tip. "Sorry, what were you sayin'?" I rubbed my eyes.

Carlo nodded. "I said I can't believe she said yes." I laughed and chucked my cigarette at him. He placed his hand on my shoulder in a congratulatory manner, "You're engaged, man. This is a big deal. You gonna tell your uncle?"

I shrugged. I didn't know what to tell Donnie or what he'd think of it. I hadn't even thought about how I'd tell him. This *was* huge. I had promised my life to somebody. "I don't know about him sometimes ...

But either way we're gonna give it a few days to enjoy the moment and let it sink in." Delaying it seemed like the best option. It always does at the time.

"Just be careful with telling Donnie too much of this shit. He doesn't seem to like it when somebody goes through a life change." Even Carlo was wise to him. It made me wonder why Donnie possessed so much loyalty from these fellas. I didn't want to stress about my uncle. He was the reason we were at this accounting firm anyway. I was here to put an end to someone's life under his orders.

"Well, I'm not his son. Besides, what about you and Larissa?"

Carlo smirked and fiddled with an old newspaper. "You heard about that, ah?" I snatched the newspaper and whacked him over the head with it.

"You're supposed to tell me everything, bello!" Then, I realized Carlo had more of a heart than I thought.

"I know, I know. I just don't wanna get anyone too excited. We've been spending every night together for the past few months. I think I'm in love with her, man."

As I opened the window and scoped the towering accounting firm, I raised my eyebrow. "Really? The infamous, courageous Carlo in love? Have you told her that?"

He rolled his eyes. "I plan to, very soon. I just gotta grow the balls, first."

I smirked. "You're gettin' soft, man."

He playfully shoved me. "Shut up, asshole, and keep this shit to yourself. You're one of the only people I can trust, so keep it to yourself, alright?"

Those words struck me like a bullet. Carlo trusted me and all the while, those exact words were being recorded by the device in the glove compartment. *Was he right to trust me?*

"I forgot to tell you. Larissa convinced me to get this bakery thing off the ground. I'm scoping out a store for rent in Brooklyn and I'm not getting my hopes up but I was gonna ask if you wanted to check it out next Tuesday with me?"

"I wouldn't miss it, my friend." I was stoked, but once again aware of the device, I kept my words to a minimum.

We approached the accounting firm from the side alley. We had arranged to meet Arnold there to avoid any suspicious transactions inside the firm itself. Well, that's what we told Arnold anyway. In reality, it was the safest place to put him down. No view from the public, no windows from above.

Carlo surveyed the area. "What a shithole to work in. Even my toilet don't look this bad." He leaned into my ear and whispered, "You packin' heat, or what? You're gonna have to hit this guy. You know that, right?"

Naturally, I tried to find any way out of it. "What if he has all the money?"

Carlo shook his head. This time, that excuse wouldn't cut it. "You heard what Donnie said. Whether he has it or not—"

Before Carlo could finish, the side door to the building creaked open and Arnold stepped out with a briefcase, cautious. "Guys," Arnold said, making sure the coast was clear.

Carlo immediately pointed to the case. "Better be some cash in there, amico."

He shook his head. "I could only get my hands on half. Next month, I can get double. I promise! Just tell Mr. Caruso to be patient."

Carlo sighed and after a few silent seconds he looked up at me. "Ay, John. The time is now."

I glanced at Arnold. He too knew what it meant. "What about the rest of the money?" I asked Carlo, still trying to find a way to avoid performing this deed.

"Donnie's orders. Either way, you gotta do it. Your uncle wouldn't know patience if it came at him like a brick."

I took a deep breath and looked around. One last glance before dropping him. By the time my hand reached into the pocket of my trench coat, Arnold was already pumping his legs down the alleyway.

"He's tryna split! You follow him, Johnny. I'll take 'im on the other side!" Carlo ran toward the street, and I went directly for Arnold.

As he scurried through the alley, he tipped over trash cans and crates to block my path, but I dodged them like it was an obstacle course. A few months before, I would've had trouble with my leg, but this time there were no excuses. I either did it, or I didn't. I noticed Carlo catching Arnold from the other side of the building, running along the public streets and past pedestrians. He knew well how important it was to finish the job.

Arnold turned a sharp corner, and I slipped on a puddle, using the adrenaline to quickly pick myself up and continue my pursuit. "Please? Leave me alone!" he yelled as he turned another corner. I pulled out my pistol as he raced into an open area. Still no windows in sight. It was the prime opportunity to do it. He then tripped over a loose pipe and collapsed in a puddle of mud. A sitting duck. "Please? I haven't done anything! I couldn't just make the cash appear! It's a system! It's a process!" The tears began streaming down his face as I held the gun, aimed between his eyes. He was shaking and biting his lips.

I remembered the week before. We were in his office interrogating him. I remembered the picture of his wife and kid, running my finger over it to threaten him—and now that idea was threatening *me*. How can I take that away from somebody? What would I be doing to that child in that photo? By taking this life, would I be ruining generations of what he or his children could've had? I'd be making a widow of his wife over a simple spat about money.

"Get the fuck outta here." I lowered the gun, and he looked up at me in disbelief.

He stuttered, "Wha—what?"

I pointed to the end of the alleyway with a faint view of the street.

"You heard me. Leave, before I change my mind. Leave the city and don't ever come back. No more deals or fucking around with us, you understand?" I needed him gone. For Donnie to believe it. I needed him to disappear for good.

He got onto his knees, praising me. "Yes. My God, thank you! You won't hear from me again, I swear it!"

I kicked his knees. "Scram! Get the fuck outta here."

As he ran away limping, I collected a few dollar notes that he'd dropped. Carlo approached about twenty seconds later, out of breath. "Fuck ... did he get away?"

I sighed. "I couldn't pull the trigger, man." I needed to tell him the truth. I'd already made too many mistakes as it was.

"Fuck, Johnny. What are we gonna tell your uncle?" Carlo said, scratching the back of his head.

"He ain't comin' back. We won't hear from him again," I muttered, just hoping to God that this wouldn't bite us in the ass.

"Better fucken not. Keep this between us, ah? Nobody wants to hear that we let a scumbag like that go." Carlo dusted himself off and lit a cigarette.

"He had a family, Carlo. He had a kid."

Carlo looked at me with a headshake as if I wasn't seeing the whole picture. "You need to get that out of your head, man. Everybody's got a family, Johnny. Some people just don't deserve theirs."

Chapter Ten

The Family

"Kick it to me!" a young version of me yelled in Sicilian. I was around four, and we were in San Leone, a suburb of Catania, back home, below our brick-paved apartment and little markets lining the street.

Isabella, my sister, six years old with tremendously long brown hair, would run out of the apartment with tunnel vision, eager to play with me and this other kid we called Federico. Isabella kicked the ball with no restraint and without looking, I chased. The horn of the small car felt like I'd be made deaf. I was stunned as the driver yelled at the top of his lungs. Upset, of course. More yelling came from the civilians on the street, screaming at the driver to slow down. It was my fault, but they defended me. As the driver shook his head and drove away, I heard another man yelling. It came from the balcony above. It was my father, Gonzalo. He was always well dressed with glasses and a slightly darker complexion than Donnie.

"Jon-Jon! Get the hell off the road. What's the problem with you?" He looked over to Isabella. She thought she was in trouble for sending me onto the road. "Get inside, now! The both of you!"

Isabella didn't want to go inside. For us, that meant playtime was over and we'd have to stop being kids for a little while. My mother, Carmela, comforted her. "Come on, baby! It's okay." She was tall, big-eyed, and beautiful with a classy Italian accent.

As we sat in the kitchen of our small apartment, I remembered the paintings on the walls of the Sicilian landscapes and buildings. I played with a toy car while watching my mother cook.

My father was on the other side of the room at a desk, sorting through papers and files. "Don will be over soon."

Carmela placed the cooking utensils gently on the table and sighed. "What for?" She didn't like him, not one bit. I couldn't tell you why. This was just a memory.

"He needs to pick something up."

Carmela shook her head and turned the stove off. "You know I don't like him coming around here."

Gonzalo shrugged, dropping the papers onto his desk. "He's my brother, for Christ's sake! He's not a bad man."

Carmela gestured wildly. "You are blind, Gonzalo! Blind and ignorant! He's trying to pull you into his business! Stop helping him! You need to stop giving him money and let him deal with his problems on his own!" She knew what Donnie wanted. It was clear. He approached my father only for his money.

Gonzalo defended himself. "You don't dare talk about my family like this! If he needs help, I help him! If he needs money, I give him money! He's only here for a few months anyway, and he doesn't ask for much."

Carmela calmed herself and began washing some of the cooking utensils she was using. "When's he gonna be here?"

Gonzalo squirmed, knowing she wouldn't like the answer. "About twenty minutes."

"Vaffanculo!" Carmela began packing her handbag, desperate to avoid Donnie's arrival. She grabbed both Isabella and me by the wrists and led us to the door. Isabella lagged behind, forgetting to put on her shoes. "I'm taking the children to get groceries." She looked at Isabella, who was taking her time. "Isabella, put your shoes on!"

Gonzalo wasn't happy, but I think he was more upset that he had to deal with Donnie by himself. And it's by yourself where Donnie is known to take full advantage of you.

Carmela made one thing very clear. "He's *not* seeing my children."

With Dr. Kumar, I had moments where I'd remember an old memory from my childhood in Catania. These were sudden instances, feeling like only half a second of memory, but each one I began to remember vividly. I wondered what they meant and why I was recalling them at these specific times. Eventually I began to wonder how random these memories were and finally I learned that they were never random, not at all.

***

Night after night, I'd lie beside Marianne, awake, staring at the ceiling. When I eventually did sleep, I was introduced to the fragments of my past, in Catania. Was it real? Who's to say? But it had to manifest from somewhere. I looked at her beside me, her bare back, sleeping softly, only hearing her exhale. We were still on thin ice—an engagement ring doesn't solve every problem. I knew something had to be done to protect her, protect us, protect what was mine. The recording device, the limbless and voiceless item that I was a slave to. Maybe my paranoia was damaging us. Maybe I was going crazy. Either way, something had to give.

Voices flooded back to me. Myself, "You trust me?"
Marianne, "I trust you."

And Carlo, "You're one of the only people I can trust, so keep it to yourself, alright?"

How could I let this happen? This device was destroying my sense of loyalty. Every day and night it drove me insane. I tried to go back to sleep but toss after turn, even in my sleep, it followed me.

I was in the driver's seat, feeling the weight of Blackjaw watching me from the passenger side. The cold barrel grazed my cheek as he held the pistol with his head tilted.

"What's it worth, Johnny?" His voice echoed. He then whispered into my ear. "*Your* life? Or your *family*?" He gestured to the backseat where Carlo and Marianne's bodies were carelessly stacked upon each other, unclothed with perfect bullet holes in their foreheads. No blood. I turned away quickly, wanting them to disappear, not to see them that way. It sickened me to my core. I was but an empty man without these people. "Are you scared of me?" Blackjaw whispered into my ear. I was shaking. His finger wrapped around the trigger as he smiled, pushing the gun tightly to my temple.

BANG!

I woke up in cold sweats, shocked and disorientated. I'd never had a dream like that before. I wiped the sweat off my forehead and got up slowly. Marianne moved over in the sheets. I didn't want to wake her. It was well past midnight. I kissed her forehead and threw a pair of shorts on. I had to get rid of it. I had to remove the device.

In the Caruso car park, I reached the Lincoln. We had numbers on all the cars to keep them in check. I ripped open the glovebox, breathing fast, nervous that I'd be caught in the act, either by Blackjaw himself, or worse, the Carusos. I felt like a traitor, but I wasn't. I yanked out the cords and all the sticky tape holding them together. I don't know why I did it. Maybe I wasn't thinking straight, but I couldn't just sit there and let him listen. I was not a rat. I'd rather die than put my family in danger. If Blackjaw wanted me dead, he would've done it right there when he had the chance. He needed me to be able pull this off. And I knew that if he killed me, it'd raise hell with Donnie and begin an all-out gang war, smack bang in the middle of New York City. I was willing to take that chance and call his bluff, even if it was the biggest chance I'd ever take.

I ripped the rest of the cords from the interior cushions and the roof lining. My heart was beating a trillion times a second. I lit a cigarette and sat back in the passenger seat with the disassembled device in my lap.

I returned to the bedroom where Marianne was waiting for me. She'd noticed I wasn't in bed beside her. "What time is it?" she asked.

I sat down beside her, removing my clothes to get some rest. "It's late. Go back to sleep, everything's alright."

She stretched out again, getting comfortable. "Where'd you go?" she said as she buried her head deep in her pillow and I got under the covers.

"I just needed a smoke, that's all."

She hugged me and fell back to sleep in my embrace. "Yeah, you smell like it. I love you."

I tried to fall asleep but yet again, no such luck. Now, I had something else keeping me up. Something more worrisome. *What were the repercussions going to be?* As she put her head into my neck, I kissed her forehead and exhaled. *Was I going to die for this?* I didn't sleep for a single minute that night.

***

The next morning was a bright, crisp day. I got up early considering the lack of sleep. Wearing a suit and sliding my sunglasses on, I was able to conceal the darkness beneath my eyes. I rushed into the car park where I'd left the recording device and noticed it was missing from the dumpster and the stack of foam I had hidden it beneath. Somebody found it. Somebody had the device. I looked around in every direction.

"Fuck," I whispered.

How could it have been collected that early? The trash wasn't taken, but the device was. Maybe some kid found it and thought it was valuable, or perhaps, somebody scrounged it for spare parts. I picked up a discarded brown paper bag and approached the bin to get a closer look, in case it had sunk down to the bottom.

An old woman mistook me for a do-gooder. "Bless you, boy. If we only had more people like you in this city, we'll be as clean as Japan!"

I nodded, playing along. As I reached the bin, it was confirmed. The device had vanished. My worst fear was if it was Blackjaw's men. I felt the world around me shrink as I looked in every direction. *I'm in over my head.* Suddenly, a car pulled up to the curb. A black Ford. I stumbled back, expecting a drive-by shot. Instead, both the passenger and the back door opened at the same time.

A tall man with a patchy beard stared at me from the passenger seat. "Get in. Don't run. We will find you anywhere." My hand ran down my jeans to grip my gun, but he aimed his own at me. "Don't even think about it, smart guy." His pistol had a silencer on it. "We're not here to hurt you. My boss just wants to talk with you, that's all. Now get in." I had no choice. It was either take my chances in the car or be shot on the street like a mutt. I couldn't help but picture where they'd take me and the possibility of them torturing me for intel on Donnie instead. A more direct approach.

I stepped into the back of the car and before I knew it, we were moving. These guys knew where they were going. I didn't. "What does he want from me?" I was shaking, expecting my blood to paint the back window at any moment or as soon as we turned into the next alley. Maybe they wanted to get me into the car first to kill me with no witnesses. Maybe I was better off on the street after all.

"Put your seatbelt on. We don't want any accidents, do we?" He aimed his gun at me as I slowly clipped my seatbelt. "That's better." He saw the sweat run down my forehead as I stared at him. He chuckled.

"Relax, kid. I'm not gonna shoot ya. My boss just wants to talk." He held his hand out to me. "I am gonna need you to hand over your piece, though. Can't be too safe around you Carusos."

"No, thank you." That's the last thing you'd do in a situation like this. Nobody wants to be shot with their own gun.

He rolled his eyes. "You wanna marry Miss Manzelli, or not? We can take that away from you, kid." These people already knew everything about me. How did they know where to get to Marianne? I took a deep breath and passed him the pistol. "Stop stressing, John. He's not *that* bad."

We drove to the suburbs of Long Island to a faded one-story home with a rusted-out mailbox. This didn't look at all like a drug lord's mansion. But I also wouldn't put it past Blackjaw to be living in plain sight either.

Romano, the passenger from the car, led me through the house where a few men were drinking coffee in the kitchen. It was definitely a joint meant for business, but they hid it well.

"Follow me. Don't touch anything." I was paranoid, afraid that somebody was going to jump out at any second and dice me like a ripe tomato. The hallway was tight as it led to one room at the back of the house. *This was it*, I thought. *This was the torture room*. But before I could confirm it, I noticed one peculiar detail. There was a small picture on the wall. It was Marianne, about six years old. You could tell her face from anywhere at any age. It was a grainy photo of her on an old swing.

I whispered to myself, "What the fuck?" Was this some kind of mind game? Some sadistic way to toy with my emotions? A youthful photo of my love on the wall.

Romano grasped my forearm and led me through the door. I was still more puzzled over the photo than whatever was inside that room. There was only a single bed and a chair with someone sitting in it. His back was to me, and he wore a checkered shirt, and was hunched. "Boss? John Caruso's here."

The man in the chair nodded and spoke with a creaky, Italian accent. "Leave him with me."

"You sure?" Romano seemed hesitant. "I'll wait right outside the door, boss."

The man shook his head. He didn't want Romano anywhere near us. "Romano, go have a coffee, will ya?"

As he left the room, the old man finally spoke. "Do me a favor and shut the door." I cautiously complied.

"Come closer." I knew this guy wasn't Blackjaw, but what if it was worse? I stood in front of him. He was in his late sixties, short and tanned with gray hair. His eyes were wide open, but they didn't look at me. I then realized, this man was blind. "Come here, so I can feel what you look like."

He placed his hands on my face, feeling every bump, curve, and wrinkle. "You're a good-lookin' kid. So, you're the man that's gonna marry my daughter?" As I heard those words, every ounce of relief in the world washed over my face.

"You're Mr. Manzelli?" I reached for his hand and shook it, surprised I'd never met him earlier.

"That's right. I would've appreciated it if you had come and asked me for my blessing before taking my daughter's hand."

I took a deep breath, having not even considered it before, but in my defense, Estevan Manzelli was a difficult man to reach. "I apologize. I hadn't met you until this point, sir. So, I'm sure you'd forgive me for thinking that I wouldn't be expecting to meet you anytime soon."

He nodded. He seemed like a reasonable man. "That's fair. Unfortunately, I've been quite busy, taking care of a few problems these last couple months. But when I hear my daughter is getting married, my priority is to know who it is, what his intentions are, and what he's going to do to keep her safe and make sure she is out of harm's way."

He loved her and I understood it. If I loved her as a man, imagine how he could love her as a father. He only wanted the best for her and to guarantee her protection. "And she is. Always."

He nodded. "How's your Uncle Don?"

"He's good, he's—"

"Still the same old bastard?" Estevan cut me off and lightly chuckled to himself.

I looked at the ground. "He's good." I didn't want to divulge too much information on Donnie since he mentioned that their relationship was rocky. I can't give any information to a potential competitor, business or not.

"I've heard a lot about you, John. Tell me, what can you offer my daughter that no other man can give?" This became a questionnaire, as if I were still competing for her as a suitor.

"Mr. Manzelli, I assure you that you have nothing to worry about. She's in safe hands." I wanted to get it right, make a stand-up first impression and claim full respect from Mr. Manzelli.

He still found ways to surprise me. "How the fuck would I know that? You're part of a dangerous business. The biggest coke movers in this city and you're telling me that my little girl is in safe hands?" He shook his head. I couldn't argue with it.

"Our business is done in a safe manner, sir." Any excuse I came up with just wasn't enough.

"There's nothin' safe about it and you know it. Try again. What can you do for my daughter that nobody else can?" This was quickly becoming an interrogation.

"Mr. Manzelli, I'm an honest guy. I make good money and she will never starve or struggle. She will live in the nicest house, water the greenest grass, and wear only the best clothing the world has to offer. That's my word." I expected to astound him with reassurance. He just sat there and sniggered sarcastically with a proud look on his face. "What's so funny about that?" My jaw tightened.

His eyes didn't move one bit, but his arms gestured to the room surrounding us. The peeling wallpaper, the crooked photo frames, and the rusted bed frame. "Look around. Does this look like the nicest place? Do I have maids and servants scrubbing my fucken feet? Am I wearing anything more than an eight-dollar shirt?" He leaned closer in my direction and whispered, "You think I live like this because I'm poor? You're wrong. With all the money I've made in my lifetime, I'd still be going strong for another six hundred years. It isn't about wealth. That's what Don can't comprehend. His life is money. I don't blame you for thinking that would make my daughter happy, John, but you're wrong."

"I'm nothing like my uncle." I sighed. "But money is important to sustain a healthy life."

"Riches aren't the be-all and end-all of everything in life. I don't give two fucks if you're broke and barely payin' the bills." Estevan sat up straight in his chair. "All I want is to know there's a smile on my little girl's face. That smile is worth more money than I've ever made or ever seen."

I nodded. "I understand."

"Come here a minute." I leaned closer to him, expecting some words of wisdom. Instead, he snatched my collar, holding me with a tight grip. "If that smile disappears from my daughter, you are gonna wish you'd never met her." I couldn't move, he had me in his grasp and he had tendons like a fucking tiger. I nodded. He pulled me tighter. "If that smile disappears from my daughter, I'll take everything from your life and kill it, slowly and painfully." He then leaned uncomfortably closer with his mouth almost grazing the side of my ear. I began to sweat. "If that smile *ever* disappears, you can count on me strapping you down myself, cutting your fucking balls off with a blunt knife, and feeding them to you. Don't think for one second that I won't do that. I may be blind, but I have eyes all over this city, you understand?"

I was shaking. I know he noticed. I nodded once more. "You have my word, sir."

He finally let go and sat back on his chair. I was still in shock over the threats. He patted me on the back with a smile. I stepped away, intimidated but glad he couldn't see my face. Although, I'm certain he heard the tremors in my voice. "I'm glad you understand. My wife wanted to have a word with you too. Will you meet her in the garage?" I thought my day was over, that I'd go back home to Marianne. Little did I know it was about to get a whole lot worse. "Don't take my wife too seriously, alright? And give my regards to Big Donnie."

I walked into the garage of the Manzelli home where Martha Manzelli had requested to meet me. Romano closed the door, having not followed me this time around. I had already developed a strange feeling about this. Was it the eerie silence? Was it the carpeted floor of the garage? Was it the smell of tobacco in the air? It must have been because it was pitch-fucking-black. For a second, I thought it was a trap, maybe even a little preview of what would happen if I were to hurt Marianne. A lighter sparked from the other side of the room. A cigarette was lit and I could only just make out the faint silhouette of a woman sitting pretty on a barstool.

"Mrs. Manzelli, is that you?" The slender figure stood up off the chair and flicked a switch, but it didn't help much, only turning a dim light on in the center of the room that hung loosely from the ceiling. At least with that, I could make out what was in front of me. Martha was about forty-eight, slender and gorgeous with long brown hair all the way down to the bottom of her back. She had a rich, elegant English accent. She was only wearing a black robe.

"I was waiting a while. You really hit it off with my husband, didn't you? I hope he didn't scare you."

I needed to be mature and charming. "It's okay, I don't scare easily. I'm glad to finally meet you. I can see where your daughter gets her looks."

I was expecting some kind of giggle, but she just smiled plainly as if she'd heard it all before. "Take a seat, will you, Johnny?"

I looked around for a chair of some sort until Martha pointed to the corner of the room at a few chairs stacked against the wall. "There are some fold-out chairs in the corner. Be a dear and fetch yourself one."

I carried two chairs to the center of the room. "Here you are, ma'am."

She glanced at me and took a seat before blowing the smoke from her cigarette into the air above her. "Chivalry isn't dead after all. You're quite the specimen to look at, aren't you?"

"Thank you, Mrs. Manzelli. You're gonna make me blush."

Things began to take a turn as she pulled her chair closer to mine and handed me her cigarette. "Call me Martha." As I took a drag of her lipstick-painted smoke, she stroked my cheek with her fingers, swift as a feather. "So, how'd you meet my daughter?"

I looked into her eyes. They were just like Marianne's and had aged like fine wine. It was like staring into the ocean. It'd consume you. "She was playin' the piano at a wedding. The most powerful but delicate tune I've ever heard. True fingers of an angel." I needed to keep the conversation about something other than the fact that she was unbearably close to me and stroking my face with her nails. But instead, she proceeded to interlock her fingers in mine.

"You know who taught her how to push those keys?" She bit her lip. The room was rising in temperature.

I began to sweat as her fingers ran down my palm. "You, I assume?"

"*Bingo.* You're quick." She smiled sarcastically, followed by a wink. "And what about the other girls? You spend a lot of time with other women, Johnny?" The interrogation had already begun.

"No, ma'am. And I don't plan to." She then untied her robe. Although it still covered most of her slender body, I knew exactly what she was doing. She wanted to plant the idea into my head.

"Ever feel yourself *wanting*, Johnny?" The temperature seemed to shoot up to a hundred and fifty degrees.

I stammered, shaking my head. "No, ma'am." She leaned into my ear, allowing the view down her chest beneath her robe to align purposely within my sight.

"'Cause I do," she whispered softly.

"I really should get going—" I tried to calmly stand up to minimize any chance of startling her, but she'd already gripped my shoulders and kept me seated.

"I'm an attractive woman, am I not?"

How the fuck was I supposed to answer that? I looked at the ground and nodded. "You're gorgeous, Mrs. Manzelli."

"What do you like about me?" Every question pushed past the boundary of the last. I looked directly into her eyes, bringing the conversation back to where it should be. "Like I said, I can see where your *daughter* gets her looks." I needed to make it clear that I didn't want this to escalate.

Martha rolled her eyes and stood up. I thought the ordeal was over as she paced around the room. "Johnny, you can probably tell by my husband's ... inability ... that I'm no longer admired or really *prized* by him anymore; at least, not the way I'd like to be. I don't get much excitement as of late."

I nodded. "He's a wonderful man."

In her overly seductive, Mrs. Robinson attitude, she turned and looked at me. "He's given me everything but ... there *are* some boxes that are unfortunately left ... unticked." Martha walked away slowly. Her robe rolled down her sculpted body and onto the floor. I quickly looked away. She was completely, utterly naked. Martha turned around. "Look at me, Johnny." Her voice was stern. I continued to stare at the floor. She was a beautiful woman. Any man would kill one of his own to admire it. However, I was completely and unconditionally in love with her daughter. "Don't make me feel ugly now, look at me." I reluctantly raised my head. Her body—there was nothing like it. Every twist and curve were cut to perfection. The irony was that her husband was blind. "Do you like what you see?"

"How do I answer that question, Mrs. Manzelli?"

She shook her head. "I told you, call me Martha." She once again approached the chair and placed one of her feet onto my chest and pressed until the chair leaned back, just enough so it didn't fall. I inhaled deeply, staring into her eyes. "It's perfectly normal for you to want somebody else, you know? Even if it's ... just a little ... *fun.*" She bit her lips, smiling and relinquishing her foot from my chest as the chair slapped to the ground. She then walked behind me slowly, whispering into my ear, "To be truthful, I'm jealous. My daughter gets you *all* to herself. Lucky girl."

She took the cigarette from my hand, stole a drag, and gave it back. This was the kind of woman who if she wanted something, she got it. And if she didn't get it, it frustrated her; it sent her insane. And by God, was she frustrated. "I'm a lucky man to have met your daughter."

"Just one night it would take, to have someone pull my hair for once, make me beg for mercy and release me from my ... insatiable yearning." She began to pull on her own hair, revving to new heights of seduction.

"Can you satisfy my desires?" She smiled daringly before swinging onto my chair and sitting on my lap, facing me, naked. She even leaned in close, grazing her lips on my chin, playing with her food. A straight tease. She then leaned her head toward my hand, smoking the cigarette as it remained between my fingers. "You're telling me, there's not the slightest, single speck of faint curiosity?" As the smoke escaped slowly through her lips, she stared deep into my eyes. A seasoned hypnotist. "You *really* wouldn't fuck my brains out, Johnny?"

I had to end this. I smiled back at her. "I'm sorry, Martha. You're a wonderful woman but I am in love with your daughter and frankly, I am *not* in love with you. I hope you can understand that."

In the span of a millisecond, her seductive smile switched before I could blink. She snatched the cigarette from my hand. "Excellent." She abruptly stood up and wrapped her robe around herself again, tying it. "I suppose I'll be seeing you at Christmas when we all get together for lunch?"

I remained stunned by the sudden change of attitude from Martha. I cleared my throat, pretending I wasn't affected. "That sounds about right. Sure."

She then smiled. "It was a pleasure to meet you, and I think you'd be a swell fit for my daughter. Thank you for stopping by." She gestured to the door. "I think you know the way out."

I left, relieved and confused over what the fuck had just transpired.

***

After the rollercoaster of a day I'd had, I needed to see the only face that made me feel at home. Although that face seemed to fluctuate between Marianne and what would sometimes be Carlo or Castello.

I shaved my beard that evening. Donnie always crapped on about how it's better for business to be clean-shaven and that we come across as more professional, and less like thugs.

As I lathered the shaving cream on, Marianne leaned on the doorframe in the reflection of the mirror. "So, I heard you met my parents?" She gritted her teeth with a smile.

"Sent somebody to scoop me up right off the street. Welcoming folk, they are," I said sarcastically as the razor began to pull the cream along my face.

"I hope they didn't act strange or embarrass you." Marianne tilted her head.

I wasn't going to tell her about her mother. She might think of her in a different way or even believe that I had something to do with it, as if I provoked it. "They care about you a lot." I turned, placing the razor down. "You never told me your father was blind."

"Well, I didn't want that to be the first thing you thought about when I spoke of him—a blind man. It shouldn't define him. He wasn't always blind," Marianne said as she walked into the bathroom, hugging my bare chest. "You goin' out tomorrow for another job?" Marianne asked as she buried her head in my neck. She didn't look at me when she asked me. Maybe it was hurting her that I wasn't around as often as I used to be, especially because Wednesdays were also taken up by the shrink.

"Tomorrow's Wednesday, right?" I asked her and she nodded. She closed her eyes, finding comfort in my chest. Sometimes the best times we had together were when we didn't speak. Silence meant comfort, but it also meant a lower probability of sparking an argument. "Yeah. Every Wednesday. I got the same job with the same guys. You know how it goes."

She looked up, wiping a bit of cream from my cheek. "I wish I could kiss you, but you've got shaving cream all over your face."

I collected some cream with my index finger. "Here, I can take it off." I dabbed the cream onto her face, and she scrunched her nose and batted me away with a giggle. "No! I just showered!"

I swiped some more off my face, and she playfully screamed, rushing to the opposite side of the bathroom, desperately darting from one side to the other. I held my arms out like a monster, closing in on her. "There ain't no way out. You best give up."

She let out a roaring laugh and scurried to the other side of the bathroom beside the shower. Her laugh was contagious. She then grabbed a bar of soap, daring to throw it at me. "I'll do it, Johnny! Don't test me!" she playfully threatened, trying to act serious but we both knew she couldn't contain her laughter.

"Come on, that's a hard soap bar," I pled with a grin. "You wouldn't do it. You wouldn't hurt me." She held the bar of soap in the air, giggling like a child. She had the power. "Don't you do it," I yelled.

She closed her eyes, laughing as I approached her. "I swear, I'll do it." I didn't believe her. She could never hurt me. Even if she wanted to. I took the bar of soap gently from her hand and placed it on the vanity. She looked deep into my eyes, and she was serious, suspended in the moment, as if I'd stolen the last ounce of laughter from her soul. It's like she had an epiphany. A sudden realization.

"I love you so much, Johnny …"

I smiled at her. She knew it was an undeniable feeling that I felt the same. I didn't even have to say it for her to know. We had something nobody else did.

"Nice try." I smiled before smearing the shaving cream right across her face as the laughter was welcomed back with a boom.

She giggled, rubbing her hands across my face, spreading the cream around in an outright mess. We made a complete mockery of the bathroom. I picked her up and swung her around, kissing her lips repeatedly.

I wondered if we were improving, if we were putting the arguments behind us. If we were to regain what she and I once had.

Chapter Eleven

The Bigger Picture

Castello and I stepped out of the car and Carlo had the biggest smile I'd ever seen on his face. This was it. His dream. This was what he was working for. An empty bakery in Queens. Rich in prospect and potential.

"Gentlemen, this is the future site of The Queen Baker."

Even Castello was impressed. "It looks spacious in there." Castello gestured to the surrounding area. "Smack-bang in the middle of Queens, too. You'll get a lotta business here, kid."

Carlo placed his hands on his hips and nodded, knowing in his brain that he wasn't going to live his life without achieving this one dream. "Ain't she beautiful? I'm close to getting a loan for it but I'm gonna need a little more of a deposit. I'm hoping it stays on the market for the next few weeks, so I can have some time to gather the funds ... Wanna go inside?" he asked. I was confused, pointing at the giant lock on the front door, assuming he was blind. "We go around the back, my friend."

Carlo knew this place well. He'd clearly been here a few times by himself before bringing us here. He expected us to jump over this prison-like fence to get to the back of the store.

Castello placed his hands comfortably in his pockets. "You're fucken nuts if you think I'm jumpin' that. I weigh triple the both of yous." I jumped over with Carlo. Turns out we *both* didn't need to jump because Carlo just unlocked the gate for Castello to stroll through anyway.

"This place isn't half bad," Castello marveled. All the appliances were still there under clear covers, ready to go.

"I've been waiting for it. You don't understand how excited I am to get this going. Even Larissa wants to work here with me." Carlo was clearly excited, but I had to bring him back to reality.

"You speak to Donnie about this?" His face changed straight away, knowing how much of a stranglehold Uncle Don had over our lives.

"I don't know what he's gonna say, you know? How can I explain that I wanna do somethin' else?"

People seemed to underestimate Carlo's potential more often than not. He reminded Castello and I that Donnie owned a fucking flour mill. Obviously for the purposes of the *real* business but a flour mill meant what it meant. At this point, Carlo was animated, almost stuttering over his excitement and the bakery prospects.

"Imagine, I cut a deal with Donnie, and he supplies my flour. The most important product to my business comes cheap right through the back door."

"I'm likin' what I'm hearin'," I said. "Just don't mix the coke with the flour from the mill, otherwise you'd get a few juiced-up complaints."

Carlo chuckled. "It's a win-win. Imagine the money we could make. Like Cas said, in the middle of Queens, barely paying a cent for the flour and having workers at my disposal. Larissa's excited and I spoke to young Giovanni, who's gonna be old enough to work soon, so I think we can pull this off, fellas."

It was a big dream, but the bigger the dream, the bigger the risk. Carlo needed a helping hand from anybody he could get. Castello then became serious. He seemed more invested in the idea now that it had manifested into something real. "How confident are you in landing this joint?"

Carlo shrugged. "I don't know. Somebody else could buy it right now if they wanted to. I'm just keeping my fingers crossed that it stays on the market until I get the funds."

Castello shook his head. That's not the answer he wanted. Not for this place, not in the middle of Queens. But reality was reality, you can't escape that. "Look, kid. I'm excited for you and I like your motivation and business plan, but I don't think this place is gonna last too long on the market. We're central in Queens, for Christ's sake. This is a hot spot with plenty of foot traffic. How long do you need to wait?"

Carlo's eyebrows lowered. "I'd say about a month until I can earn enough for the deposit."

"In all honesty, I'd barely give it until the end of the week to be snatched up by a franchise or some rich investor." Castello sighed.

Carlo's heart broke in front of us. He glanced over the appliances and blank walls, scratching his head.

"Tell ya what." Castello placed his hands on his hips. "How 'bout I loan you the money for it and you march your ass down there today and purchase this hot property before some other schmuck does."

Carlo's face lit up brighter than the lights of Las Vegas. "Are you fucking around or what?" Castello was dead serious. I couldn't believe it either. "Don't you fuck around with me, Cas. Don't you tease me with that shit." Carlo could barely control the excitement running through his veins.

"I'm as real as the hairs on your nut sack, kid." Castello pointed at Carlo. "It's your dream and we all deserve the best shot at achieving our dreams. Right?" Carlo jumped on Cas like a hug from an ape. I couldn't help but smile. This didn't just mean achieving a dream for Carlo, but it meant liberation from the reality of our business.

"I'd do anything for the both of ya, you know that? Anything to get you a head start on the rest o' your lives."

Carlo was still dreaming and his eyes were still closed in Castello's chest. "I can't believe it, man. We're actually gonna do this."

Castello chuckled. "It's no longer a dream, kid."

"I knew there was a reason I only brought you two here. You are the two men I trust most with my life, and I am fucking glad that I am sharing this with you guys." Carlo looked around the bakery. It was his. He could already picture the customers, the bread, the passion in his baking. "If my old man could see me now."

Castello then broke the silence. "What are ya waitin' for, a celebratory blowjob? Somebody could be buyin' this place right now!" I looked at Cas and he shot me a wink. I responded with a smile and a nod. Castello was a different kind of family. He actually cared about us without expecting anything in return. No ulterior motives, no expectations, no bullshit. Without question, these fellas were the only two guys who I knew wouldn't screw me when push came to shove.

Small businesses were a popular trend in our circle. You had Chester Marchetti, one of Donnie's oldest friends, running a strip joint downtown. Robbie Oatmeal—don't ask me where he got that name, must've been a nickname from when he was younger or something. *How am I to know everybody's history?* He owned a small restaurant in Harlem. We'd go there every few months to have dinner, meetings, and sometimes to collect what was Donnie's. Which is where my uncle came in. As much as he let somebody believe they were making it on their own, or liberating themselves from our lifestyle, he found a way to keep them involved, whether it meant funding their business and expecting major financial return, using their business places for meetings and laundering, or simply providing the flour for their bakeries. They were all fooled by the promise of freedom, but Donnie kept them tangled in the web; mind you, he even profited heavily, considering their businesses as an extension of his own. Whether it was a loan, a lending hand, or a beating hand to outrun the competition, Donnie would always be "pulling favors" in expectation of a bigger favor in return. People preferred to view his generosity through rose-colored glasses.

***

That night, as I stared down at the take-out noodles in front of me, I came to an odd realization. Marianne stopped eating and looked at me.

She smiled politely. "What's wrong? You haven't touched your food, baby."

I didn't know if I should have brought it up. "I've been so busy with work these last couple days. I think it's just becoming a lot to handle."

"Maybe if you eat, you'll feel better." Marianne seemed happy. By God, I loved when she was happy, but there comes a point where you know so much about a person that when their behavior changes, you can sense it a mile away. "I'm sorry that it's just Chinese tonight. I was gonna cook lasagna, but the oven stopped working a few days ago for some reason."

I glanced at the oven. It was a lie. She lied to me. I knew the oven worked. I used it that very morning. Why would she lie? Was she embarrassed that she hadn't cooked? Was it just an excuse? Or was there another reason? "I'll get Vinnie to take a look at it tomorrow."

"Besides, I don't mind Chinese," she added. "It's a nice change of pace, I guess."

As she dug her fork into her noodles, I could tell she was keeping a constant busy rhythm. A usual tell when it comes to hiding something. I needed to keep it to myself a little longer. "So long as it ain't Indian. You can't beat the taste, but that stuff sets me up on a week-long date with the bathroom." Marianne giggled but still didn't take one look at me. I placed my fork down and looked up at her with a squint. I couldn't sit there any longer. The curiosity was bugging me. "You haven't been beggin' me for sex lately. What gives?"

She shrugged and sipped her water, again keeping busy. "I'm not some kind of animal. I just get sick of askin' for it when I know it won't happen."

I continued stirring my food, although I was too distracted to enjoy it. "So, you don't feel like it as much?"

"Of course, I do. But ... a woman can have fun on her own as well." She poked her fork back into her food. There wasn't even a three-second gap where her hands weren't busy. "Besides, it's all about when *you're* ready. All I care about is you."

And that was it. It was too understanding of her. I know that Marianne wanted sex—she'd made it clear many times. The more I couldn't give it to her, the more she asked. Suddenly, she stopped asking. Something changed. I could have taken it as a positive like she'd hoped. Less yacking, less whining about me not satisfying her. But no, I think it meant something else. "Thanks, I know you understand." I kept it to myself. I didn't need another argument. Marianne continued eating her food. I stared at her. I wasn't hungry anymore.

Days went on like this. Work, Marianne, the drop-offs. My life was starting to become a loop.

***

Monday: Weekly drop-offs with Carlo to this motherfucker named Jerry at the docks—wouldn't be his real name but I didn't blame him. We'd barely ever see his face and if we did catch a glimpse, there'd be a different guy the following week.

Tuesday: Meetings with Donnie and the douchebags, telling us where to go, what to do, and how much green we were bringing in weekly. He would hand out warnings to those who'd slip up or didn't come back with what they agreed on. There were no second warnings in this business. Rule number one: Keep your nose clean. Every day was like a new first impression. One fuck-up and it's a permanent stain on your reputation. A *single* fuck-up could mean you're never trusted again. And if it's a bad enough fuck-up, you're never seen again.

Wednesday: Attend evening sessions with Dr. Kumar and make any little progress we can. Let me tell you, it's not easy to open up and unlock memories with somebody you just met a few months before. You feel like they judge every word that exits your mouth. The hard part is tiptoeing over the subtle details that might incriminate you. There was one time I almost mentioned the pizza parlor incident. I had to trail it off with a cock-and-bull story about how much I couldn't stand Asians running a pizza joint. I'm sure it came off as racist, but I didn't bother to correct myself, so long as I was safe. As much as confidentiality is promised, you could never be too careful.

Thursday: The only day where I felt like I could spend some quality time with Marianne and properly talk to her. Some days, we'd make progress, and some days it'd feel like we were only going backwards.

Friday: The day we'd celebrate what we put together throughout the week, catch up and have a few drinks. Donnie would set up the bar upstairs just for the men. Sometimes, he'd even surprise them with a stripper or two. They'd have a laugh followed by a few more drinks and they'd all stumble back to their apartments with smiles on their faces, laughing about something stupid that Frankie did.

Saturday: We'd help Carlo set up his bakery business. Marianne and Larissa would come along and lend a hand. We seemed to work well as a team of four, each giving our own ideas and opinions on how we could better the business. I'd stand there with Marianne and watch Carlo and Larissa's relationship flourish over this business they thoroughly planned together, talking about how their children were going to work with them one day. To Larissa's surprise, she didn't expect Carlo to be thinking about children already. It only made her love him even more.

Sunday: The only day I had off to rest. I would be so fucken tired from the week that I wouldn't even be able to get up and go outside. Even taking a leak would feel like a task. That one day I had off, I'd always be looking forward to it. But when that day finally arrived, I'd just sit around and watch the time go by, feeling guilty that I didn't spend my day doing something productive. Until Monday came back around.

This loop went on for a few weeks. The same shit. The same jobs.

Everything.

***

Central Park on a Thursday. She was wearing an oversized gray jumper. Although the day was dull and so were the color of her clothes, Marianne's face was by far getting more beautiful by the minute. In this busy period, she stopped taking ballet and began teaching it full time at a studio a few blocks over. That meant more hours, more friends, and less time for me. It made me appreciate the rare moments with her, and as much as I'd hate to admit it, I believed that the time apart could heal us.

I leaned in to hug her, but she stepped back with a smile. She was hiding something beneath her jacket.

"What's got you so excited, beautiful?" I smiled.

"I've got a surprise for you. Close your eyes, pretty boy."

I closed them, hoping I'd feel her lips on mine before I opened them.

"Okay, open up!"

As my eyes opened, a big black nose hovered in front of me, furry with big brown eyes. No, I wasn't talking about Marianne. It was the fluffiest little dog I'd ever seen in my life. I really was surprised.

"What? Who's this?" I scratched behind the dog's ears and picked it up, looking close into its eyes. I was an animal lover, but I didn't know to what extent. He was beautiful. It was almost like a physical manifestation of what I had with Marianne. Now we had something to care for, maybe even a distraction in the household to deter us from arguing.

"A friend of mine at the studio asked if we wanted him. I couldn't say no!" Marianne was bubbly, excited as much as I was.

"What did I do to deserve such a compassionate woman?" I asked. She shook her head with a smile. "We're a family of three now!"

I kissed her lips and then her forehead, holding the dog in between us. It was a special moment, one that'd last forever, and definitely a step in the right direction for us.

"What's his name?' I asked as I tickled its nose.

"I thought you could name him." Marianne shifted a strand of my hair as she looked into my eyes.

"Bernie," I muttered.

"Bernie?" She squinted. "What's Bernie?"

I shrugged. I don't know why I named him Bernie. "For some reason, it's the first name I thought of."

Marianne giggled, admiring my impulsive name choice. "Bernie it is! I love that." She laughed as she ruffled Bernie's fur. The sight of her was incomparable. Within this continuous loop of my life, she was the only thing to break the tension, the only thing keeping me sane.

***

This life has undeniable disadvantages but in life, everything has a balance. A risky business meant an excessive amount of income, a gorgeous woman meant more attention from other men, and a life spent without regret is a life spent in sin.

At a tailor in Newark, Carlo and I were trying suits on in front of a mirror. We weren't there for suits, but it was one of the perks of the job. The tailor, Leon, was a small, chubby, and greedy man but very kind and generous if you were the person he wanted to see. He hobbled toward us with two folded suits in his hands. He seemed to only address me, knowing I was Caruso blood.

"Mr. Caruso, can I interest you in one of these prestige designs? Brand-new arrivals from San Sebastian." He placed them out on a chair.

I shook my head. "I think I'm gonna go with this one, my good sir."

Carlo nodded, impressed by the suit I'd chosen. "Azzurro." He winked. Leon turned his head, disgruntled. Most of these guys never really liked it when we spoke in Italian. They had the strange idea that we were keeping something from them. Carlo corrected himself. "The blue one. I like it."

As Carlo threw on a gray version of the same suit, Leon looked at me, clamping his hands together. "And about the small matter of payment?" I picked up the orange suitcase behind me and handed it over. We never went anywhere for no reason or no motive.

Although Carlo wanted out of the business, it's not something you could simply bid farewell and wish a swell day to. Carlo was one of the regulars. And Donnie would rather hang on to an old dog who knew the game than bring somebody in and teach them the tricks of our trade. The work continued regardless. Even if it meant closing the bakery for a day to cover the suitcase swaps. There were so many places we had ties with that the clients would come in quicker than the product. Donnie and the guys would then cut the coke with flour ... plain fucking flour from the mill—only in desperate circumstances, of course.

As Leon tasted the cocaine on his lips, he smiled, shutting the suitcase full of small, cut bags and nodded at Carlo and I with a smile from cheek to cheek. "Happy to do business with you, Mr. Caruso."

I nodded back, gesturing to the suit I was wearing. "There's a little extra in there. Consider it payment for these." When you have something that somebody wants most in the world, they'd almost let anything slide in order to get it. With the business we were running, there'd be nothing that nobody wanted more than coke, and with that, we had the power.

"And don't forget to send your uncle my regards," Leon shouted as we walked right out of there.

I was about to light a cigarette as we exited the store. Before I could reach for my lighter, a black Lincoln swerved onto the curb. I dropped my cigarette; Carlo reached for his gun.

Vinnie poked his fat head through the window. "Get in."

Surprised and shocked, Carlo protested, "What the fuck, Vin? It's not cool to swing up on us like that."

Vinnie pointed to the backseat with his thumb. "Just get the fuck in the car, I'll explain on the way." Usually, a response from Vinnie would be humorous or cheerful at least, but this kind of introduction meant it was serious.

Carlo was still caught off guard. "What about our car, we can't just leave it here."

Vinnie stared at him with a thumb still aimed at the backseat. "I don't give a fuck—get in. They nailed Riccardo. We need to move." This meant trouble. Big trouble.

The Lower Manhattan Courthouse. I waited outside with Carlo and Celestino, who had a handful of cigarette butts at his feet. It was his brother who was nabbed. Whenever one of us got pinched, it meant any information about any one of us was at stake. These instances would catch you off guard at any time and any date. It all depended on that one person who was caught. You just had to hope and pray that they had enough balls not to say anything. Number one rule about gettin' nabbed by the pigs: Don't. Fucking. Say. A. Thing.

Carlo scratched his head in confusion and looked over at Celestino in disbelief. "Stealing watches? How far could your head fit up your asses? He's gonna get us all collared."

Celestino stood up quickly and pointed intensely at Carlo. "Hey, shut the fuck up, bastard. You weren't there, alright?"

As expected, Carlo didn't quite shut up. "What are yous doing in New York, anyway? You should be staying where you belong in Boston until you hear Donnie's whistle—"

Celestino stomped over to Carlo. "Do I look like a fucken dog to you? We do *what* we want, *when* we want. If I wanna go to New York, I don't need to ask Donnie's permission. If I wanna go to Disneyland, I don't need Donnie's permission. If I wanna screw your *mother*, I—" Carlo immediately threw a punch, but Celestino began shoving him against a wall. I had to separate the both of them.

"What the fuck are you doing?" I stood between them both. "We're in front of a courtroom, for fuck's sake!"

I looked at Carlo as he dusted himself off. "Carlo, he can go wherever he wants." Celestino thought I was taking his side, but I don't take sides when it comes to perspective. "And when you two travel, you need to keep your noses clean." I was stern to Celestino as he unwrapped yet another packet of cigarettes.

"Who put you in charge?"

I pointed in his face. "I'm not the one in the fucking courtroom, alright?" This wasn't the first time the Boston Connection found themselves treading hot water. As you could probably tell, this shitty situation puts everyone on edge, knowing that we could simply be drowned at the end of that court session. By the time Celestino was up to his thirteenth cigarette, the boys walked out of the courthouse. Riccardo was between Donnie and Louie, with a right smug look upon his face as if he beat the feds. As arrogant as it was, it meant good news for the rest of us, and we could finally breathe a sigh of relief.

Celestino walked up to his brother and asked how it went. With a smirk, Ricky said, "Slap on da wrist!"

Donnie jokingly wrapped his fingers around Riccardo's neck. "You got us scared for a second there, I'm telling ya." It was funny; if he had let any information slide, Donnie's grip would have been tighter and not a single breath of air would have escaped that mouth of Riccardo's.

Vinnie chimed in, "Especially when they asked about the flour delivery in Yonkers. That was a close one. I was sweatin' bullets!" We all walked back to the cars, wiping the sweat off our foreheads.

These close calls were sometimes for the better, reiterating the fact that we needed to stay on our toes in future dealings. It wasn't only the information that was on the line. We saw these fellas so often that we didn't want them locked up and put away. After all, they were our family, and we were theirs.

Chapter Twelve

Monday, Bloody Monday

Pictures. Pictures and objects—and even sounds—can spark specific memories in your mind. I wasn't aware of the magnitude until one particular session with Dr. Kumar. I slouched on the chair in his office and as he flicked through a set of pictures, I stared outside to the city, feeling like these sessions were my one-hour-a-week hideaway from the world. As if I were backstage and stepping back on the street would mean I was required to be Johnny Caruso again. I would have to put on the mask of my character and be the man everybody knows I am. These sessions as Abraham were an escape for me. A commercial break in what would usually be a life of confusion, moral dilemma, and stress.

"Okay, Abraham. I'm going to ask you to flick through these pictures and tell me which one impacts you the most."

I flicked through the booklet he'd given me. There was a picture of a handgun, a cartoon ghost, a black door, and a toy truck.

"That one." My finger made its way to the toy truck. I was uneasy looking at it. It didn't quite make sense to me.

"That's very interesting, although unsurprising," Dr. Kumar said, stroking his beard. He wrote something down.

"What's it supposed to mean?" I interrupted. I couldn't make heads nor tails of it. "What are you writing down? You keep saying these things are not surprising, but I don't feel myself overcoming anything here, Doc."

"I remember you telling me last week you used to have a toy truck in your bedroom when you were younger," he said as he placed the booklet on his office desk. "A red one … I had my assistant bring in some photos similar to what you described."

"What is it about the truck that makes me feel uneasy?" I began to think it was bogus. I had these suspicions before. I was paying big bucks for this guy, and knowing it was confidential meant he could drive up the price whenever he wanted, and I was the sucker who got wrapped up in his reel. I also wondered if it was why he never gave me a straight answer—to keep me coming back, take me for a ride, highlight random pieces of information to give them some sense of false significance.

"The truck suggests that what happened would have been when you were much younger. Probably younger than we suspected." He was puzzled. "Do you remember anyone around you that weren't your parents?" I stared at the ground for a second.

"Zio ..." I mumbled.

"Pardon me?" He couldn't hear what I said, and I didn't expect him to understand it in Italian.

"Um ... my uncle. He used to babysit me and my sister sometimes."

Dr. Kumar sat up in his chair as if he'd struck oil. "What do you remember about him?" He placed his glasses on and readied his notebook. I shrugged, having not yet connected anything with Donnie from the present to my interactions with him from the past. To me, they were two different people. "Well, when was the last time you saw this man?"

"Monday."

Dr. Kumar raised his eyebrows. "He's still around? You're in contact with him, are you?" He seemed desperate to know the answer. I needed to be careful. This territory was like a minefield when mentioned.

"I work for him." I tried to contain the elaboration to avoid any slip-ups about who we were.

Dr. Kumar crossed his legs on his chair, taking off his glasses and cleaning them. "Of course, of course. This is progress, Abraham. I think we're getting somewhere." All I could say was that I was confused. "Now, let's start digging into your uncle, shall we?"

***

A toy truck, a red one. It was another memory. I could've been about four.

"Jon-Jon, Isabella, get up!" My mother, Carmela, ran into the room, yanking me away from the truck and my sister away from her dolls. She rushed us to a bedroom, opening a tall cupboard and forcing us inside. "Stay in here until I tell you to come out." There was trouble. Something had happened. "You understand?" I stared at her and nodded. Isabella put her arms around me, and I felt safe. But I think she was just as fearful.

We stood there, watching through the thin gaps in the cupboard as my mother paced in a circle, biting her nails. It almost looked like she was running away from something. Another door from inside the apartment swung open with a bang and Carmela flinched.

"Carmela?" It was Donnie's muffled voice from another room. Carmela leaned as naturally as she could on a desk and neatened her hair. Donnie strutted into the room, skinnier with slicked-back hair, wearing a white shirt and a bright gold watch.

"Where's Gonzalo?" He was agitated, possibly drunk.

Carmela shrugged. "I think he's out getting groceries."

"You think? Are you lying to me?" Donnie almost seemed like he'd been lacking his fix of some kind of dangerous, addictive drug.

"Come back tomorrow, Donnie. Please? The house isn't clean enough for visitors." Carmela kept herself busy, tidying up. You could tell she was riddled with fear.

"I own this apartment. I'm the reason you're not on the street! When

I visit, I don't care whether it's clean or not. And I know you don't care either," Donnie said as he ran his fingers down the faded wallpaper.

"Okay. Make yourself at home. You want me to cook you something? I've got leftover risotto." Carmela changed the subject in an attempt to seem hospitable.

"Where's little Johnny? Out with his father, too?" Carmela took a moment to answer and kept her glance far away from the cupboard where we were hiding. "You look at me when I'm talkin' to you. Where is Johnny?"

"Out with his father. Why do you need to know?" Carmela nervously muttered.

Donnie slapped her with force. I could feel the sting of her cheek from where we spied. Carmela looked at him, frozen.

"Why don't you look at me the same way you used to?" Donnie ran his fingers through her hair.

Carmela turned around and faced her back to him. "That was years ago, Donnie."

Donnie then pointed his finger in her face. "I was too broke for you, wasn't I? It's funny how things change. We had somethin' and you killed it. Because Gonzalo was the richer one, right? *He had his head screwed on straight!*"

Carmela tried to turn away from him. "You're drunk, I can smell it!"

Donnie ignored her. "We had something growing and you killed it, didn't you?" A vein emerged on his forehead as he stared at her with intimidation.

The tears began to fall from my mother's eyes. "I didn't do anything—"

Donnie pointed at her, cutting her off, tormenting her. "Didn't you?"

Carmela frustratingly began to pull on her own hair, yearning for the conversation to end. "Stop it, Donnie! Stop it!" Donnie grabbed my mother and bent her over the coloring table. Her face was flat against it as she glanced at us through the cupboard. Donnie lifted her skirt and began untying his belt. "No! Please? Not now. Not here. Donnie, not here!"

He stopped, leaning over her and talking into her ear. "Oh, how the tables have turned. I got da cash now, bitch! My selfish brother is now struggling to keep a fucken roof over his head! I remember when there was a chance for us, Carmela—you and I. Back when we were young, back when we had our dreams of getting outta here ... back before Gonzalo got his dirty fucken fingers inside your—" She turned and slapped him before he could say it. At that point, he pounced on her, shoving her petite body up against a bookshelf. I stared at them as the children's books fell to the floor, one by one. I couldn't do anything. She'd told me not to come out of the cupboard. I began to cry, thinking he'd kill her. He kept pushing her up against the wall, constricting her. She tried to yell but he covered her mouth. "I don't wanna hurt you, Carmela. You know I don't. But you must be punished. Everybody gets what they deserve in the end. If the men aren't here, then where is Isabella?" She couldn't help it. It was just a reaction. Her eyes glanced quickly through the gaps in the cupboard before looking away. Donnie sighed but he wasn't done. He grabbed her by the neck as she shrieked, and walked her to the door, throwing her out before locking it behind her. Carmela began banging her fists on the door like a caged animal.

We were alone in the room with Donnie. He'd already begun pacing. "Isabella." We stared at him, staying quiet because we were told to, and staying quiet because we were scared of what he'd do if we showed ourselves. "Isabella, I know you're in here. Come out and give your Zio Donnie a kiss, will ya? I haven't seen you in weeks." He didn't know I was there but both Isabella and I were breathing fast, covering our mouths so he didn't hear. Carmela's banging and screeching continued on the door but the confrontation with Donnie felt much louder. Donnie spoke to the walls surrounding him. "Please, Bella? Make this easier for the both of us." He quickly spun his body like Clint Eastwood, staring directly at the cupboard we were contained within. Isabella flinched as Donnie employed a daring smile. "Open the door, Bella. I'm not gonna hurt you."

He began pacing again. He knew where she was, but he wanted her to come out by herself. Carmela's cries continued, wailing against the door. Donnie continued. "Open the doooor, Bella." Donnie became impatient, stepping closer to the cupboard and shaping his hands into fists. I breathed in deep, knowing we were both about to be caught.

"Open the *dooooor*, Bella!" More intensely this time. He turned and slammed his fist on the table in anger. I was jolted from the scare and Isabella was hyperventilating with tears. He then yelled, "Unless you want me to pull you out here by your fuckin' ears, I suggest you open that fucking door, Isabella!" Donnie was out of breath after yelling. Even Carmela was quiet. He was still staring at the cupboard as we stared back into his eyes through the slender gaps. Isabella turned to me, placing a finger over her lips and telling me to be quiet. She covered my face with a hanging jacket. There was a short silence before I heard the cupboard door creak open. He suddenly looked calm, as if she were the drug that he needed to be happy again. He smiled politely as she stepped out slowly. He tilted his head sideways. "Now, why didn't ya come out when I asked?"

The second he said that Carmela started again, banging and throwing herself against the door, knowing Isabella had given herself up to him. "No, nooo! You stay away from my children, bastard!" Her voice was still muffled from behind the door.

Donnie glanced at the door and then back to my sister. He unclipped his belt and unraveled it from his pants. I stared at him, unable to swallow as it felt like my throat was blocked. "You know, it's not very polite, Isabella, to ignore a man who's speaking directly to you. I thought your father woulda at least taught ya that." He cracked the belt onto the desk like a whip, creating a shockwave of noise. Carmela had given up, resorting to a mere sobbing behind the bedroom door. "Where

I come from, there's a little somethin' called respect." He stepped closer to my sister and cracked the belt against the cupboard door. He smiled, standing above her.

***

A black belt hung on a chair across from me in the living room of my New York apartment. I stared at it, forgetting I had Bernie sleeping on my lap. On TV, most channels were bombarded by the news. A second assassination attempt on Gerald Ford in just seventeen days. It made me wonder what kind of world we lived in when being the president became the most dangerous job in the world.

The only thing heavier than the thoughts in my mind was the knock on the door. I jumped up, retrieving a pistol taped beneath the coffee table. In this business, you learn to look over your shoulder, around every corner, and prepare yourself for the worst. Anybody could be behind that door. Your neighbor, your best friend, your grandmother, or your worst enemy. I cautiously opened the door and there stood Castello, Louie, and Vinnie. "What the fuck?" I yelled.

"Got bad news for ya, kid," Castello murmured as they welcomed themselves into my apartment.

"Why you got your piece out for? Who you afraid of?" Louie

gestured to the gun as I slid it into my pocket, outraged over the surprise.

"You wanna tell me what's goin' on? You think you can just barge in here without askin'? What if Marianne was naked or somethin'?"

Castello nodded. "Exactly. Where *is* Marianne, Johnny?"

"She's teaching ballet, what's it to you?" I had my hands on my hips, trying to retain some sense of privacy. Louie began walking through the apartment, fiddling with photo frames and magazines.

"We noticed you've been out on Wednesdays," Vinnie said under his breath.

"And? I'm just goin' out for somethin' to eat. Sometimes, I see a movie. Why does that matter? What is this shit?" I fiddled with my hair. I was defensive but rightfully so. I worried they'd find out about the shrink. All three of them were in my apartment which meant the matter was serious.

"Look, Johnny, we're not here because you've done anything wrong. Whatever you get up to alone is your business," Louie said as he looked closely at a hairbrush Marianne had left in front of the mirror.

Vinnie glanced at Bernie on the couch and then back to me. "We've noticed Marianne leaving the building at exactly six every Wednesday evening. Sometimes, a couple minutes later. But *always* at six."

I shrugged, confused. "That doesn't make any sense. She's here, preparin' dinner."

Castello sighed, knowing I wouldn't like what he was about to tell me. "Look, I don't like to be the bearer of bad news or anything, kid, but we sent Frankie to follow where she went."

"Why the fuck are you followin' her?" I said, defending her privacy.

"Calm down, Johnny." Louie placed his palms in the air. "She's from another family, so it's a little difficult to trust these ones, no matter how long they stick around. We gotta keep a close eye, you understand?"

I gestured wildly. "And who the fuck is Frankie?"

Castello nodded. "You know Frankie! He's Louie's nephew."

I glared at them all, as if they'd gone out of their way to ruin my week. "So, what exactly did *Frankie* find?"

Castello walked over to the window and looked over the city beneath us. "He followed her to a motel downtown. She went in. Frankie got a burger. She came out about forty-five minutes later." He neatened his collar.

I shook my head. "You think she's cheating on me?" The news was unbelievable. I just assumed they'd made it up because Donnie had some stupid argument with Estevan Manzelli and they wanted to cut ties. "You people make me sick to the stomach. Do you understand how bullshit this sounds? What the fuck gives you the right to go following my fiancée around, ah?" I was ready for a fight, I felt just as attacked as she would have. Castello tried to talk but I didn't give him a second of space. "You are pryin' into my personal life when I know she wouldn't do that shit! You know how much she loves me? I bet you don't even fucken know, do ya?" I pointed at the three of them, shaking with frustration. "You people need to stay the fuck outta my business and have some respect! *Frankie did this, Frankie found that*—fuck Frankie! I barely ever met the guy. I can trust him as much as I can remember his fucking face!"

Maybe I wasn't mad at them, but mad at the cruel possibility that it may have been the truth. They all stood in silence. Castello sighed and stepped forward, sincerely placing his hand on my shoulder. "Her hair was messy, Johnny ..."

I exhaled, trying to calm down as Vinnie patted my back. "Just thought we ought to inform you. You're family to us, and nobody fucks with family, ah?"

"I wanna be alone right now," I whispered. "Thanks for stoppin' by."

Castello, Vinnie, and Louie walked out of the apartment as I stared ahead of me in an intense gaze. I hoped it wasn't true. I hoped to God that there was some kind of misunderstanding. I wracked my brain to make sense of it, but the more I thought about it, the more the jigsaw pieces fell into place.

The next Wednesday came around. Behind the wheel of my car, I lit a cigarette in the darkness as I watched Marianne step out of the Caruso building, neaten her hair, and get into her car. I didn't want it to be true. I had to turn the headlights off so she didn't know I was going to tail her. Something about it was wrong, treating my fiancée like she was one of our gang targets. It sickened me. I even had to skip a session with Dr.

Kumar because of all this.

I jammed the key into the ignition but before I rotated it, I noticed a few polaroids on the passenger-side floor. Confused, I picked them up, startled over the fact that they were pictures of myself. Pictures of me taking the recording device out of the car, pictures of me disposing of it in the dumpster. My heart dropped. I inhaled quickly, looking left, right, and behind. They were watching me. Blackjaw's crew knew I disabled the device the second it happened. And with the confrontation of polaroids, it was a simple statement to tell me I was no longer a free man. They were watching me at that very moment, too. I knew it. It was the last thing I needed that night, but if I didn't follow Marianne at that moment, I'd have to wait another week. I had no choice. A bright-red beam lit the interior of my car. Marianne's brake lights were on, and she was about to leave. I tried to tear the polaroids, but they were plastic, so I threw them onto the passenger seat and was about to start the car. I stared at the key, daring to turn it. These photos were recently placed in the car, which meant the lock wasn't the only thing they could have tampered with. Marianne had begun driving and I was still torn between starting the car and delaying her confrontation for another seven days. I looked back down at the ignition, squinting as I slowly turned it, hearing each click, louder than the last. As her car left the parking garage, one last click fired up the ignition. Relief washed over me as I took a deep breath and began the chase. I followed her down the city streets. She was driving slow, so I had to drive slower. I kept a safe distance as the city lights swept over her car and over mine a few seconds later. I glanced at the scattered polaroid prints on the passenger seat, knowing it was a problem I had to shove to the back of my mind to focus on the issue at hand. I wiped the sweat off my forehead, hoping it wasn't true, almost trying to convince myself that the guys were crazy. However, Castello wouldn't lie to me. Not him.

She parked her car in a motel parking lot downtown. I drove past, keeping my distance and surveying the rest of the car park. I had already noticed Castello and Louie sitting in a car with its lights off on the other side of the lot.

"What if she is cheating? You ain't married yet, so maybe she thinks it's okay?" It felt so surreal that I began reasoning with myself out loud in the car. I looked in the mirror, whispering intensely, "Are you going insane, Johnny? What are you even gonna do if there's somebody else?" I wondered if I could live with the lie, turn around, go home, and tell myself it wasn't happening—live in ignorant bliss. I glanced at Cas and Lou, nodding at them before they nodded back, lighting their own cigarettes. Marianne finally stepped out of the car, applying lipstick as it began raining. I shook my head. "Oh, Mary. Don't do this to me ..." She entered one of the motel rooms. I looked over at Louie, who stepped out of the car with a suppressed pistol. I quickly jumped out and gestured for him to stop. Louie was ready to whack her, right there and then. He pocketed the pistol and walked back to the car, somewhat disappointed as if he had missed out on some fun.

I decided it was time. Enough had gone past for whatever it was to unravel inside. I shut the door of the car and walked over toward the motel through the puddles of water. Each step I took felt like I was further and further away. It was as if I had walked a hundred miles to this motel room door. My footsteps felt louder and louder as I approached Room 3. I dropped my cigarette in a puddle and stepped on it with a sigh. "Fuck ..." I then walked faster and faster until I finally reached the door.

I kicked the thick motel door open and it slammed hard against the wall. My worst fear was realized. Marianne was naked, in bed with some scumbag. He was in his late twenties, maybe early thirties, and short with a bald patch. All their clothes were scattered around the room as if I'd missed the part where they'd vigorously made out beforehand. I was lost for words. I literally could not find the words to speak, quite possibly still hoping for there to be some outrageous explanation for it. It felt like my insides had turned to charcoal and if I'd opened my mouth, only black dust would escape.

Marianne jumped in shock. "Johnny! What are you doin' here?" She said it as if I was the one intruding over her life. She sat up, covering her breasts. Covering them from me ... *me*. The man she promised her life to, as if the scumbag had more of a right to admire her physique than I did. He must've earned it. I tried within these four seconds that'd passed to keep my head screwed on, until the air escaped the scumbag's mouth.

"Who the fuck are you, asshole?" My eyes darted to him as he rolled quickly off the bed to retrieve his shorts. I launched at him, and he tried to speak. "What the fuck?" he panicked.

I don't know what to tell you and I don't quite know how to explain this part. Where do I even start?

His head slamming against the wall, cracking the cheap motel plaster?

My fist, puncturing his face repeatedly with my rings until his teeth were dislodged?

Smashing the bedside lamp over his head until it was left in small shards of ceramic and patterned material?

"No! Johnny! Stop!" I heard the muffled screams of Marianne on the bed. I couldn't see her as my eyes were glued to the scumbag like a dog with lockjaw. But I can tell she was seeing something she ain't never seen before. I proceeded to snatch the telephone from the bedside table, beating it against his fucken head until it snapped into cheap plastic bits. His bald patch was no longer visible due to the gouges in his scalp and the rapidly escaping blood.

But it wasn't enough. I stomped on his head with my heavy boots, over and over. Over and fucking over. Over and over until the sound of the relentless stomping became merely a part of the environment.

Marianne tugged on her own hair in sheer panic as if she were going insane, as if what was happening before her eyes wasn't even real, hoping for the nightmare to be over. But this time she wasn't going to wake up. The smell of blood would prove that this was all too real. "You're killing him, Johnny! You're killing him! It's not his fault!" she screamed helplessly.

It still wasn't enough. My boots hadn't had enough. I continued to stomp, this time hearing cracks and clunks. I couldn't help but picture his bones breaking and snapping as I stomped, further crushing his jaw beneath my heel. Marianne was in hysterics, not knowing whether to cry or scream. "You fucking killed him! He's already dead! Stop it! Stop it! Ahhh, God!" The scumbag stopped responding; in fact, I think he had already stopped long before that. Never will it be enough. "No, no, no, no, no, no, no ... No, no, no, no, no, no, no, noooo ..." Marianne was mindless, as if all the juice from her brain had been squeezed out of her and that was the only word she could muster in an endless loop. Traumatic at the very least. Although, it was still more than the scumbag could say as I was no longer controlling my own body, stomping on the unrecognizable pulp of human flesh, splattering on the surrounding walls. I finally stopped, out of breath and realizing that the scumbag's nose was more than a few feet away from his lips. I stepped back with a blood-drenched shirt and chunks of skin and clumps of hair hanging loosely upon it.

I took the gun out of my pocket with dull eyes, looking over to

Marianne as she glanced back at me in sheer horror. She'd never seen anything like this before. Not in the movies, not in nothing. She didn't even know a human body could crumble like that under a force like mine. I fired a shot in what used to be the scumbag's head. The rage I felt. The fucking rage I had inside me. I fired five more until the clip was empty, pulling the trigger even after there were no rounds left. It was a purge, a line that when crossed—cannot be *uncrossed*. I then dropped the gun, unable to create expressions with my face anymore. I was no longer a man, but a creature spawned from sheer evil and terror. I was finally what my uncle wanted me to be. Marianne stumbled off the bed and onto the floor, scrambling to the nearest corner and curling up into a ball. She began lightly bumping her head against the wall repeatedly. I broke her. I'd ruined us. She closed her eyes as she continued, hoping to wake up, but again, she knew she wasn't going to. I stared at the artwork of human flesh against the wall and glanced down at my hands, drenched in blood. Some may call it psychopathic, others may call it love—which for me, could be the same thing. What I *am* entirely sure of is that it was a complete mutilation of another human being, whether he deserved it or not. Although, I don't think his mother would ever want to see him like that.

Castello and Louie barged in soon after they heard the shots, expecting to break up two men in a gunfight. Instead, they found a monster, standing in a pool of another man's blood. I stood there, still frozen, glaring over the mess I'd made. Marianne was still curled up in the corner, but her eyes were wide open in horror, desperately attempting to register what had just unfolded. She simply couldn't.

Louie lowered his pistol, examining the room. "Blood all over the fucken walls, Johnny ... What did ya do to this guy?"

Castello walked slowly over to me, holding my arms and bringing me down to the blood-soaked bed. I was emotionless, but a shell of what I was before. Donnie arrived soon after and closed the door behind him. He glanced at the human sludge on the floor and looked up at me, surprised. He turned to Louie. "Get her outta here, Lou." Louie took his jacket off and threw it around Marianne, lifting her up and walking her to the door. What I could never quite grasp about Louie is that before this happened, he was ready to blow a hole in her skull, and now he was comforting her with a jacket. I learned quickly that he was a real yes-man. A yes-man only exists for the means of their superior. Donnie looked over to Castello, who was already picking up pieces of blood-soaked clothing. "Remind Frankie about the noise outside." As Vinnie entered, Donnie took a second to glance at me, still trying to work out what had transpired. He gestured to Vinnie. "Get the car ready, then come back and guard the door." As Louie dragged Marianne out, she held him close, only covering her breasts with Louie's jacket. Donnie walked over and began neatening what furniture could be salvaged around the dead scumbag. I sat there, still in shock. Even if I wanted to move, I couldn't.

One of the only respectable things about Donnie is he helped out when he could. But it makes you wonder if he's doing it for you, or to cover his own ass. I thought my brain had been playing with me when I heard gunshots outside, but it was Frankie across the street pounding a baseball bat on an empty trash can as if it were a gong. Donnie put him up to it to make some noise to account for the gunshots and act mentally challenged if somebody were to confront him. This pulled attention directly away from the clean-up, and would make the residents in the area question whether they really heard gunshots, or if it were just some loony banging on a drum.

It took a while to recover from cleaning this guy—even though it was anything but clean. I had nightmares about it for months after that; I couldn't sleep.

As Castello slid on a pair of gloves and readied a trash bag, he and Donnie began dragging away the remains. I glanced out the door to Marianne, crying and screaming into Louie's shoulder. Louie held her, glancing back at me before closing the door.

The sleepless nights that followed weren't the only problem. What did I do to her? Maybe I was the reason she cheated, and it's my fault. So, now some poor scumbag gets beaten to death and shot up, just because some doe-eyed dame needed an outlet.

Chapter Thirteen

The Point of No Return

With a quiver upon my lower lip, I sat on the chair in front of Donnie's desk in dead silence. I couldn't look up. The carpet was my only comfort and staring into nothingness was my only escape from the events that'd just hijacked my life. Donnie sat on his chair and stared at me with his fingers interlocked on the desk. I wasn't looking at him, but I knew he was staring. I could feel it.

"I'm proud of you," Donnie said under his breath. I looked up, outraged.

How could he be proud of that?

How could anybody be proud of taking a life?

He pointed at me and placed his glass of whiskey on the desk. "For defending something that's yours, Johnny. I am truly sorry you had to go through that."

I looked down again. I didn't deserve to hold my chin up high. I didn't deserve to respond to somebody over such monstrous actions. "I am, too."

Donnie stepped away from his desk, beginning to pace. I prepared for some kind of lecture. I was expecting him to tell me to grow a backbone and accept the business I was a part of. I was waiting for him to tell me my balls weren't big enough.

"The first few times are always the worst, no matter who it is, but especially when it involves someone close to you. Not sayin' that it gets easier, but it just doesn't affect you as much." Donnie walked as he let the cigar burn between his fingers, looking over the framed photos on the walls. The scumbag was the first soul I claimed but to him, it wasn't. Donnie was still under the impression that we'd offed Arnold nearly six months earlier. He assumed I was broken up over the fact that it involved Marianne. The truth was, I was distraught over taking a life regardless. "I still remember the first person I whacked. I was doin' a job for this guy named Blackjaw," Donnie said as he swirled and sank his whiskey. I looked up, recognizing the name but he thought it was the first time I'd heard of it. "He forced me to take out his assistant. He heard she was skimmin' the top of his earnings or some shit ... They never told us much." He passed me a cigarette. It was refreshing not to have the attention on myself. I took a lighter out of my pocket with my shaky left hand, igniting the tobacco strands.

"I remember every single detail. Her last facial expression, what she was wearing, the items in the room, and what color they were. I was thinkin' to myself—I saw her two days earlier and she smiled at me. I smiled back; in fact, I was kinda sweet on her, not knowin' that I'd be blowin' her brains out through the front of her head in just forty-eight hours." I looked up at Donnie as I could've sworn he was holding in a tear or two. It surprised me. There was some kind of similarity between us, probably for the first time in my life. He quickly turned to me. "And you know what? It ended up bein' his nephew who was skimmin' the entire time." Donnie sniggered sarcastically, shaking his head over the senseless life he'd taken due to Blackjaw's poor judgment. "Poor girl didn't even put a foot wrong."

There was a moment of silence after that, as if Donnie had stepped right into his past and all the tremors from that moment had come flooding back to him. This was a rare occurrence for my uncle. He'd always held a front, a mask to cover his true self. Maybe the more I became like him, the more I came to understand him. "I'm sorry to hear that, Zio."

"You see, Johnny, we're not so different. You're gonna remember this guy for the rest of your life. This is nothin' like that string bean you whacked from that firm because this situation is personal. Like I said, this shit doesn't get easier, but over time it just doesn't affect you as much."

I looked up, hoping he'd finally see my side of things. "The fact is, I don't wanna kill nobody, Zio."

Donnie immediately shook his head as if I was the one misunderstanding. "You don't get it, do you? This is part of the business. You don't get to choose. You know how it goes, either kill or be killed. It's a fucken shit-show, I'll tell ya that part for free." He didn't say it to straighten me up, but more to empathize with me over the business, something we couldn't change.

I was never prepared to accept this as a way of life. "I didn't ask for this."

Donnie matched the tone, pointing at me and stepping closer to the chair I was sitting in. "None of us did. We were all just born into this business. If you're gonna take my place one day, then you better let it sink into that thick skull of yours."

"What makes you think I wanna take your place?"

At that point he'd stepped close to me, almost at eye level as he glared with intensity. "Because ... I can see it in your eyes. You crave control. You crave the power. You crave the validation." He was almost shaking. Was he right? Of course not. Everybody wants control of their lives. Power was for an individual to define. For me, maybe he was right about one thing: validation. Some of us just crave acceptance and the feeling of belonging.

"I don't care for none of it," I said to him with my firm chest.

Donnie then stood up straight, walking away and smoking his cigar. "Everybody wants fame. Everybody wants fortune. Everybody wants to be somebody, Johnny!" As he sipped his scotch, he leaned on his desk. "Either way, it's critical that you get used to this life. You've experienced the highs. Now it's time to accept the lows. We can live the sweet life, but we must make sacrifices for it."

I slouched into my chair. What else was I going to walk out of that room with? There was no point fighting him on it. Maybe it was my only option. Maybe that was the only way to thrive in New York. I glanced over to a painting of Donnie—a lot more flattering than reality—with a group of men raising their glasses. Blackjaw was amongst them.

"So, what happened with Blackjaw's nephew, in the end?"

Donnie looked at me, then down to his newly poured glass of scotch with a few ice cubes on the surface. As he swirled it, he stared into it as if it were a window into his past. I waited for him to speak, desperate to hear how the story concluded. "Piece by piece ..."—Donnie stared at his reflection in the glass of his office window—"he was fed to the pigs."

***

After that day, my mindset switched. A full one-eighty. It became part of who I was and how I dealt with the senseless noise in my head. The gunshots seemed to shut them the fuck up. And for the people who deserved it, it was effortless. The fact was—as much as I hated to admit it—taking lives *did* get easier every time. Especially when they weren't looking at you when you cleaned them.

Running down an alleyway and taking down a dirtbag in a hood made us feel like we were the police, but with no boundaries and no backlash, this may have been even better. A silenced shot through the back of his head meant three keys of Donnie's coke were secured and returned. This meant saving money for the crew, gaining credibility with the guys, and most importantly, cutting off a loose end. Carlo was surprised at my sudden change in rhythm. He didn't expect it and neither did I. Taking a life was like a seal that was broken, and once broken, I felt unstoppable. The power felt like something infinite was inside me—a sense of invincibility, perhaps. I could do anything and especially in this life—as Donnie explained—it was either kill or be killed. I was forced to adapt and if I was to thrive in this city, I was going to do it in style and become the best version of me there ever was. Why struggle and protest so much against something that feels so right? Going with the current was more comfortable than going against it. It could've been Donnie speaking through me, but if this was the way to live, I was just getting started.

A few weeks later, we tracked down the middleman between a group we called "El Blanco" and our own Boston connection. He'd been given a case which never made it to the clients. This meant trouble. That case could've been anywhere. Whether it was sold to the scummy street consumers, snorted up by himself, or in the worst case, delivered to government organizations, we had to track it down. A lost case is an open case.

We had him strapped to a chair in the same warehouse Donnie had welcomed me to a couple years back. "Where's the case?" I stood over the nervy man, about thirty-six and scruffy. I thumped him over the head with the pistol. "Give me the fucking case!" Instant blood from his forehead.

"I don't know where it is!" he yelled into my face. So, I moved closer.

"Why are you screamin'? It's a simple question. Where is the fucking case?" I leaned closer, Donnie-esque. He stared at me, afraid. I knew he was lying. "It's a simple question, that requires a simple answer." He kept his mouth shut as my patience was running thinner than the strands of hair on his forehead. I aimed the pistol. Anything to do with missing product was a "code red" in our books. "I ask where the case is—and you give me a location."

He looked up at me, exhausted as I cocked the gun. "Fifteen sixty-three, Union Street, Crown Heights. Second floor. But don't—" A bullet traveled quickly through his brain before he could finish the sentence. This was the first time Carlo looked at me in shock. Even *he* was disgusted and astounded. We got our information and I learnt that this was the quickest way to get it. I don't know why it was easier after the situation with Marianne. Was I realizing who I was meant to be? Was this in my blood? Or maybe it was my own fucked-up way of dealing with what unfolded at the motel on that fateful night. I believe it changed me forever.

I became relentless. Carlo couldn't keep up. What I didn't know was, I was making enemies. See, when you take a life, you think the problem is dealt with. Killing someone isn't killing the problem. You don't think about who their connections are and what consequences lie beneath. It's all too easy until the shit hits the fan at six hundred and fifty miles an hour.

In the same week, we had another guy we had to clean. I don't know what was going on, I must've been on a rampage. These jobs kept getting fed to us. Either it was because we'd get the job done quick with no questions asked or because Donnie wanted me to hit the ground running. Once again, I was with Carlo. We slowly creaked open the door to one of the Caruso hotel suites on the west side of the building. Amongst the crew, we'd called it the Wild West. This usually meant that these guests would enter the building with a smile on their faces and exit with their eyes closed, and that's if they ever came out at all. As Carlo and I vigilantly made our way down a narrow hall, we heard a noise coming from the bathroom, so we moved across to the laundry that shared the same wall. There was a photo frame in the laundry with a view into the bathroom, strategically placed by whichever pervert had lived there previously. Carlo was the first to peek inside, gripping his gun tight in case he was caught out. Gustav, a chubby, greasy, bearded man was sitting on the toilet, jerking off to a nudie mag.

"Go on, do it," Carlo whispered in my ear. He relied on me to put people to sleep in those times, considering my newfound lack of conscience. His own seemed to grow thicker while mine was almost non-existent. I looked at Carlo and back at Gustav through the hole in the wall. "Take the shot, what are ya waiting for?" Carlo wanted to get out of there, for obvious reasons.

"The guy's jerkin' himself off, I can't do him in like that," I said to Carlo with a shrug. I was more than happy to blow the brains out of the poor bastard, but I at least wanted him to retain his dignity. Nobody wants to be shot with their pants off and their Richard in their hands.

"You joking me? I wanna get outta here, Johnny." Carlo was getting impatient, whispering louder.

"Not while he's doin' that, it's not the gentlemanly thing to do. He's doin' his business. Who am I to disturb him like that?" I protested, unsure of how long we'd be there for. "We'll wait 'til he's done. What's the big hurry, anyway?"

Carlo's gestures were animated but remained in whispers. "I'm fucken hungry and watching him is making me lose my appetite." I continued waiting as Gustav's breaths became shorter and louder. He even began to smile at whatever he was looking at on the magazine in his left hand.

"I can't believe you right now." Carlo was almost in hysterics, desperately wanting me to get the job done.

"You wanna do it?" I asked Carlo and he shut up. "Look, I wouldn't wanna be killed while I was doin' that either. It's not a noble way to go."

"But you'd rather be killed right after?" Carlo asked.

"It's just not comfortable, that's all. And it's kind of embarrassing and disarming. We're waiting 'til he finishes," I repeated.

"So, we're just gonna watch this guy jerk himself off? You're really gonna wait 'til he comes?" I began to ignore Carlo as he was becoming more and more like a broken record. "This ain't no fuckin' peep show that I've been to before. Maybe Frankie, but not me. You wanna join him? Finish him off, big guy? Do the guy a favor in his last few minutes?" Carlo sarcastically muttered.

I continued to wait until Gustav reached a certain point of satisfaction, moaning to himself, free and loud, assuming he was alone. I began screwing a suppressor onto the pistol before Carlo made another smart remark. "Well, there goes *my* appetite."

As the toilet flushed, I stood up and walked into the hallway, awaiting Gustav's reveal as we heard his belt being clipped. The door opened and I finally pulled the trigger. This guy was so much bigger face to face than staring at him through a hole in the wall. As Carlo emerged from the laundry, Gustav's corpse was already sliding down the stairs by itself. I must admit, it was one of the messier jobs we had to do, right from the get-go.

As we stepped into the carpark shortly after disposing of Gustav, we walked over to the Lincoln.

"So, you hungry? Or is your stomach still weak?" I asked Carlo after the ordeal.

"What do you think? I haven't eaten all fucking day. Gotta have something to get that picture outta my head," Carlo said as he was enjoying a breath of fresh air. As I unlocked the car, Carlo leaned on the roof. "Hitting the bakery later, right? I gotta set up a few posters and signs before the grand opening."

I smiled, opening the door and nodding. "Yeah, we'll grab a bite to eat, first. I wanna try out this place called Giuseppe's, downtown."

I got into the car and noticed a stunning red C3 Corvette parked a few spaces away. A 1981 model. Quite probably the sexiest car I'd ever seen. "Hey, it's one of those new Corvettes. Wouldn't mind me a ride in one o' those."

Carlo agreed. "It'd be fun to drive, but I heard it's the most dangerous road-legal sports car in America."

I winked and grinned with my newfound persona. "That's why I like it. She's fast and not afraid to be a little risky."

He laughed and clipped his seatbelt. "My kind of girl, ah?"

Now this is the part that hurts. As I sniggered, I turned the key, but before the usual pre-ignition clicks, there was a very discernible tick.

My eyes darted over to Carlo in the passenger seat, and he did the same to me. We both knew exactly what it meant. We'd both heard the horror stories. We rushed to throw ourselves out of the car. Having not clipped my seatbelt, I dove onto the pavement before the inside of the car went up in flames, followed by a small interior explosion designed to scorch the driver and their associates. I rolled over, dusting the loose flames from my sleeves, and looked up at the mass of fire and debris hitting the ceiling of the car park.

"Ahhhhh! Fuck! My fucken legs! Ah!" Carlo screamed. Even though he was screaming and writhing in excruciating pain, it was a relief to my ears for the fact that he could even speak at all. I slowly rose to my feet, limping around the car to find Carlo on the ground in flames. His legs were half blown off, both of them, up and past his knees. His blood had painted the asphalt beneath. He continued rolling around as if he were being tugged side to side by a gang of fiery demons.

That right there ... That is what happens when you get too confident. I couldn't close my eyes or look away. In contrast to Carlo, I was frozen, shocked, even though I shouldn't have been surprised. Not one bit.

Carlo faced the ceiling as he was rolled into the hospital. I could only imagine what was going through his head. He would've been thinking about his future at the bakery, his legless life with Larissa, and the prospect of his own burden. Maybe even his children and if he could even have any after an incident like that. The last thing on his mind would be the business with Donnie. When you're so close to death, you think about the things you care about the most, the important things that mean the world to you. Some part of me hoped that I was important enough for him to think of our friendship. The problem was, in a business like this, you're forced to think about work in this situation. Anybody asks you an incriminating question, you must not open your mouth or shed light on anything that happened. If you're involved in an accident, you have to act brain-dead, because if you don't, it won't be the police that take you down, it'll be your own guys.

Carlo became unresponsive while being wheeled down one of the spacious hallways in the hospital. I tried to go in with him. "Sir! You can't go through!"

I pulled out any excuse I could. "Let me through! I'm his caretaker." I never meant for this to happen. Somebody targeted me and the car I drove and Carlo was the one paying big for it. Not an arm, but two legs. "I know it's difficult, but by you getting in the way, it's slowing down the process of us helping your friend in there!" the nurse said sternly as she placed her hand on my chest.

I held my hand on my forehead, piling on the guilt. It was eating me alive. "Fuck! Is he gonna be alright?" I begged, looking over at Carlo and his lifeless eyes.

"We're not sure yet. We need to see how severe the damage is first, aside from the burns. I know this is a hard time. Just be patient and go to the waiting room, understand? Get yourself a coffee or somethin'," she said as they wheeled him through the doors. I wasn't allowed to go with him, as much as I wanted to know the full extent of his injuries. It's funny because Donnie would have wanted me to go in with him—not to make sure he was okay or anything—but if he were to spill any information, I'd be expected to take care of it. That's the humbling reality I lived, knowing that the spillage of tight information could mean I'd have to execute one of our own, let alone Carlo. Maybe it was better that I didn't go in with him.

The beeping sounds and the pens writing on paper had already driven me insane by the time I ordered a coffee and sat beside Castello in the waiting room. He was the first to get there, worried over Carlo's condition as if an immediate family member. We were both stressed out of our minds. I was twiddling my fingers while Castello was stroking the last strands of hair on his balding head.

"It's all my fault, Cas," I whispered.

"Shit happens, Johnny. At least you're alright."

I shook my head. The weight of remorse was a heavy load. "I was being reckless."

Castello quickly turned to me, outraged that I was blaming myself, "You were bein' reckless by steppin' into a car? You couldn't have known that would happen. Nobody would've."

I pointed to myself, stabbing my index finger into my chest. "It was *my* car, not his. That should be *me* in there."

Castello took a deep breath and looked me in the eyes. "Are you gonna check every vehicle you step into? That'll be living in fear. When the big man calls your number, then it's your time to go. Let's just hope it ain't Carlo's time, that's all." He adjusted his chair and leaned back again, still with a worried look on his face as if it were his own son on that operating table.

"I'm gonna find out who it was and I'm gonna clean 'em for this." I could feel Castello turn his head and look at me, surprised over my sudden bloodthirst. We both knew the last few months had changed who I was after the ordeal with Marianne.

Castello sighed. "Relax, Johnny. We'll get to that part. Just take a breather for a second, okay? Don't put so much pressure on yourself, kid. Like I said, shit happens, and we deal with it. It's as simple as that."

I bit my lip, yearning to find the perpetrator and put them in the ground, but where the fuck would I start? The doors suddenly swung open, and Donnie walked in with Vinnie by his side like a bodyguard.

Donnie stood right above me. "Stand up." I stood up, quickly. He put both hands on my shoulders. "Are you hurt?" I shook my head. "You know who was behind this?"

I shook my head again and looked at the ground. "No, Zio."

"Did you tell *anyone* what happened?" I shook my head again. The good thing about Donnie is that he thought fast and precise in any tricky situation that could get him into trouble. He looked quickly over to Vinnie. "Go home and bust open an empty gas can in the car park. We don't need no feds involved. They already got their noses in our guts as it is." Donnie then looked at the receptionist and back at Castello and I. "If anyone asks, he was tryna start a barbecue and the can was damaged."

The nurse approached the four of us, looking at me, knowing I was the one who was with him when he came in. "Good news, your friend should be okay for now. We're going to keep him here for a while until he recovers. He's lucky to be alive." She looked around between Donnie, Cas, and Vinnie. "I'm going to need somebody to fill out some forms, though."

Castello stood up straight away. "I can do that." As he followed the nurse to the reception desk, Donnie glanced at me with a sigh.

***

The sun shined brightly through the curtains of Donnie's office window. Louie, Vinnie, Castello, and I stood up in front of Donnie's desk in a row. Donnie sat there, hunched in his chair with a hot, steaming short black in front of him. He still hadn't taken a sip. Instead, he shrugged.

"I don't understand. You're sayin' you got nothin'? Bupkis?"

Vinnie gestured outside to the fresh air. "Boss, they can make it in and out of that garage whenever they want to. The only thing the cars are safe from is the rain."

Donnie shook his head. "So, we got no leads on this fucker that's tryna off us in our own fucking territory?" He shrugged again, expecting a better answer. He looked around at the four of us. "You're tellin' me, that any dingbat off the street can just waltz right into our garage and rig our cars? Is that how it is? Are you fucking kidding me? Why aren't the gates closed?"

Castello looked at his feet. "They *are* closed at night. Anybody can still jump over it or slide underneath. The gates only stop cars, not ... *dingbats*."

Louie cracked a smirk. Donnie's eyes darted directly to him. "What, you think this is funny? Are you mocking me? Am I some kind of joke to you?" Donnie fumed.

Louie's face straightened. "No, Don. I just—"

Donnie pointed at him. "How would *you* feel if I waltzed on my merry way into your apartment while you were sleepin' and rigged your toaster to explode when you made your mornin' bacon and beans?" Louie nodded and scratched the back of his head. This was no laughing matter. One of us was now missing two legs, and someone had been able to reach us—hurt us. Donnie continued to address the four of us. "From now on, we check every car, every morning before ignition. Comprendere? I don't give two fucks if it takes us a half hour to get movin'. I'm not takin' any more chances."

Vinnie nodded. "Yes, Boss. We'll assign Frankie to it."

Donnie tilted his head sideways in disbelief. "*Not* Frankie. One of yous."

Louie rolled his eyes, but Castello got the message well and clear. "Got it, Don."

Donnie then leaned back in his chair, shaking his head and picking up his short black, about to take a sip. "Now, we're down a man *and* a car. If any of you get the slightest sniff *or* hunch on who was behind this, you come to *me* first. I want them buried. I want them at bedrock."

Chapter Fourteen

Suspicion

There are many risks that come with this life. Whether it's the drugs, the rival gangs, or the dangers of your own men. Every day is a gamble but one threat always remains a constant: the mighty law.

While Carlo was recovering, a new problem had emerged. See, Donnie had six mattress stores pinned around Manhattan. We didn't even sell mattresses; it was all a laundering scheme. In each store, we had about six prestige mattresses for sale, but they were way too overpriced to even consider a purchase. Although, if a customer *was* willing to spend that kind of money, it's still profit in the Caruso bank. This idea worked great in most ways for Donnie. Low maintenance and low interest in the product would usually mean no interference. As Santo, our "cashier" at NYC Mattresses Inc., stacked the cash in the bags, a black car was waiting outside the lot on the street. I stepped out of my car, suspicious. I could make out a pair of binoculars behind the tinted glass. I walked toward the car and the man whispered something into his walkie-talkie and drove off. This was a common issue, but it was never as consistent as this. All the signs were pointing to an eventual sting, likely flagging the joint due to the lack of consumer interest. I took the last puff of my cigarette as the car disappeared down the block and parked in the distance. I flicked the cigarette onto the concrete and squashed it beneath my boot.

Towering over an office table in one of the Caruso building meeting rooms, Donnie stood there with the nub of a cigar wedged between his fingers. He was always holding something. "We gotta throw 'em off, somehow. If they breach the place, they'll find bullshit for stock and so much money, they'd think we're printing it."

Louie shrugged. "We got six stores and no customers. They're bound to start wonderin' how the business is surviving."

Donnie looked around to Vinnie and me. "Any suggestions? I can't just close down the joint. You think we gotta hire some fake customers or something?"

Vinnie placed his cup of coffee on the table and shrugged. "The less involved, the better. I checked with Santo downtown and he said the same guys show up in the same car every Tuesday to monitor the place. They're seeking out patterns."

Donnie leaned on the table, gesturing to Vinnie, expecting more. "What's the suggestion here?"

Vinnie straightened himself up and adjusted his jacket. "I think we should have us a sale event."

Donnie seemed impatient. "We got no stock and our prices are sky-high. What's a sale gonna do for us, Vin?" He wanted this problem solved yesterday and forgotten tomorrow.

"To show that we're active." Vinnie eyed all of us. "We gotta make it seem legitimate. Who cares if we run out of stock? First come, first served. Like Lou said, we ought to start—"

Before Vinnie could finish voicing his suggestion, we were interrupted by an uninvited guest. Angela barged through the door; face still caked as per usual but this time the icing was running down her cheeks. Donnie turned in his chair. "What the fuck is this all about?" He was more rattled by the fact that she entered without knocking than what her issue was. Understandable, considering the sensitivity of what we discussed in there on a daily basis. "I ought to put a lock on that door."

She was distraught. "I needa talk to Louie." We all looked over to Louie for a response. It seemed to me like Angela saw Louie the same way that I saw Cas. Somebody to confide in. Donnie was outraged. It had to be serious. "I'm sorry, I just need help from Louie." Angela pled. Louie sighed, fiddling with several of the rings on his fingers, somewhat embarrassed over being summoned by a young girl with no authority.

He gulped. "What is it, darling?"

Angela turned a cheek and amongst all the makeup in Paris smeared upon her face, it was clear to see. A bruised eye—resembling a raccoon with no sleep after a bareknuckle boxing match. She began sobbing dramatically in front of us all.

"He hit me, Louie. He fucking hit me!" She pointed to it, and you could tell Louie was enraged. It was clearly a story he'd heard before, but nothing had gone so far as this. He wanted to stand up, but it was Donnie's call over who enters and leaves these meetings and at what time they did so.

Donnie palmed his own forehead and sighed, knowing this was another matter we didn't have time to deal with considering the circumstances. "Fuck. Louie, you go deal with that. We'll continue the meeting without you."

In a split second, Louie got up and rushed over, taking Angela through the door. "Who did this to you, sweetheart?"

After the door closed, Donnie looked over at the rest of us. "What does everyone else think? Am I the only one that thinks this idea is a load of horseshit?" He went straight back to the matter at hand.

"I say we give it a try. Those feds are there every week, waitin' for somethin' to change." Castello interlocked his fingers and rested them on the table. "This might clean our noses a little and make them think they got better things to do than monitor some plain-Jane mattress store. They could be spending their time chasing drug-dealers."

All of us sniggered at the comment before Donnie slammed his palm on the table, causing us all to flinch. "Okay. It's settled. I'll get Frankie to print out some signs, and we'll all go there and grill a couple sausages or somethin'. How's that sound?"

We all nodded, satisfied with the idea, but I couldn't help thinking about a certain somebody ... Frankie, Frankie, Frankie ... All we heard about was useless fucking Frankie.

***

Short, skinny, bug-eyed with a patchy beard. About twenty-six. Frankie was a clumsy fool. Only in the business 'cause he was Louie's nephew. There were many names that I could have used to describe him: useless, pathetic, a halfwit, rat-like ... you name it. You wouldn't trust this guy to hold your drink while you were taking a piss, and I mean that with all my heart. It's not that he wasn't trustworthy, it was simply the fact that he was a clumsy motherfucker with a peanut for a brain and a dishonorable waste of space. Frankie would cop all the shit jobs—the ones nobody wanted or even cared to do. But even those jobs, he'd fuck up somehow; like bringing platters to the boys on comedy night in the Caruso building, he once spilled a platter of champagne twice in one night—one of those times on Vinnie's brand-new Armani tuxedo.

"Ay! Ay! What the fuck, Frankie?" Vinnie squealed as he was showered in bubbles. Frankie would then attempt to soak up the mess he made but it'd somehow make things worse, spreading the mess to

Vinnie's tie and shirt. And this wasn't your regular booze, this was champagne and *authentic* champagne from the region in France of the same name. So, he wasn't just making a mess, but he was costing us a few coins here and there. So, we tried to find other work for him, something less hands-on, like guarding the door to our meetings. A pointless job but it gave him something to do and feel important about. Even when he made mistakes, Donnie didn't give two shits because he wasn't doing anything too important to really fuck up, anyway. The second I met Frankie, I didn't like him one bit. The guy never knew what time of day it was, and I mean he was whacked out of his brain most of the time. He ended up working in the flour mill in Salisbury, moving the loads of flour we got while unintentionally "guarding" the coke we had, disguised as flour in the backrooms. We couldn't wise him up to that. The information was too sensitive to crawl through a fragile brain like his.

I'd often find myself visiting him at the mill while he was unloading the bags just to make sure he wasn't mixing them up; even though it seemed impossible, we'd never put it past him. "Frankie. That's the *outgoing* pallet. These bags just got delivered, we're not gonna send them back out." I stood there with my cigarette, gesturing to the loading zone and shaking my head. But really, how many mistakes can you make with a few bags of flour, right?

Frankie sighed. "Are you serious?"

I nodded. "Yes, I'm fucken serious. We're wastin' time, double handlin' everything over here. Check the labels, man." Somebody had to keep him in check, even over the most basic jobs. I gestured to the pallet he was moving. "Unstack them and restack them on the rack at the back. Okay?"

As I dabbed my cigarette ashes on the floor, Frankie sighed. "Alright, Johnny." He didn't want to be there, but neither did I.

As Frankie got back to the back-breaking hard labor, which was the only thing he was good for, I noticed the door at the back, ajar. "And why the *fuck* is that door opened?"

Frankie started stammering, "I don't know. I mean, I needed a clamp for the crates, and I thought I'd find some in there."

"You just said you don't know. You clearly opened that door, right?" I pointed to the door, awaiting a response from his shaky lips. "Close it right now and lock it. The Barresi brothers are comin' to do a pickup at eight. We don't want this place to be a fucken pigsty when they arrive. We respect these fellas, andiamo!"

Frankie nodded, rushing over to close the door. "Sure, Johnny. I'm sorry, Johnny—"

"Nobody touches the flour in there but us." I made sure he locked it. We could never be too safe and frankly, he was the wrong person to be guarding such a sensitive product, even if he wasn't aware of it. I was always reluctant to shake his hand because he never deserved the respect ingrained within the sweat of my palms—but unfortunately it was in our culture to always shake another man's hand, unless of course, he'd killed your mother or raped your daughter. Aside from that, Frankie was what we'd call ... a weak link. The less he knew, the better. He was easily the dumbest bastard I'd ever met.

***

Back to the mattress store and the overly colorful display of advertising. Only one thing was for sure: *It was a fucking blowout.* People came from all over the city for these mattresses. Turns out Frankie set the price about six hundred dollars too low, and buyers far and wide came to collect. The retail price on one of these premium mattresses was fourteen hundred dollars—rich people shit—and I'm not talking Donnie-rich, I'm talking presidential shit. Frankie pinned them up for peanuts. These people showed up as if they'd been sleeping on concrete slabs their whole lives. We had to cover it up by saying we sold out before everybody showed up. The shop was so packed that we were even running out of hot dogs, and we'd bought hundreds of them. We had traditional Italian music playing and people even brought their families along, and even if they didn't score a mattress, they hung around for the festivities. Vinnie stood there in blue uniform, apologizing to the customers who didn't get a chance to purchase the goods.

He guided them out the door and back onto the street. "I apologize for the inconvenience, folks. We didn't expect to sell out so fast! Why don't you grab a bite on the way out? It's free."

Yes, the barbecue was run by none other than—you guessed it—Frankie, serving the customers one by one. And yes, a few unfortunate sausages went to waste due to his clumsy handling of the tongs. A weapon far beyond his capacity. As he bent over to pick it up, he ended up dropping the tongs on the ground, too. The Barresi brothers couldn't help but laugh, being their first time witnessing his embarrassing shenanigans. "Get a load of butterfingers, over there," said Celestino.

Riccardo still couldn't get enough. He was the more aggressive of the two. "You clumsy motherfucker, you. If you drop a sausage, leave it on the fucken floor. Don't pick it up, dumbass. Give it to the birds or somethin', nobody's gonna eat dat shit."

As I had a chuckle and a sausage of my own, I looked over everybody in front of the store. This wasn't just a cover-up, it almost felt like a celebration. The whole scheme was initially a stunt, but apparently, everyone in New York and their brothers needed mattresses. We even made a few grand out of it from the couple display mattresses that we actually had in the store. It was almost a cheap shot at the feds, a raw display of arrogance and pride. Louie would've loved to be here for it, but instead, he was out on his own errand.

***

We were told the story of Angela's fiasco in dramatic detail. A Western cowboy-style song was playing on a set of speakers in an old, mangy apartment in Elizabeth. The junkie, about twenty-eight, skinny, balding, and wearing a stained singlet was injecting meth over his chipped coffee table. Little did he know he was about to be paid a visit, an expensive one.

One by one, Louie's boots stepped up those stairs to the second story of the apartment block. The water dripped from each tread that was stepped upon with his thick boots. Behind him followed Angela in her light-footed heels. The railing shook as Louie made his way to the stained apartment door. *Thirteen.* I guess it really is an unlucky number.

Louie kicked open the door as it swung with force, startling the junkie—stumped in shock. Louie grasped Angela by the wrist and showed her to him with force. She was still in tears with her bruised eye. "You!" Louie pointed at the junkie.

"What the fuck, dude?" sputtered the junkie, panicked and probably paranoid enough as it was.

Louie threw Angela onto the floor in front of him and pointed at her. "You do this to her? You responsible for this?"

The junkie was still in shock over the sudden visit. "Do what? Who are you?" he stammered.

Louie then pointed at Angela's eye. "Look at her, you fucken crackhead. Look at her fucken eye!" Louie yelled as the junkie stepped backward, shaking his head, surprised by the caliber of Angela's connections.

"That was an accident! Ange, tell 'im it was an accident!" he begged.

"You hit me, you fuck!" Angela wasn't taking none of it.

Louie then grabbed the junkie by his singlet collar and yanked him down to the crumb-littered floor, right beside Angela. "Take a closer look! Look at her fucken face! Look at her *fucking* face. Does that look like an accident to you?" Louie yelled as he forced the junkie to admit to what he'd done. Louie then swept all the drugs off the glass coffee table and shattered it with his boot, grabbing a sharp piece of glass. He then approached the junkie and pulled his head up by his hair, forcing him to look at Louie, holding the shard against his throat. "You think you can touch my girls, you scum-sucking prick?" He moved the shard closer to the man's eye, about half an inch away. "You think you can leave a mark on my Angela, you fucken dirt-bag fucker?" Louie proceeded to beat the junkie's stomach in with his boots. He really liked these boots of his. "This look like an accident? Does it? You slimy motherfucker!" Louie turned around and dropped the glass on the floor. Although the junkie may have thought the ordeal was over, Louie had other plans, grabbing the stereo that played that wonderful Wild West music and dropping it onto the junkie's legs. "You stupid waste of a human being! You lousy junkie—piece of ass!" Oh, Louie could be a dangerous motherfucker, and I mean he wouldn't stop until he was satisfied. Louie began kicking him in the head, over and over, while the junkie tried to protect himself with his hands, until he finally pled.

"I'm sorry! Stop! I'm sorry!"

Louie pointed right in the man's face. "You stay the fuck away from her, you fucken hear me? You filthy … cunt." He was almost spitting along with the words exiting his mouth.

Louie looked at Angela. "Go wait outside, sweetheart."

Angela finally spoke up after realizing Louie did more than she would have paid for. "No. I'm not leaving—I don't want you to kill 'im, Lou! He learned. Look at him! Pathetic bastard!" She gestured to the scrawny ex-boyfriend on the floor, reduced to less than pig's waste.

Louie looked at her with a blank stare. We all knew Louie had a soft spot for Angela, and some of us even wondered if there were deeper feelings involved. He was going to make this man pay dearly—he simply didn't want her to witness it. Once in the zone, there was no stopping Louie. He'd seen too many of these guys before. "You don't wanna see this, Ange. It's not gonna be pretty and it'll be the same outcome whether you're here or not." Angela gulped before shaking her head. She decided to stay, in hopes that he'd stop. He didn't.

The junkie began trembling as Louie approached him with dead eyes. "Please ... please don't do this?"

Louie sniggered, approaching him slowly. "After what you did to her, you've lost every right to speak, you clown-nosed fucker." Louie pulled out a pistol and stuck it between the junkie's teeth, pushing his head against the wall. "This wall's lookin' pretty faded, you think it needs a new coat o' paint?" The junkie rapidly shook his head. Ange backed up to the door, quite possibly regretting her decision to stay. Louie forced the gun harder into the junkie's mouth. "You want me to spray this fucken wall? I'll fucken do it, you fuck-bag! I'll spray the fucken wall! You want that?"

"No," the junkie yelled. "No, I don't want it!" Tears began to stream down his face, and urine began to stream down his legs. He'd had enough.

Louie then whispered into his ear, "You go within fifty feet of her again and I'll cut your stomach open, drain the blood, and drown you in it. Understand? I've done it before." Louie glared into the man's eyes. The junkie nodded quickly. Louie then smiled. "You like that nose of yours? You want me to smash it in, big fella?" Of course, the junkie shook his head. "I can break it so fucking hard that you won't be able to snort that coke through it ever again." Louie pointed to a loose bag of coke on a rickety bookshelf. "That's right, I spotted your coke ... and I'm takin' it with me. Maybe I'll be doing you a favor by takin' it off your hands." The junkie closed his eyes, shivering. Louie continued. "You gonna thank me for my services?" Louie ground his teeth as he pulled the barrel of the gun out of the man's mouth. "I'm helpin' you get clean. You gonna thank me or do I gotta break somethin' else on that face?" Louie angrily tapped the pistol on the junkie's temple.

He nodded, sweating, still with his eyes closed in terror. "Thank you," the junkie said reluctantly.

Louie was quite chuffed with that one. I remember him telling us how he finally got somebody to thank him after taking a beating. It was on his bucket list. He really got a kick out of it. He yanked the junkie by his hair and pulled him in close. "Speak louder. I can't hear a fucking word through those crooked junkie teeth o' yours," Louie whispered at point blank.

The junkie sobbed loudly, "Thank you! Thank you!"

Louie nodded and released his grip, knocking the man's head against the wall again. "That's better. You're welcome." Louie took a small bow and whacked the junkie over the head for good measure, grabbing the coke and stepping over him toward the door. "Made me miss a barbecue for this shit." Louie picked up the wrecked stereo and plugged it back into the wall, continuing the badass—now crackly—Western music. Angela took a final, awkward glance at the wreck of a man she'd been tangled with before following Louie to the door. Louie stopped before leaving. "Now you have yourself a swell day. And if you show your face again—you'll see *me* again. And it'll be the last thing you ever see, fucko."

***

Back at the mattress barbecue, I stood there with Donnie and a glass of orange juice. By this time, it became such a fiesta that we had the girls come by, bring some homemade Italian sangria, and have a bite to eat. Nonna Francesca, Larissa, Nicky, and Sophia. It was satisfying for such a cover-up stunt to be so successful that it turned into a celebration.

Donnie subtly leaned over to me. "They still watchin' us, or what?"

"Like vultures," I whispered. "Wouldn't be surprised if they call in a chopper."

Donnie smirked, knowing that the longer we drew this out, the more they'd believe the story. "Fucken ridiculous." Donnie squashed a cigarette under his shoe. "Feel like I'm in a zoo. Can't imagine what prison's like."

As Donnie walked away to greet a few of his associates who'd also come for the festivities, Francesca hobbled over. "Johnny. Mangia mangia?" she yelled. I gave her a kiss on both cheeks.

"Yes, I've been busy. I'll eat in a minute, Nonna." She didn't believe me, raising an eyebrow and patting my flat stomach.

"Magra." She'd always catch me being the one who didn't eat at these things. I guess I didn't have the appetite that the next guy did, or maybe my brain was always too occupied. She walked away but that space beside me was quickly filled by Larissa. She looked worried; I already knew the thoughts that resided in her mind. "Tell me he's alright at least. Nobody's talking to me. Why haven't I heard from Carlo?" After an incident like getting your legs blown off in a rigged automobile—things would get quiet. It couldn't be spoken about, especially to the girls. As much as they didn't have a handle on things, they saw each other even more often than the men did, which meant information traveled twice as fast and with an incident like this, we couldn't take any chances. If it were up to me, she would've been the first to know.

I leaned over, kissing her on the cheek and whispering in her ear, "He's gonna be okay. We gotta get him a wheelchair but that's it. Don't you worry, alright? How are you two, anyway?"

Her heart must have sunk the second I mentioned the wheelchair. She tried not to cry in front of anybody else, but it was difficult to imagine her love being so harshly disadvantaged without shedding a tear or two. She inconspicuously wiped the tears, knowing she couldn't share that information with anybody. Being a woman in this life is no easy feat. There's a whole other side to it. You're not in control and you're kept in the dark. Carlo had presumably told her plenty about the business in private, but since I wasn't Carlo, I had to act like we were strangers in front of the crew, regardless of the moral compass.

She looked at the ground, waving the tears from her eyes. "I wanted to announce us this week, officially. I've been asking him so much about it and he keeps on delaying it—and now, this happens."

"Look what happened to him, Larissa. Do ya blame him for not wanting to make it public? The less people know about these things, the less chance you'll be in danger." I placed my hand on her shoulder, and she looked at me.

"It's just ... I wanted us to be like you and Marianne. It's a perfect relationship—a fairy tale. Everyone knows about you guys. Everyone loves you guys. There's no sneaking around, so your love has room to flourish and grow."

She had a point, but the timing couldn't be worse. My relationship with Marianne was a shithole at that moment in time—and things were bound to get worse after what happened at the motel. She wanted nothing to do with me. It wasn't quite the prime example of a steady relationship. "Look, Carlo's only hurt because he was with *me* that day," I said with regret. "It was *my* car that they rigged. You really think he'd want you to be with him if somebody targets him one day? Of course not."

"You're right. I know." She sighed and nodded. "I feel so selfish talking about this after what's happened ... Thanks, Johnny. Just make sure he's alright and send him my love, will ya?"

She really loved him. They had found each other in this cesspool of a system that we lived in. With the bakery involved, they were even helping each other escape. Sometimes I wondered if their bond was stronger than mine and Marianne's. Or maybe it was just a matter of time until they ended up like us. "It'll all be fine, okay? You'll see him in no time. I'll give him a smooch for ya." I winked and she laughed. I'm glad I reintroduced a smile to her face. She really needed it. And she really needed Carlo back in her life.

As Larissa walked away, I lit a smoke and saw the car across the street drive away. The feds must've been tired, thinking they were just spectating a barbecue. Surely, they had better things to do than that. I glanced at Donnie. He was standing close to the entrance of the store. He raised his glass of orange juice to the feds as they circled around the corner. He looked at me with a smile and I nodded. At least we could say the heat was off our asses ... for now.

Chapter Fifteen

Diary Entry: 017

My heart tries to sing but it's bound by an inescapable cage. The bars, solid steel. The floor, a stage for the spectators to watch, amused—entertained. I almost feel like some kind of mime, a performer. I'm expected to look my best, always. I'm expected to listen to him, always. I'm expected to shut the fuck up and stay hospitable to somebody I thought couldn't change—couldn't be corrupted or brainwashed, but did.

I'm a contortionist, bending, flexing, and twirling, almost to the point of snapping until my body crumbles beneath the weight of what I've been subject to. As I dangle on the string on stage, in my cage as the spectators watch and laugh, I yearn to wrap it around my neck and let my body collapse. I yearn to see if they continue to laugh when my skin becomes pale.

Marianne Martha Manzelli. The name I inherited from my parents.

Almost comical. A joke which reflects my waking life at this very moment. Who am I? What will I be remembered for? Will I be remembered at all? The fiancée of a killer. The future wife of the infamous John Caruso. He becomes more and more like his uncle every day. The more he molds into Don, the further I feel we part. I still love him. I always will. That's the trouble I find myself in. Do I love him for who he currently is, or do I love him for the man I fell for at the start? Even if it lay deep inside that mere vessel of what he has become. I know my Johnny is still in there ... somewhere. Is it simply too late to mend the trench between us?

The woman inside me tells me to leave. How can I? He can change. He just needs to learn the error of his ways. And why should I be the one to leave? This is my life; I don't want to escape it. I still love him. I've never loved anybody more in my entire life. He's everything to me.

It can't be his fault that I made a mistake with Richard, was it? After all, it was my decision to go to that motel every Wednesday. Richard wanted to see me more. He wanted me to leave Johnny. I should have left one or the other but now it's too late. Richard's dead, at the vengeful hand of my eventual husband. Did I underestimate my fiancé? I didn't know he was capable of such ... slaughter. Sheer, vicious, animalistic behavior. He mutilated him, right in front of me. I watched as Richard's face was torn to pieces, as if he were attacked and ripped—mauled by dogs, hounds, wolves, beasts. I don't want to write about it, but I need to get it out of my fucking head and put it on paper. It's surreal—

horrifically surreal to see a person's face destroyed. I didn't love Richard, but he tried to liberate me from my life, whether it meant for good or just that one hour every Wednesday evening. A temporary fix. A way to keep my head on straight, a way to take tension from my waking relationship. It's my fault he's dead. I thought about cutting him off a week earlier. I was in too deep. Moreover, he didn't know the capabilities of the people I associated with.

Do I leave? He'll hurt me just like he did Richard. He'll get Louie or one of his goons to keep an eye on me—if he hasn't already. After all, that's how he found out about the affair. What about Leonard? I cut that off a few months before. He was becoming too attached and wanted to know too much. My life wasn't meant for him. Ronnie? He was only in it for the money—he seemed to think that if I were persuaded to leave, I'd take my parents' money and run off into the sunset with him.

Johnny isn't like that. He loved me for me, and I think he still does. Although, when he came home last night, he seemed cheerful but it disappeared when he noticed me sitting at the kitchen bench. I couldn't look him straight in the eye. Visions of what he did to Richard flashed into my brain every time I laid eyes on him. That gnarly, disturbed look in his eyes made me sick to the stomach. Maybe that's why the emotion crept from his face when he saw me? Maybe he remembered what he'd done to Richard and thinks of it whenever he sees me. I'm hoping he feels remorse, some kind of regret. Maybe it's too much to ask and maybe he's too far gone.

I needed to get out of the house after he returned home. We weren't speaking, so there was no reason to hang around and watch him resent me. "I might ask Angela if she wants to do dinner."

"No," Johnny said. I was taken aback. He'd never declined that abruptly, especially not so stern. He'd become strict, keeping a close eye on me.

"Can I ask why?" I placed both my hands on my hips as my lips quivered. I didn't want an argument, but I also wasn't prepared to lie down and become a doormat for him.

As he packed a few things with intent to head off somewhere himself, he stopped and looked at me again. "Angela's in no state to see anybody."

I knew it. This attitude was going to bubble up to the top sooner or later, given hints of who he spends his time with. I shouldn't even be asking him to let me go. I'm my own person and I should just go. He obviously thought I was planning to cheat on him again, seek another man as if I had ever been so desperate. As he left, I wondered if I'd deserved this treatment. It felt like house arrest. And if I'd disobeyed his orders to see Angela for myself, he'd think I was being unfaithful. Either that, or he didn't want me tweeting information to the other girls. I feel forced to stay at home and prove my loyalty, prove that I'm his, and his only. I even asked him a few times if I could take a part-time job at the cafe across the street. It could be fun. I could make more friends, feel less alone, and actually feel productive. Sergey's asked for my resume a few times, but Johnny insists that it's too dangerous. He even told me to stop doing ballet. He says it's imperative that I stay home. Is it true? Or is he regulating my lifestyle? Restricting my movement, afraid that I'd slip up for a second time.

I didn't mean for it to get this far. I needed somebody, somebody who understood me, somebody to make me feel loved. I don't want to be the wife that cleans and cooks until Johnny gets home from his deeds. I want a life of my own. I have aspirations, ambitions, goals. I want friends, I want to paint, I want to travel and feel love again as I did once before ... I want a child.

Dear God, I want so badly a child.

Is Johnny the stem of this issue? His inability to satisfy my needs. Not that it's a pivotal part of my relationship with him, but it still counts for something. Some part of why I feel disconnected with him. I don't like finding it with other men, but it's the only way I can reset my brain to be the best girl I can for Johnny. My father is blind and yet my mother stays for him. But is it because she wants to, or because she must? I must stay. I must do it for him. I love him and I can't hurt him again.

Larissa's been calling but Johnny keeps intercepting the phone. He whispers to her, mentioning Carlo. I did initially wonder if he'd been seeing her in private which would account for the secrecy, but I really don't think he would. Then again, his characteristic changes have surprised me of late.

Chapter Sixteen

Mephisto's Waltz

I opened my eyes, and I was twelve years old. My father had lost all his hair and was arguing with somebody over the phone. It seemed the older he grew, the more impatient and aggressive he became. Perhaps, the absence of my mother took a toll on him.

"Go upstairs, Johnny. Please?" He'd usually wait until I reached the top of the staircase to really scream his guts out over the phone. "You wanna blackmail me, you sonofabitch? After everything I've done for you?"

This time, it wasn't the separation of floors that drowned my father's yelling. It was the blaring music coming from the bedroom of my sister. I knocked on the door a few times and there was no response. The music must've been too loud. I opened the door, covering my eyes in case Isabella was getting dressed or talking to a boy. Standing in the doorway of her room with hand-covered eyes, there was still no response. I removed my hands and my sister was on the floor—her body jerking, saliva streaming from her mouth. I didn't know what to do. My body couldn't move. Call my father? The music was too loud. CPR? I didn't know how. I noticed a bottle of pills, tipped over on her desk. I had to think quickly. I rushed to that same desk and snatched a pencil. I opened her mouth and stuck it as far down her throat as I could until I felt a reaction from her esophagus.

"Papa!" I yelled over the music, which somehow seemed louder. "Papaaaa!" Isabella's body convulsed and seven pills flew out of her mouth in a puddle of saliva. Some of them almost fully dissolved. "Paapaaaaa!" I screamed at the top of my lungs, crying and wondering if it was too late to save her. I turned the music off and ran to the staircase, screaming for my father again.

Isabella tried to kill herself. In school, I was learning about Romeo and Juliet at the time and wondered if she was being dramatic regarding a boy at her school. They had to pump her stomach, and she survived but she never told me why she did it, why she wanted to escape this world. She later developed a form of schizophrenia. Maybe my mother's death weighed on her more than it did me. After all, Isabella was older than me, and she'd spent more time with my mother and gained more memories with her than I ever did.

I needed another session with Dr. Kumar.

***

I had a few months break from the shrink after the Marianne-motel incident, so it'd been a while. I returned to Dr. Kumar with a few things I needed to get off my chest. These memories were all too real to be imaginary. There needed to be some explanation.

"Okay, Abraham. Over the last few months, you've clearly been able to unlock some of your repressed memories. Are there any others?"

I looked at the floor, interlocking my fingers. I didn't know what to do with them. I was more fidgety than ever. "In what way?"

Dr. Kumar cleared his throat and sat up straight. "Usually with my patients, we dig through their old memories and in their time out of session, these memories are naturally unlocked due to a string of other memories that had been explored through our previous sessions."

I stared at him. He spoke way too fast over something I knew nothing about. "I didn't understand a single word of that."

He smiled and reworded it. "Apologies. So, after our sessions, some memories may be unlocked when you're alone." I told him there was nothing else I could pick out. I couldn't explain what I saw to him, or mention figures from my past or my family. It was far too sensitive to divulge and I feared that I'd slip up. "We're making good progress, anyway—" He closed his notepad. It sounded like he was ending the session early, but I wasn't done. I needed more. I needed answers.

"Wait. There are a few things that I can remember sometimes. Short recollections." I inhaled deeply. Dr. Kumar looked up, intrigued. He'd been waiting for me to willfully bring these memories up. "Like my sister overdosing on pills, or my uncle being at my childhood apartment. Most of the time, he was unwelcome."

Dr. Kumar nodded, cleaning his glasses. "Are you just seeing the actions of this man or hearing his voice in these memories as well?"

"I don't know if this means anything but the words 'Shut the fuck up and don't move' keep coming to mind. I don't know why. In my memories, he's talking but how do I know if they're real?"

He slid his glasses back on and slouched into his chair. "It's true that the mind can fabricate a memory, Abraham, or even mistake one for a dream. But even in a fake memory, these circumstances you're experiencing aren't happening for no reason. You see, *my* father was good to me but in the instance that he had beaten me when I was younger, I may not have dreams of him beating me per se, but instead he could be doing something as simple as throwing a baseball at me with *force*. Either way, my mind would develop negative connotations to the person who was abusing me. Therefore, the physical abuse progresses into mental." He leaned back on his chair, fiddling with a pen and staring at the ceiling.

"So, you're saying I was mentally abused?" I asked, hoping to take something away from this session, something valuable, some kind of explanation.

"I can't say anything for sure. But as for the vividness of these memories, once access is gained to something that has been locked away for so long—your brain may relive these events as though they are occurring in real time." He stared at me as he spoke, explaining my own brain as if he'd pulled it apart with a scalpel and stitched it up again. "But after all, memories are similar to dreams; they can be altered and interfered with beyond comprehension."

I knew by this time that something was sour about Donnie. It was clear that he wasn't a good man—everybody was wise to that much. But there was more to it. I could guess by the memories that he had sexually abused my mother. But did they have prior exchanges? Was I mistaking it for abuse? Regardless, something was still suspicious about him. Something deeper was hidden in the depths of that man's soul and in my memories. I was so close, I could almost taste it. I just needed to put my finger on it once and for all.

***

The way her legs twirled, the way her body was conveyed to express emotion aside from her facial muscles, it's what made the live scene in New York just that little more special. Over there, the talent was kicked up a notch. The dancers were more agile; the moves were quicker and precise. The audience was bigger. Even the music was more dramatic.

Sofia Alvarez. A South American ballet dancer with just about every bit of talent you could physically extract from the human body. It was mesmerizing to watch, and she made two hours feel like twelve and a half seconds. You'd be lost in a trance when she performed at the Koch Theater, the most picturesque place to see a show. But Donnie, Castello, and I weren't there for the entertainment.

As Castello made his way across to our seats among the audience, he scooched over their legs while trying to get a view of Sofia during her first number. "I'm sorry—'scuse me." I was sitting between Donnie and Castello, all dressed up for a show, but whenever we were with Donnie, things were never as they seemed. It was rare to see Donnie on the town doing something unrelated to his work. I wouldn't believe it for a second. There was always an ulterior motive. "What are we doin' here'?" I whispered, leaning slightly into Donnie's ear.

"Just watch the show," he said, staring directly ahead, watching Sofia perform. I sighed, turning to Castello for answers but he shrugged. I decided to sit back and enjoy the show. The gears in my brain were constantly moving, so I needed to slow myself down and enjoy something for once. After all, the tickets were maliciously overpriced.

Sofia moved always with perfect timing and balance. Even Castello was hypnotized beyond understanding. "She can do just about anything, my friend. You could say she's a jack of all trades, but in everything she does, she still outperforms everybody else."

I nodded, watching her move across the stage in harmony with the heavy strums of the violins. "Mesmerizing. The *Queen* of all trades."

Donnie nudged me in annoyance. "Can you two keep it down?"

I whispered to him again, "What are we doin' here, Zio?" I never liked surprises. I guess it's a security thing.

Donnie finally looked over to me. "Take it easy for a second and enjoy the show. It's not every night that we get to be enticed by a piece of what Manhattan has to offer. We've performed enough for this city, now we can watch her perform for us." As the other dancers joined Sofia, the piano and brass instruments began to rise with intensity, faster and faster as the dancers moved in a perfect circle. The other dancers, you could see the expressions on their faces; this stuff was difficult. *Sofia?* Not a chance. She was just getting started—she hadn't even broken a sweat as far as the eye could see. After hitting the crescendo, the lights dimmed, and the music lowered in volume. Donnie leaned over. "That skirt on stage. She's only eighteen and she's already got the lead," he said as I nodded. "She's the niece of a very powerful man," he continued. "He's sitting in the front row." Immediately, I glanced toward the front row. It was too far to see but I knew that this was the reason we were here. It was something to do with the man in the front row. "That man is among the richest people in America. He is the reason our Perico sales are declining."

My blood ran cold. I knew who it was. I knew the second he

mentioned the product. "Blackjaw," I said to myself. It just slipped out.

Donnie looked at me, confused. "How the hell do *you* know?" I shrugged and gestured to Castello. After all, he was the one who wised me up to Blackjaw.

What was I supposed to do? Scamper out of there in case he saw me after ripping his recording devices from my car and ignoring his warnings? No, why would he bring that up in front of Donnie? That wouldn't be a smart move, no matter how powerful somebody may be.

"Good. Saves me a bit of explaining. Heriberto Alvarez—the man I used to work for. If you ever have the chance to shake that man's hand. You shake it, Johnny."

He didn't have a fucking clue of what I'd been through. How could he have? He was blinded by the business and wasn't even aware of the snake-like capabilities of the man with the black beard. "Why should I shake his hand when we're not supposed to like the guy?" I debated.

Donnie shook his head. It was the wrong mentality, at least to his knowledge. "Because his backbone is based on respect and trust. At least, that's what he tells you. But one day, who knows? You might need a favor. You'd rather stand beside this man than in front of him."

I looked at Blackjaw, only seeing the back of his head, looking up at his niece on stage. "You shake his hand if he sees you tonight. But you don't ever make a deal with a man like that. You'd either get killed by the end of it, or you'd get the opposite of what he promised you."

Maybe Donnie knew him better than I thought, but he still wasn't aware that I'd already met him. "How do you know all this?" I asked, curious to hear more, curious to see if there was a way for me to uncover some kind of weakness in that jaw for any advantage, if I ever needed it.

"I told you, I used to work for him, Johnny. He's the one that ordered my first hit. He was the one that whacked his own nephew; I know how this man works better than anyone else. This is a man that makes his money for himself and nobody else. He doesn't care who he fucks over, as long as he's makin' bank. He'd probably chop his own wife over a cash dispute." As Donnie leaned back, he sighed. I knew well and true that Blackjaw was becoming a real thorn in his ass. "He's becoming more possessive over this business. Seeing us here is gonna remind him that New York is *our* domain. It's a friendly way of showing that we're watching him. No need for guns or threats ... just a simple appearance to make a statement."

As Sofia completed her performance, the theater erupted with applause. I'd never heard one louder than that. "Life seems mundane now after that," Castello said, getting up before Donnie placed a firm hand on his chest.

"Wait a minute."

As the sea of well-dressed theatergoers surged up the aisles, the three of us stood stationary like rocks on the seashore. I noticed Blackjaw with two of his men also walking up the aisles. This was when I started to sweat. There had to be some confrontation. Somebody's going to find out about that night in the car and the recording device. If Donnie did, he'd probably kill me for not telling him, but if I had, it could've started a war with Blackjaw. And I'd be the first person he'd want to put to sleep. I watched every step he took up the aisles with one bodyguard in front of him and another behind. I was nervous, breathing faster and faster until I wracked my brain for any excuse to leave. Being dead center between Donnie and Cas made it all the more difficult. Even by the time I thought of staging a bust for the bathroom, he'd already come upon us. "Don Caruso. Am I seein' a ghost?" spat Blackjaw as he stopped at the end of our aisle, readying a cigar to light outside. I stared at the ground. I didn't want eye contact. Not with the man that held my own pistol to my head.

"It's good to see you, you old bastard." Donnie wasn't shy at being playful, especially when it meant business.

Blackjaw smiled. "Since when do you come to these things? I always thought you were into the racehorses and such."

Donnie chuckled with a shrug. "Oh, you know me. I like to dabble with different interests. It keeps me young. I'd like to introduce you to my nephew, Johnny."

I was forced to look up at him. He looked even more evil than before with his cocky grin. The way he looked at me. He was speaking with his eyes. He knew exactly what I was thinking. He knew I was keeping the secret of that night in the alley. And I knew that he knew that I ripped that device from my car. But Donnie didn't. He didn't know a goddamn thing. Blackjaw and I just had a conversation with our eyes.

He reached to me, playing the game. Donnie looked at me with concern, waiting for me to shake his hand like the rest of my life depended on it. It probably did. I played along, as if I'd never heard of the guy. "I don't believe we've met," Blackjaw said with a smirk.

"Your niece was wonderful on stage. Truly phenomenal," I said with a nod.

Blackjaw smiled, seeming somewhat disarmed but managing to keep that grin on his face. "You fellas have done your homework. I'm glad you enjoyed the show! She's really shapin' up to be a talent for the ages." Blackjaw placed his hand firmly on my shoulder, squeezing so hard that it almost felt like he was screaming, "You're a dead man for ripping out that recording device." He looked at Donnie, still with his hand on my shoulder. "This your new driver, then?" Blackjaw asked, keeping a tense grip.

"Something like that, yeah," replied Donnie.

Blackjaw stepped back and looked at me, and me only. "I hear the new Corvettes are nice … Well, I better get going! Can't show my face around here too long. You know how it is, Don?" Blackjaw winked as he began moving.

Donnie nodded. "That I do."

Blackjaw then disappeared into the crowd. As we made our way out of the seats, Castello muttered, "That guy gives me the creeps."

As we stepped out of the theater, I wondered why he asked if I was a driver. He knew I wasn't. Then I wondered why he mentioned a Corvette. I found it coincidental that I told Carlo just a few weeks before that I fancied those new models, right before his legs were blown off. It then hit me like a steam train. It was Blackjaw's way of telling me he was listening. Still listening, even after the recording device was removed. There must've been another one, but there was no way to find out because the car was blown to smithereens. I didn't know the extent of it. Was it just a recording device? Was he the one who rigged my car?

From what I heard, Blackjaw liked to play mind games. One conversation and he was already in my head. I didn't want to have another one with him. I never liked picking apart conversations after they were over. Unfortunately, it wouldn't be our last exchange.

***

During the usual Friday evening meeting at the Caruso building, Donnie stood high above us. Everybody was there—Castello, Vinnie, Louie, Gigi, and a few others. Carlo finally resurfaced with a welcome smile from everybody. He was in a wheelchair. He had no legs. It was awful to see him that way. I was just glad he was alive, to see his face again. That cheeky grin everybody loved.

"Go on, make ya jokes, laugh at me!" Carlo spat while the boys gave him a pat on the back as he wheeled past them to his place at the table. "Legless—I'd probably still get double the work done that *you* clowns do!"

"We did alright this week." Donnie quickly stopped the laughter. "There's only one problem," Donnie said as he passed out wads of cash to each of us individually. Small gifts for putting our asses on the line week in and week out. Mine was always a bit thicker than the others. I always appreciated that but didn't say nothing about it to nobody.

"What is it, Boss?" Louie asked. We all hoped that the "problem" Donnie was referring to wasn't any of our fuck-ups. But it had to be somebody.

"We're missin' two pounds of angel dust."

We all looked around at one another. This was unheard of. Our Yayo was so tight, nobody could get a sniff without being caught. Two pounds is a major loss. It wasn't even about the product; it was the risk. Other drug dealers could've had it, the feds, Blackjaw … anybody.

Castello shrugged, looking around. "Who was in charge o' that?"

Donnie shrugged back, but with a pinch of sarcasm. "I don't know. Looks like it's been lost in transit. I have a buyer needin' one pound and somehow, I'm down two."

He picked up a cigar he'd been smoking and flicked the ashes off before taking a long, stress-induced drag. He began to walk around the table with a slow pace. "First, I have another issue. I wanna talk to Johnny and Carlo now."

I felt a chill go straight down my spine. Was this about Blackjaw? Did he find out? It couldn't be. Carlo wasn't even aware of my dealings with him. I gulped, looking at Carlo but he was already looking back at me. "Yes, Boss?" asked Carlo, quivering under his breath. He'd just returned to our graces, and he was already under the chopping block in front of everybody.

"Does the name Arnold Richards ring a bell?" My blood ran cold. I shook my head, hoping to God that it was by chance another Arnold. Donnie looked at Carlo. "The cocksucker from that accounting firm? Sound familiar at all?" It was the same Arnold. Out of everything that's bitten me in the ass, this had to be the one of the worst. Carlo looked down at the table. He'd never give me up, or the fact that I let that bastard go. "You look at me when I'm talkin' to you!" Donnie spoke sternly. Carlo looked up. "Carlo. You told me this guy was in the ground. I told you to whack that fucker that's been hoarding my investment and I hear he's still tryna keep my money?"

Carlo looked at everybody else. The attention was all on him. A lot of pressure for his first day back. "Boss—" he stuttered, "we gave him a warning and told him never to come back." Carlo didn't believe in pointing fingers. That deed, we did it together, even though it was *my* fuck-up.

"Is that what I told you to do? Well, he came back. You got no legs and now I'm startin' to think you ain't got no brain, either." Donnie shook his head and turned his back, walking over to his desk.

I stood up out of my seat. "Zio, I'm the one that let 'im go—"

He spun around, pointing directly at me with a stern yell. "Sit the fuck down and shut the fuck up! Do not interrupt me when I'm speaking, you fucking coward. I don't wanna hear it." Being spoken to that way in front of the others felt degrading. I felt my fists clench and my eyes twitch. But I sat back down, because after all, he was right. I fucked up. Donnie turned back to Carlo. "Carlo was the one that lied to my face, claimin' that this bottom feeder ain't comin' back."

Carlo looked down at his wheelchair, seeking any way to distract himself from Donnie's piercing glare. "I'm sorry, Boss."

Donnie then took a deep breath. A much longer pause than usual. His fingers began to twitch. He was upset. I'd never seen him this upset before; obviously I'd seen him lose his shit, but this was different. He couldn't control the tips of his fingers. "Louie. Take Carlo with you on that errand I told you to run tonight. I don't wanna see his face." He wanted Carlo out of his sight. I only had myself to blame. Louie rolled Carlo out the door. Carlo looked at me and we knew we'd made a grave mistake.

After everybody left, Donnie placed an extra wad of cash in front of me. "Don't *ever* lie to me again."

I didn't like the special treatment. It felt dirty, like I hadn't earned it.

I deserved to be treated the way Carlo had been. In fact, I deserved it more. "That wasn't fair. I'm the one that didn't kill Arnold."

"Carlo lied." Donnie pointed to the door. "You may have withheld information from me, but Carlo's the one that misled me. That's much worse." I stood up, throwing my jacket on and pushing in all the chairs—noticing a free spot where Carlo parked his wheelchair. "Wait up a sec." Donnie interrupted my exit. "I have a theory, and it checks out." I inhaled deeply, wondering if, and hoping that he hadn't foiled my web of lies pertaining to his nemesis, Blackjaw. "Johnny. I know I haven't been the best uncle. I know it hasn't been easy working together, but I can see how far you've come. You're loyal, you're a man, you're strong. I stand here in front of you and see my nephew—even better than I wanted you to be. I don't tell it to you enough, but I'm proud of you."

At last, I felt accepted. Was it another play at deception, or was I finally able to lower my guard and accept the fact that I'd adapted to this life in a way he wanted? "What's that theory you were going to tell me?" If it were anything incriminating about me, he wouldn't have just said those wonderful things.

"I think Blackjaw was behind the car attack. I think he tried to kill you, Johnny. He's a sick character and he wants us to play his sick game." Donnie began pouring us both a scotch.

"How can we be sure it was him?"

"Because nobody gets underneath us like that. I need to ask you a favor, because you're deep in this now—he has single-handedly reeled you into this problem."

"What is it, Zio?"

Donnie sighed, drinking down the entire glass in one gulp. "We're going to play Blackjaw's game. He isn't just a threat. He's an emergency that needs to be harshly dealt with, and I need your help." It was the first time Donnie ever said anything like that. "We're gonna take him down, together. And I don't mean in the market. We need to kill 'im, Johnny. So, between you and I, there are to be no lies. You and I are now equals, and we are in this together. We're gonna put Blackjaw to sleep."

I nodded, almost exhilarated by the fact that I could put that sonofabitch behind me. I wanted his blood. I wanted him and his crew dead, especially if they were to blame for the car and Carlo's legs. He deserved pain, and with my uncle, we couldn't be stopped.

"I'm in."

***

Catania. My mother nervously rushed around the apartment, snatching handbags, keys, and fetching small wads of cash from hidden places like empty diced tomato cans and behind cupboards. I was playing with a few toys on the floor with Isabella before my mother kneeled down to the both of us.

"Now, you two wait right here. I'm going to get your father and we're leaving, tonight," she said, exasperated.

Isabella was concerned. "Where are we going?"

As she tried to hold in her tears, she held my sister's hand. "Somewhere else, baby. Somewhere safer than here. We'll be okay. I promise." She stood up straight and walked toward the door of the apartment, turning back and glancing at us both. Isabella was older than me, so she could better sense the weight of what Carmela was feeling. "Just be ready when I come back," my mother said. As she left, I proceeded to play with my red toy truck.

I felt a presence. Something wasn't right. Remembering back to these moments was peculiar, because unlocking it would feel like the memory was untouched, meaning these fine details were vivid, as if they happened yesterday because they were preserved in the vault for so long. I glanced around the dark room and there emerged a figure I hadn't expected. It was Donnie. He employed the face of dejection. "Did you even bother to say goodbye to your mother?" he said in a croaky voice, as if heartbroken. I was confused over the sentence. Suddenly we heard a loud explosion outside on the street. Isabella screamed, covering her ears. I began to cry, standing up and forgetting that Donnie was even there as I walked slowly to the one window that viewed the street below.

My mother's car was in flames. The burning wreckage was engulfed. I could almost hear her screaming, but I couldn't tell if it was her, Isabella, or the pedestrians. The screams would've told me she was alive. At least I would have hoped she'd have a chance. As I looked below, I couldn't believe what I was seeing. My brain wouldn't register it among the chaos. Suddenly an arm rested on my shoulder—Donnie's. "Oh, my poor boy. Don't look ... Don't look out there," he cried.

Was he pretending? Was he trying to win me over as a new parental figure in my life? I continued to stare at the street as passersby and onlookers crowded the area, some throwing water onto the wreckage, but all hope was lost before they arrived.

I pushed my head into Donnie's shoulder. He was there for me, either way. He held me tight and amongst the confusion over what had just happened, I needed somebody there, and he was. He ran his fingers through my hair, rocking me back and forth in his embrace. He was in pain, too. Whether he was attached to her murder or not, it destroyed him. "Donnie's here ... Zio Donnie's here." I couldn't tell what it all meant. *Did he do it? Did Donnie murder my mother?* If he did, then why? Were these flooding memories just figments of my imagination? Was I getting it completely wrong? How could I possibly believe some piece of information that had resurfaced in my brain after two decades? Especially in such vivid detail. Could I be getting it completely wrong?

***

I was asked to go for a ride with Louie to the sticks. It was regarded as a sensitive situation. We came to a stop at the usual bridge over the usual river. I couldn't tell you how many problems were buried there.

"You okay, kid?" Louie asked, looking over at me and pulling the handbrake up.

"Yeah, why?"

"I know it's been pretty rough for you lately," he said as he looked in the rearview mirror. I liked it, the comfort. It was rare coming from Louie and it was a good change of pace at the time.

"Shit's not great at the moment, Lou. Marianne hasn't spoken to me for weeks. I don't even know what to do anymore. To be truthful, I'm feeling a little lost," I admitted, staring out the window into the darkness.

"Look, after we get rid of the luggage, we'll get Mama Vero to make some cannolis." Louie nodded before opening the door. "Luggage" usually meant some scumbag, dirtbag, or junkie without a name. It was easy to make guys like that disappear.

"Sounds great, Lou." As we made our way to the trunk, I felt a slight breeze. Winter was coming in and boy, was it cold when it arrived. Wherever I went, a jacket was the one thing I'd forget, every time without fail. Louie opened the trunk, dragging out a body wrapped in plastic—likely the plastic they use to cover brand-new furniture after purchase. It was nice not to be wasteful. I flicked my cigarette into a puddle and grabbed one end of the package. Louie grabbed the other.

"This one's lightweight. We usually dump the fat fucks," I said with a grunt, letting the body hang between us like a hammock strung between two trees. It was eerily small, as if a child's corpse—but even Donnie wouldn't be *that* inhumane.

"Just bring him over to the river," Louie muttered under his breath.

Now, this is the part that fucks me. Halfway to the river, we caught the moonlight as it emerged from the clouds. I took one glance down at the plastic and noticed something shockingly familiar. Carlo's face. Carlo's innocent, youthful, lifeless fucken face wrapped within plastic like he was a pig in a butcher. Carlo's body, lighter weight than expected because he wasn't accompanied by his own legs. Carlo's body I was unknowingly disposing of in our usual routine luggage. Carlo, treated just like any other pill-popping, rule-breaking, cash-owing scumbag Donnie cleaned on a monthly basis. My best friend … killed by my own. I couldn't register it at first. To me, it wasn't real. It was him. I dropped the body. I stumbled back, covering my mouth in disbelief. Louie's eyes widened as he quickly approached me, knowing I'd wised up to it.

"Now, Johnny! Relax!" Louie said with his palms facing me. I couldn't help it. I instantly fell to the ground and threw up in the grass.

"What the fuck? What did you do?" I howled. "What did you *doooo?*" I stumbled backward. Something wasn't letting me get to my feet as I stared at the plastic wrap in horror, sheer terror. I panicked, shaking with rage, confusion, surrealism, and sickness. My stomach was retching, although there was nothing left to purge.

Louie slowly approached me, cautious. "Let's not ask questions, okay?"

I launched at him, striking his face three times, smashing his nose with my knuckles before he regained his footing. I tackled him again and he fell to the ground. I scratched at him like a cat; I couldn't think of anything else to do. The only thing I wanted was to cause pain—as much as I could in the smallest amount of time, over and over. Louie threw a punch but missed me; his arm was lodged in my ribs, so he couldn't extend his fist all the way. I continued striking him, knowing that if punching was my choice of combat, he'd do the same the second he broke free. The tears streamed as I beat him over and over. Louie was like a brick wall. Each strike would feel like you were dealing no damage. It was almost as if he'd been absorbing the damage to use it against you when you were done. As soon as I let my emotions take over, it was his turn.

Louie pushed me off him and I stumbled backwards; drunk in the midst of mental anguish, I collapsed in a pit of mud. Louie went for the stomach, over and over, striking about four times harder than I ever could. I instantly coughed blood. It felt as if my insides were churned into a sack of sludge and that the next time I expelled urine, it was bound to be a dark-red color. Louie stood up, dusting himself off and limping away from me. I got up to continue. I was far from done. That's when I realized how hard a body-hit could be. I couldn't even deal the next blow. I collapsed into Louie's chest, bringing him back down to the ground as the mud and loose dirt painted us. Louie caught me in a stranglehold, and it felt like I was being constricted by a python. I squirmed side to side until I had no more breath to spend on my physical capabilities.

"What did you doooo? What did you fucking do? He didn't deserve it! It's Carlo! He's innocent—it's fucking Carlo!" I cried to the moon, coughing up spit, blood, and sweat. I don't even think I was talking to Louie that time. I knew who was behind this. Donnie called the hit. I thought about everything. Carlo's business, his family, Larissa, the future of what could've been his children. All the desires, all the steps he'd taken to escape this business, and all the time we'd spent together. They weren't strong enough. It engulfed his life. The amount of pain I felt for Carlo, the multitude of opportunities he had, the places he could've gone, the life he could have led. It all disappeared with a single bullet in the side of his head.

In this business, I guess you don't think about the big picture until it happens to somebody close to you. Every single person we'd waste, they'd have a family, they'd have something to live for. But just because we didn't see that side of it, doesn't mean it didn't exist—and it doesn't mean they didn't have families that grieved at their loss. It made me wonder how many lives we'd ruined and how many branches we'd blindly severed from the family trees we never ever considered thinking about.

Louie held me tight as I flailed in his arms. "You gotta understand, Johnny. It was for the good of the family—" Knowing Louie, he would've done it with no questions asked. Like I said, he was a yes-man.

I threw weak blows, unable to land a hit, but Louie overpowered me. "You killed him! You fucking killed him!" I continued to scream to the clouds above until Louie held me down in the dirt.

"Quiet! Shut the fuck up!" He stared at me. I could almost see a sparkle of a tear, as if he did feel some kind of remorse for it. He ground his teeth. "I know how it feels. I know ... just relax." He exhaustedly relinquished me as I looked back at him with hatred. I covered my eyes with my forearm. I couldn't bear to look at that plastic-wrapped bag with my best friend in it. Louie held me close as my head fell into his chest.

"I know, I know. I know how it feels. I know ..." he whispered gently.

***

I knew he was a monster. Everybody knew it. I was accepted by him, finally after so many years of belittlement. A so-called "equal" to Donnie. As he made me feel complete, he dropped the axe on Carlo. Was it an act to stabilize me for a hit like this? Was it a way to warn me of what he'd do if I fucked him over? He was no ally—he was drunk with power and was willing to take down his own men to prove a point.

What kind of family is that?

What kind of monster could commit these deeds and feel nothing?

I tried to wrap my feeble brain about why he did it, and that brain even tried to convince me that Carlo must've done something to deserve it.

Did Carlo lie to Donnie on more than one occasion?

Did he have secrets that I didn't know about?

Was it a mistake? Was he framed for doing something he didn't do?

This entire time, I'd been a pawn in Donnie's game, a mere chess piece to manipulate and turn into his own, personal soldier. He wanted me to fight with him against Blackjaw, but I think the real creature of the damned was right beside me, and I knew I'd have to strike at the right time, whether I made it a poisoning, a staged suicide, or simply a bullet to the back of the head.

Blackjaw may have been the diversion, but Donnie needed to fall. And what better way to do it than to pretend I was on his side?

TO BE CONTINUED...

Acknowledgments

As my second publication and first series publication, I'd like to thank the readers that have followed me from the beginning and continue to follow me through my career. *Killing Donnie* was a very different style compared to my usual philosophic/introspective entries like *Honeybird*. I appreciate those who were able to adapt to my different writing styles and hope those readers have enjoyed *Part One* of *Killing Donnie* enough to read *Part Two*.

I would also like to thank anybody that spared a mere second of their lives to glance upon this book, pick it up, borrow it, purchase it, skim through it—or actually read it. Thank you for giving my words your time.

To my family: My father, my mother, my sisters and my brother-in-law. Having these incredible humans in my life encourages me to shoot for the skies, deny myself a mundane life and realize that there is more to our existence than what the world, and society, expects from us. Thank you for being so supportive and encouraging of the words I write. Sometimes, I find that through my writing is the only way I can express myself. But my family make it that little bit easier.

I would also like to thank RLC Motion Pictures – specifically Russell Cunningham, Clayton Watson and Felipe Teplitsky. Without these three incredible individuals, *Killing Donnie* wouldn't have evolved into the massive project it has become. What began as a feature film with a three-hour duration—I was given the choice to shorten the feature to one and a half hours, or lengthen it to a limited mini-series; six episodes—one hour per episode. I decided on the latter, to add depth to my work instead of cutting it short, and by sharing this work with the team at RLC, I was able to refine the project to strengthen character arcs, inject more emotion, create backstories and morph *Killing Donnie* into what it was meant to become. If I hadn't had the motivation from these creatives to push the project further to its destiny—there's a chance it would exist merely as a shelved feature script. Thank you, RLC—for everything.

I'd like to thank my friends for supporting me through this project since it was conceived, specifically Aidan and Marco.

I'd also like to thank Michael Lake – who was originally cast in the film project and has stuck by me and believed in my work since we made first contact. Thank you for reading my scripts and my other books. I promise you a role if *Killing Donnie* ever makes it to the screen.

Once again, thanks to Anita for the magnificent editing.

Last but never least, I'd like to give thanks to my mother, who is the reason I write, and is my motivation to achieve the dreams I never thought I could reach, knowing that there is no expiry on a dream, nor are we too old to chase them. You are my biggest inspiration and will continue to be so for the rest of my life.

About the Author

Born in Melbourne, Australia, Dean 'Rafael Francis' Paniagua wrote *Honeybird* at the age of twenty-four and had it published at twenty-five. In the six years prior, Rafael began writing screenplays for film and television, gaining a taste for storytelling under a heavily restricted format, and received multiple accolades for his works as a screenwriter. At twenty-six, he finally published *Killing Donnie: Part 1*. A project five years in the making.

Rafael is well known to articulate his stories in a manner that is easy to visualise. Timespans in his scripts and novels are known to dilate and slow down, almost to a momentary halt—or speed up, to the passing of three months in a single sentence. A common trend is the bittersweetness. The protagonists don't always win, and the most hated, worst-behaved characters don't always fall. It's the realities of life and knowing that every story isn't always a three-act fairy tale.

"There is no *correct* way to write. Creativity has no rules and knows no bounds. If I can impact my intended audience—make them feel something— then I consider my purpose fulfilled."
— Rafael Francis